To Jim

Best Wishes
Hope you enjoy
Gordon Taylor

About the author

Gordon Taylor's first novel, *Cometh the Man,* represents the culmination of a long standing ambition to prove himself worthy as a fiction author.

He has worked in the advertising media profession for more than twenty five years, and is the ghost writer of ITV's Hell's Kitchen winner chef, Terry Miller's autobiography.

Having written factual articles for regional and national magazines such as *Best of British,* it was a logical progression to pen his first novel.

Cometh the Man is the first part of a trilogy surrounding the exploits of the Davidson family of Northumberland, beginning in the early 1800's.

Gordon Taylor lives in the outstanding county of Northumberland with his wife and daughter.

COMETH THE MAN

DEDICATION

The writing of any novel requires time, patience and dedication. While this is true of the author, it is equally true of the family who see their loved one burying themselves alone in a room, agonising over the plot of their work.

To my wife Lynda and daughter Lesley.

I would like to dedicate this novel for their unstinting love and understanding during its conception, and unwavering support until its completion.

I would also like to mention my very good friends, Roger, Ian and Mike who have supported me constantly throughout the years.

Gordon Taylor

COMETH THE MAN

AUSTIN & MACAULEY

A CIP catalogue record for this title is available from the British Library.

ISBN 978 1 84963 032 0

www.austinmacauley.com

First Published (2010)
Austin & Macauley Publishers Ltd.
25 Canada Square
Canary Wharf
London
E14 5LB

Printed & Bound in Great Britain

CHAPTER 1

Pulsing veins stood out on the animal's neck as it reared and bucked against the unbreakable cord. Nathaniel Davidson clung desperately to the rope as the horse did all in its power to escape the bond, forcing his heels into the earth for purchase. In a second he knew it was no good. The ground, saturated from overnight rain, gave way and he slid crazily over the lush turf. Tumbling over in the process, he managed to retain his grip but the hemp bit fiercely into his hands. The aqueous stickiness of blood escaping from between his fingers told him he wouldn't be able to hold on much longer.

It was a battle he couldn't afford to lose if he was to break the horse in on this first attempt, a conflict of wills he wasn't prepared to forfeit. The animal was both running and bucking now, pitching Nathaniel onto his face in the grass. As his nose hit the ground there was a crack as the bridge shattered and all that stopped him passing out, was the reluctance to lose the fight.

He looked up to see the fence approaching at terrific speed, somehow finding his feet once more to run alongside the animal. With little time to avoid further injury of more serious nature, the man formed an instant plan in his head. The only complication was the unpredictable nature of his captive. Nathaniel couldn't base his plan on that, however, and was relieved that the horse's path wasn't deviating.

At the last minute, the horse veered away from the wooden fence but Nathaniel's inertia and the length of rope, carried him into the barrier. Winded, he looped the restraint around the top of a fence post, the horse careering to instantaneous halt with a terrifying howl of pain.

With the horse now restrained by the strength of the fence, Nathaniel slumped to the floor, holding tight to the rope. It was now the pain set in, waves of excruciating intensity almost overwhelming his consciousness but he held on fast to the rope in case the animal should slip the fetter.

As he looked down to examine the damage done to his hands, a great globule of red escaped from his nose, followed by a steady stream dripping onto his trousers. Instant fatigue enveloped him, although he had the presence of mind to rise and tie off the rope more securely.

At sixteen, breaking a horse was a task which should have been beyond him, older men would find the animal he had tackled demanding but Nathaniel had a motive for undertaking the job.

Nathaniel's father was a harsh man who, over the years, had been far happier beating his son for minor indiscretions, than praising the boy for success. The moment Radcliffe brought the raw animal; Nathaniel had resolved to break its spirit before his father arrived back from London.

He had learned over the years to cherish the moments when his father was away, enough to endure the assaults and chastisements when he was in residence. Thankfully those times of occupancy were becoming less and less frequent. Since the man's election as MP for the rural constituency of Gorseland in Northumberland, his duties required his attendance in the capital on a regular basis.

Nathaniel relished living in Northumberland, the county was as beautiful as any in the country and Thistlebrough estate with its magnificent hall, stood out as one of the most striking properties in the land. His mother was the antithesis of his father. A woman of great warmth and love, who idolised her son. The dignity with which she bore the conduct of her husband never ceased to amaze Nathaniel. Had it not been for her affection and the times of absence which his father undertook, he doubted whether he could have survived.

Looking over the magnificently manicured gardens of the hall and surrounds, he saw the coach sweep through the gates and on towards the house. He had been hoping for a few more hours of relative peace and calm but now his heart sank, his father had returned earlier than expected and his presence would inevitably be required.

Nathaniel's father stood with his back to him as he entered the book lined library. He faced the massive, ornate fireplace, a faint but unmistakable odour of pine drifted around the room, vying with the musty smell of long disused tomes. As Nathaniel entered, the man turned slowly to face him, one look at the expression in the craggy features told the boy everything he needed to know about his father's mood.

"Good Day, Nathaniel," the tone was as icy as the face. "May I ask what you have been doing to yourself; you look as though you've been in the wars?"

The sixteen year old gingerly touched the bruised flesh of his nose, pain from the lacerated fingers combining with the discomfort from the proboscis in overwhelming magnitude, "Radcliffe brought you a new horse sir; I attempted to break in the wild steed but the animal got the better of me."

"That kind of work should be left to the experts Nathaniel; I see that the animal outfoxed you well, a little pain will do you no harm."

His father crossed to the salver on which the decanters lay. Pouring himself a generous serving of whisky, he settled himself behind the prodigious desk which dominated the room; he looked Nathaniel disconcertingly in the eyes.

"I have given your future much thought Nathaniel, you are of an age now where a career which will develop your character is required," the man smirked. "I think it's fair to say that we both know you are a sensitive boy, no doubt too much influenced by your mother. During my recent visit to London I spoke to contacts I have in the military and you have been commissioned into the army in my old regiment; your training begins in one month and I sincerely hope you can mature into a son I can be proud of. From now on, you'll be in the wars in the literal sense."

"But Father, I don't want to go into the army," pleaded the boy, who could see the bullying of one man turn into his intimidation by many. "My character won't fit."

A look of loathing crossed the features of Sir Toby, "Stop snivelling, you've always been an excuse for a man, Nathaniel, but I am determined that you will develop into someone of which this family can be proud."

Nathaniel was desperate, inside he was in turmoil, "Father I will do anything you want me to do, if only you will change your mind on this; please spare me from enduring something which I cannot manage."

The older man rose from the desk and walked around the room, the expression on his features even more loathsome than before, "Save your protestations my boy, it is all arranged."

"I won't do it, Father," Nathaniel could barely believe the confrontational tone in his voice, "you can do everything you can in your power to make me join the army but I won't do it; it's what you want and not what I wish for and no matter how much you bluster, I won't join the army and there's an end to it."

An eruptive volcano would have demonstrated less violence than the appearance on the estate owner's face, purple lines of vein stood prominently on his forehead and neck. Nathaniel could see the man was about to explode and moved away from him rapidly.

The older man seemed astonished at the brazenness for a moment, but only a moment. "You are going to regret that Nathaniel," he shouted menacingly before rushing across the floor with his hand raised. The sixteen-year-old grasped the limb before the hand could come down on him and held it as tightly as a piece of metal in a vice.

Sir Toby turned purple with rage but, despite effort, he couldn't break his son's grip. It was the first physical act of defiance from Nathaniel and he delighted in the feeling of power, knowing the days of ignominy were over, expelled forever. Significantly, he saw the same in his father's features, the man was broken. Nathaniel could see failure in his father's eyes for the first time in his life, a realisation that nothing would ever be the same.

"No Father, you will never hurt me again," he hissed, "do you understand?" and with that he left the room to the astonishment of his stupefied parent, clashing the door behind him.

CHAPTER 2

The breeze cooled Nathaniel's face as he headed for the stables; his demonstration of bravado inside the house had been a pretence. Inside he shook like a leaf and the realisation dawned that he would have to leave Thistlebrough. It was a catastrophe; he wanted to cry but to break down in sight of the house and the possibility of his father's eyes, was an odious prospect.

The moment he entered the stable block and realised he was alone, the weeping began. He sat dejectedly on newly strewn straw, dust particles from the creamy stalks danced merrily in the light from the door as the tears flowed. The young man tended to his injuries the best he could, a nearby trough afforded him the opportunity to wash some of the caked blood from his hands and face. He was especially careful as he pressed a cooling rag to the bridge of his damaged nose.

A noise disturbed Nathaniel's thoughts, his head twisted toward the door of the stables where the face of Sally, the scullery maid, peeped cautiously from the exterior of the block. The girl's face was a picture of cherubic beauty, not fat but well filled out; the lips moistened and her eyes sparkled as the sunlight reflected from the vivid blue irises.

She was vaguely familiar to Nathaniel, from his fleeting visits to the hall's kitchens. Seeing her up close for the first time, he realised she was a rare beauty with inky hair and lusty form, disconcerting was the apt word to describe the girl's impression on Sir Toby's son.

Sally confidently approached him, a nervous smile playing around the dimples at the extremity of her lips. "What happened to you, Nathaniel?" she remarked, distress clouding her eyes.

"A battle with an unruly horse," advised the boy, "and the horse emerged victorious."

The kiss instigated by Sally, seemed to be the most natural consequence, Nathaniel abandoned himself to the brushing of her abundant mouth.

What followed was spontaneous, beautiful and powerful; the boy surrendered his body and soul to the sensual aura of the girl. It seemed Sally knew instinctively that Nathaniel needed the consolation which intimacy rendered.

The next half hour was filled with tenderness as the two young people explored each other until their energy was depleted.

"Sally," he began but she placed her finger to his lips and stared into his eyes. It was a look of pure love. There was no mistaking the adoration and Nathaniel was shocked. He'd no idea the girl felt so much for him but it was evident she did and he pulled her naked body close to his, the sweet smell of cheap soap filled his nostrils but to him it could have been the most expensive of perfumes and he knew whenever he thought of her, that smell would overwhelm his senses.

"Nathaniel," she confided, "I have always loved you; I know that nothing is possible between us but I saw and heard the conduct that your father inflicted on you through the open door of the library and I just needed to show you that life doesn't have to be so unfair, that there is also love and that someone, even as low as a scullery maid like me, could show you the pleasure there is to be had in life."

Nathaniel was stunned. He had never had an inkling the girl felt this way about him, but as he thought more he realised many times she would be near him when her duties were elsewhere and the realisation began to dawn on him.

"You must get away from here, Nathaniel," she continued, "if you don't he'll eventually break you. His drinking is worsening, all the servants know that and his violence is erratic. One day he will lose control completely and I fear he'll injure you badly or even kill you when he is in a rage."

"I have my mother to think of Sally," replied the young man, "I can't leave her in the hands of this bully, I need to protect her. If I wasn't here he may change his attention to her and I cant bear to think of him maltreating her."

Concern showed in Sally's face as she weighed up her next words carefully but there was no choice except confide in him the knowledge that she knew about the relationship of his mother and father. "Nathaniel," she began gently, "there are things I think you ought to know about your father's treatment of your mother." She faltered but carried on after a moment, "It's common knowledge in the servants hall that your father beats your mother too; oh, he's wise enough not to let the marks show visibly but he's often violent to the point of lunacy, it's a miracle it hasn't got completely out of hand."

Nathaniel raised himself on his elbow and looked down at the girl, "How do you know this?" he questioned her.

"Through Mrs Beattie, your mother's ladies' maid," Sally added, "your mother has confided in her time and again. He's an animal in drink; the savagery is beyond description and your mother copes with it despite the pain she must be in, almost constantly."

Nathaniel's eyes pricked with tears as he heard the news. He boiled inside, his desire to confront his father overpowered him and he made a grab for his clothes. Sally could see the look of mania in his face and she grabbed him by the arm, preventing him from rushing off immediately. "Nathaniel no!" the girl's voice betrayed her concern, "think before you act, take time to consider your actions."

The man wrenched his arm free and pulled on his clothes in a haphazard fashion, rushing out of the stable block toward the house. He stumbled in a blind rage across the yard and into the servants' entrance, startling the people there as he rushed into the entrance hall of Thistlebrough. Systematically, he searched the downstairs rooms for his father, realising that he wasn't there; he dashed up the stairs to his father's bedroom, tearing the door almost from its hinges as he entered.

The man stood in a state of half dress, preparing to get some sleep after his long journey from the metropolis. Nathaniel's hands went to his father's throat and he began choking the shocked man. Sir Toby's hands flew to the boy's arms trying to undo the grip but it was that of a madman and no matter how much he strove to force them apart, it was impossible.

Nathaniel pushed him onto his knees and squeezed dementedly, the life ebbing from Sir Toby; consciousness dwindling away like a gambler's luck on his forlorn last throw. Sally's voice broke into his reason; she had followed her lover from the stables, standing aghast in the doorway of the bedroom,

"Don't Nathaniel," she screamed, "you'll swing if you kill him."

The grip loosened a small amount and one hand released the neck altogether; the son looking down into his father's terrified eyes, drew his hand back and with a monumental energy, struck him hard in the face.

"If you ever touch my mother again I'll kill you, I promise you that," and he punched Sir Toby again, leaving him unconscious on the floor, blood pouring from the older man's mouth where teeth had lacerated the inner cheek.

He faced Sally and swiftly made up his mind, "Sally," he begged, "come with me. I must leave this place now; I have no money and no prospects when my father lets it be known what I've done, but I want you with me. I'll look after you and I promise you one thing, you will never be in service again."

The girl looked him in the eye with undisguised affection. "I would like to Nathaniel, I really would but we're too young to survive, here I have a roof over my head and a position and food. Out there would be a challenge to survive and perhaps we'd fail; odds would be against us." The practicality of the statement hurt her more than she knew possible. She longed for this boy so much but she knew in her heart that her words were realistic.

He felt as though his heart had been physically torn from his body. Their lovemaking was the greatest sensation he had known in his young life and he knew inside that the feelings he was experiencing were a deep love and respect for the girl.

21

"I…I have to get away now," he stammered, trying to mask his feelings of regret, "I will come back for you Sally if you want me to; when I have made my way, we will be together."

She barely succeeded in keeping her tears at bay, "Please," she breathed hard, "come back for me as quick as you can."

They kissed. One wild passionate moment of attachment and then he swept away from her, heading to his room.

As he left the scene of the altercation, Nathaniel saw his mother climbing the polished oak staircase. The boy tried to move past her but she grasped his arm pulling him to face her. "What has happened, Nathaniel?" she demanded. He could never deceive his mother; the woman knew his temperament too well for that.

She guided her son into her bedroom and closed the door. "Something's wrong, what has happened?" the woman asked.

Nathaniel looked earnestly into Lady Celia's imploring eyes; he felt as though he couldn't go through the horse incident again, "Father and I have come to blows; I've heard how he treats you; why didn't you tell me what was going on?"

The revelation did nothing to prick the woman's cool exterior. Crossing the room, she sat in the chair at her dressing table. "The relationship between a man and his wife is not necessarily the business of their children," she advised the boy, "besides you are still too young to be told of such things and the man is my husband, so I have my duties and loyalties to him."

"But that doesn't include allowing him to beat you," Nathaniel asserted, "no human being has to endure that."

Lady Celia smiled. "So tender," she stated, rising to cup her son's face in her hands.

"Mother, I have to get away from this place, I want you to come with me."

"Leaving my husband is something I can never do son," his mother explained, "but I agree that you must leave; he has told me of his plans to enrol you in the army despite my opposition, and you are not the type for such a regimented life."

Nathaniel's heart sank, he wanted the opportunity to save and look after his mother and her resolution to stay in such an abusive relationship, deflated him,

"Very well, mother, I'll go but I will get word to you wherever I am and I will hope you'll join me if things here get beyond your ability to cope." He kissed her and left the room, knowing it was probably for the last time in his life.

CHAPTER 3

Nathaniel studied Thistlebrough Hall, bathed in glorious evening sun glow, its gardens overwhelmingly beautiful, a testament to his father's wealth and something Sir Toby's vision had accomplished to his credit.

The horse whinnied as he tugged the left rein, turning the animal away from the home he knew he might never see again. Before he could dig his heels into the animal's flank he saw Sally standing alone outside the servants' entrance, gazing in his direction. Nathaniel raised his hand, kicked the animal on and in a few seconds he had rounded the tree lined drive and was heading out into wild Northumbrian landscape.

Despite the circumstances, Nathaniel felt free for the first time in his life. His mother had provided him some money but precious little, enough maybe for three nights stay in reasonable inns. After that he would be at the grace of God and his wits. It was a worrying prospect. From that moment he knew he would never forget Sally, never lose sight of the passion she had afforded him and he wept on his horse to know that it would be sometime before he would look at her exquisite face again and kiss the lips, which he could still taste in his mind.

Where he was going was a mystery but Newcastle seemed the best idea to begin with. It was forty miles away and Nathaniel decided to stay the night in the market town of Alnwick. He cantered the horse in the right direction and spent the journey deep in thought until he came on the town in darkness. The windows of the houses and inns were gloomily illuminated by lanterns, their murky, yellowish glow suggested warmth and Nathaniel searched out a coaching inn, the Traveller's Friend. It was a place he had visited with his father years before and was reputed to be the best in the area.

As he rode through the arched entrance into the main courtyard, the heavens opened and rain bucketed down. A boy ran from the hostelry and took the reins of Nathaniel's horse as he climbed from the saddle, "Go inside," the boy advised, "I'll stable the horse for you."

Inside, the smoky atmosphere of a myriad of pipes made him cough violently. He looked through the low fug to see a mixture of clientele. Townsfolk and travellers merged as one, several games of cards were in progress and copious amounts of ale were being swigged by men of dubious character, Nathaniel was sure. Several serving women were negotiating their way expertly between tables, avoiding the sweaty grasps of men's hands. It seemed this was the pastime that was prevalent in ale houses and inns throughout the land. Suddenly one of the men got lucky and his hand stroked the backside of a particularly busty waitress. She spun on her heel and slapped his face with a force that made the sound exceed the din of the room. The man's friends collapsed in convulsions of laughter, as the perpetrator rubbed his cheek in embarrassment.

Like a ghostly apparition, a barrel of a man emerged at Nathaniel's elbow. His dirty white apron was daubed with the stains of his trade, ale, fat and general filth seemed to struggle for ascendancy of the cloth, the rest of his apparel fared no better. "And what can I do for you?" boomed the man, who was eyeing the boy with suspicion.

"I'd like a bed for the night if you don't mind," replied Nathaniel, "and some food," he went on.

The coaching inn proprietor shifted on one leg, "I'll need to see the colour of your money first," he sniffed. Nathaniel took some coins out of his pocket and waved them in the sweaty face of the man, whose expression immediately turned from suspicion to goodwill.

"And that colour is perfect," the man fawned as he eyed the glint of silver, "come in and sit yourself down and Mary will attend to you," this to a girl passing the two men. As he led the boy into the interior of the premises he turned, "Will lamb stew be alright for you?" he enquired.

He thanked the man and chose a table close to the fire. Peering into the flames, watching them dance and flicker he lost himself there until Mary clashed down a plate and a mug of ale in front of him. He attacked the food ferociously, abating the hunger which had built up over the journey. While he ate he thought of Sally's face and how long it might be before he saw her sweet features again.

When the meal was finished, he noticed two unkempt individuals staring intently at him from the next table, a threatening look in their eyes, which disconcerted him. The first, a stick insect of a human being with a shock of red hair and fingernails encrusted with dirt, which Nathaniel noticed on the hands, clasping a pewter tankard.

Number two was likewise slim but no where near the plight of his friend. His features were angular in the extreme, the head almost square and in his case the eyes were bright and suggested a trace of intelligence.

Nathaniel was sure this was the dominant one of the pair, the way he held himself demonstrated a confidence the other could never aspire to. It was clear to the boy that they had some felonious activity in mind and he decided to make himself scarce, rising from the table to seek out the inn landlord and his bed for the night. As he walked from the table the men's eyes followed him intently.

The innkeeper sat in a corner with four men, obviously friends, sniggering over some ribald story and his podgy features changed as Nathaniel approached the group.

"I would appreciate it if you could show me to my bed now Landlord," the boy demanded. The owner didn't move from his stool but called across the crowded room.

"Mary," he bawled over the increasing din, "show this young gentleman to number 6." And without another glance at Nathaniel, the man turned back to his companions and their banal discussion.

He followed the girl up the unstable staircase and into a tiny room. She stepped inside first and then turned to face him as he crossed the threshold.

"Would you like me to stay?" she drawled provocatively, and Nathaniel knew immediately the connotation of the words.

"I don't think so," he said, urging her towards the door.

"Don't you like me?" she coaxed and placed her hand on the front of his breeches. "Wouldn't you like to spend some time with me?"

He steered her out of the room and closed the door. Looking round, he noticed the depressing atmosphere of the shambolic chamber, made even more dour by the guttering candlelight. Weeks of accumulated dust draped everything and It was obvious to him that he had not been afforded the best room in the house.

The lack of cleanliness was truly staggering but he needed a bed for the night and he had no stomach for an argument. There was little doubt that the rooms for the more affluent clientele would be far superior.

Wearily he began to undress, his back facing the door when it creaked open. Believing Mary had returned to ply her trade once more, he turned, intending to eject her a second time. Instead he came face to face with the two characters from the tap room below.

The wiry one bolted towards Nathaniel, forcing him back on the bed, pummelling him as he hit the lumpy mattress. Nathaniel was struggling to fight back and vainly tried to gouge at the man's eyes. As he did so he noticed the other assailant searching his jacket pockets, removing the few coins he found there. From somewhere he found strength and forced the man attacking him from his body, raining manic blows to the man's head. What little money he possessed he intended to keep and, at the very least, he wouldn't give it up without a bloody good fight.

Through the open door a third man entered, grabbing the thief by his collar and dragging him to the ground. With one almighty blow to the head, he laid the individual out cold and turned his attention to the second ruffian. Dragging him away from Nathaniel he offered the man a similar fate to his compatriot. In an instant the two would be robbers were lying unconscious on the dirty floorboards.

"I owe you a great debt sir," panted Nathaniel, "may I know your name?"

His saviour was stooping over the robbers, ensuring they would not wake imminently, he looked up smiling, "Captain Christian Davenport," he advised, dragging two tassled chords from the curtains and expertly securing the men's hands with them.

"Well Captain Davenport," Nathaniel continued, "I think I owe you an enormous drink for the service you've just rendered me." Davenport's lips spread into a huge grin,

"That would be most acceptable but I think we should get the innkeeper to send for the constable first."

Twenty minutes later the captives had been marched away from the coaching inn. Nathaniel and his new found colleague sat at the same table the boy had occupied earlier in the evening. The inn was much quieter now, the travellers had taken themselves off to bed and most of the local populace had unsteadily set off for their homes.

Davenport was staring moodily into his brandy, his mind wandering; Nathaniel sipped his own, feeling the warm liquid cut a savage pathway to his gut. He was loathe to break into the man's thoughts, so kept silent.

Presently the Captain looked up from the alcohol and smiled into Nathaniel's eyes, "I trust your experience has not shaken you up too much?" he enquired.

"No sir," advised the boy, "although I have to say the outcome could have been quite different but for your timely intervention."

"Think nothing of it, it really was quite fun."

"What brings you to these parts sir, do you live here?" queried Nathaniel.

The Captain drained his glass and called to the serving girl to fetch two more. "No," he said, "I am on my way to Newcastle to board a ship bound for Africa. It appears my presence on these shores is no longer required."

"Why would that be Captain?" asked the boy, downing the residue of his first drink.

"I have been dismissed from the army," the man advised, "accused of a crime I did not commit and not charged with, the army doesn't appreciate scandal associated with its officers, hence my hunt for a new land, where I hope to make a new life for myself," he looked quizzically at Nathaniel, "And you Nathaniel, what plans have you? What brings you to the Traveller's Friend this night?"

Briefly Nathaniel recounted his tale to the Captain, explaining his need to get away from his father but having no fixed idea what he was going to do or how to acquire the fortune that necessity demanded.

"But this is fortuitous," exploded Davenport, "I have a suggestion for you and I hope you will consider it most carefully," he laughed. "Why not join me and together we will seek the best that life has to offer, and if we don't find it then we will at least have some adventure and experience along the way."

It took Nathaniel less than a second to make up his mind,

"Yes," he agreed, "I would be honoured to join you."

The two men shook hands and ordered another round of drinks. Their course was set but Nathaniel would have lied if he said he didn't feel just a little anxious regarding his future at that precise moment.

CHAPTER 4

Newcastle Upon Tyne was bustling, heaving with the human traffic every city possesses as Nathaniel and Davenport guided their horses into its boundaries. A market was underway, the exotic aroma of vegetables and fruit heavy in the air, stall holders calling out their prices in ever increasing loudness, screeching manically to outdo their rivals.

Beside a makeshift counter selling hot soup, a fight broke out between two inebriated customers, so drunk that the only chance of hurting each other was if they caught a cold from the misdirected blows passing their heads. Several bystanders moved in to break up the brawl, dragging the men apart and moving them well away from each other. Like most clashing paralytics, the argument seemed to be instantly forgotten and the men collapsed affectionately into each other's arms.

Davenport turned to his companion, "Typical city life," he laughed, "straight to the quayside I think."

"Yes," Nathaniel agreed, smiling at the scene.

Fifteen minutes later the men rode onto the road adjacent to the river Tyne, its typical river smell prevalent in the strengthening breeze. Several sailing ships were moored to the quay along with much smaller vessels, mainly fishing boats. Scarcely an inch was devoid of people going about their business. Stores were being lugged up gangplanks by sailors engrossed in their work. The noise was truly formidable as Nathaniel and Davenport sought out a riverside inn, eventually settling on the Crown and Anchor. It seemed a good name to find a captain of a ship bound for foreign lands.

Inside, the inn teemed with sailors, seeking out their last drink before boarding. The two men headed to the beer swilled bar, searching out the landlord who had a huge stomach and remarkable side whiskers. Great forests of hair sprouting from his pockmarked skin, evidence of some former disease. He fired a globule of phlegm expertly into a convenient spittoon as he approached the would be voyagers,

"Can I help you?" he said gruffly, directing his look on Nathaniel.

"We're looking for passage on a boat to Africa," exclaimed the boy. "Do you know of any captains heading there?"

"Perhaps," he replied, "it will cost you if I do though."

Davenport interjected, "I thought it might," the captain sneered, handing over several coins into the man's grubby fist. "Is your memory improving now?" The landlord pointed out a curtain.

"The back room, Captain Ebenezer Smith. He's heading there this evening and if your money is sufficient he'll be your man." The back room was filled with pungent smoke from the Captain's cheroot. He sat at a table with several other men playing dice for money and it was clear by his expression that he was winning and handsomely. The massive grin beneath the beard was in stark contrast to the crestfallen faces of the other players. Looking up he greeted Nathaniel and Captain Davenport.

"Ah some more players, welcome gentlemen," his enthusiasm infectious, "pull up a chair and we'll get on with the game." Davenport looked at the stash of money in front of Smith.

"Actually we are not here for that," he explained, "and looking in front of you, it's evident that's a good decision of ours."

"Then what is it you seek gentlemen?" the dice had been thrown again, more money was being swept to the Captain's growing pile of silver.

"We understand you are sailing to Africa Captain and would like to buy passage there," Nathaniel was astonished at the man's fortune in the game. He had won yet again.

"It is true we are calling at Africa on the way to Bombay and I will consider your request but the game is occupying me at the moment. If you can amuse yourselves in the tavern for an hour, I

31

will talk to you then gentlemen," and with that he tidied his money, preparing to throw the dice again.

Nathaniel and Davenport had seen two tankards of ale off before Ebenezer Smith approached their table.

"Now then friends, we have some negotiations to get through, do we not?" stated the Captain who called for three more tankards of ale while seating himself in the hard chair opposite the two men. "My price for passage to Africa is fifteen guineas apiece, paid in advance."

The price seemed scandalous to Nathaniel but Davenport extracted his money pouch and counted out the sovereigns and some silver, "Then we have a deal Captain," the ex army officer stated, passing over the money and taking the captain's proffered hand in a firm but strange looking shake. Smiths eyes flickered over the currency, counting it almost in an instant.

"Indeed we do gentlemen, you will be honoured guests aboard the Lady Bamburgh and we will make our way to her directly after we have finished our ale, for I intend to sail immediately on the tide." The man looked intently at the two of them, "I trust this meets with your approval gentlemen."

"Nothing could suit us better," exclaimed Nathaniel, warming to the hint of adventure on the high seas.

Davenport was infinitely more practical. He questioned Smith, "What is the purpose of your voyage Captain? I trust piracy is not a word in your vocabulary."

Smith guffawed, "No Captain Davenport, I'm afraid my vessel is a company ship and our final destination is Bombay, but first we have a cargo of port to obtain from Lisbon, which is bound for Cape Town and that is where we will put you off." He lit a cheroot and continued, "And from what I detect it will not matter which part of the continent you alight, am I correct?"

The Lady Bamburgh was a sturdy vessel with a length of one hundred and ten feet and a beam of thirty. She lay at harbour bobbing gently on the swell. Three masts towered above the deck and some sails were already unfurled, announcing imminent departure. Her shape was almost sensual in its creation, reminding Nathaniel of Sally's curves. Sally, he had not thought of her since meeting Davenport and now with their coming departure he fell into a black mood. How long would it be until he could hold her once again, he mused? Would she wait for him, could she wait for him? It may be years until he returned to England. Could he expect her to hold onto her affections for that length of time? It was something he could not afford to think about so he made a pact with himself not to imagine a life with her until he returned, his fortune made.

Smith, Nathaniel and Davenport made their way up the gangplank and set foot on the decking boards. It was the first time Nathaniel had boarded a ship and the commotion on deck of sailors running to prepare the vessel for sea, seemed to him like a colony of worker ants. Each had his task and each performed that task with gusto. It was a well-disciplined crew, that was obvious. By this time the provisions had been quartered, all hands had boarded and the ship was ready to get underway.

Smith moved to a position next to the wheel, which was tended by the Helmsman, "Cast Off," the order clearly given was heard by everyone on the ship. Mooring ropes were thrown into the sea and the Lady Bamburgh edged majestically away from the quay, her captain scanning the surrounding vessels, ensuring any collision was avoided. She cut away into the centre of the river, her sails burgeoning in the wind and picked up speed.

People on the dock waved the craft on its way. Some sailors returned the gestures of women on shore. Nathaniel wondered if they were true sweethearts or ladies of the night, but then again he deliberated, maybe a sailor could only expect to have a transient relationship and had to love whenever and wherever it offered itself and in whatever form.

The pilot was disembarked as the Lady Bamburgh eased past the black rocks, off North Shields, the last hazard before open sea. A small boat rowed out to receive the man who climbed expertly down the rope ladder and stood in the interior of the vessel waving the ship away to sea.

Nathaniel noticed a shift in the work rate of the crew. They fell into a well worn routine, efficient and methodical. The haste had gone, replaced by professional seamanship. Sailors snaked their way down the rigging now that full sail had been ordered, not a man of them was unhappy at being on deck again. They knew as every sailor did, the perils of working on high and everyone of them had seen a man fall to serious injury or death.

As Nathaniel watched the everyday life on board, a sailor came up on deck with a canvas bucket. He tossed the slops over the stern rail. A screeching hoard of ravenous seagulls congregated near the stern and battled over the expelled fragments.

Davenport turned to him, "The adventure starts here Nathaniel," he stated. "Still happy to have come along?" he questioned.

The boy looked around him, "Yes," he affirmed, "there's nowhere I'd rather be Christian." It was the first time he had used Davenport's first name but it seemed appropriate to do so now.

Smith made his way down from the wheel, "Gentlemen," he requested, "I would like to see you in my cabin if you please." They followed him below, ducking their heads to avoid the low beams. Smith's cabin was small but exquisitely furnished, there was a cot in one corner and an oak table shined to perfection. He lived well as befitted the Captain of a vessel of this company. The Morgan line was famed for its treatment of its masters and Smith was the principal Captain as well as a shareholder in the company. With eighteen vessels, the Morgan line was the leading maritime concern in the north of England, the diversity of its vessels ensured that it could carry almost any cargo to any destination.

"Be seated gentlemen," the Captain proffered two chairs at the table and seated himself opposite. He yelled, "First Mate," through the open door of his cabin.

A powerful individual entered the room. He was the fittest man Nathaniel had ever set eyes on. Possessing a set of shoulders so wide he had to enter the cabin sideways, the two travellers were amazed at the sheer size of the man. The cabin door was six feet tall and this character stood at least five inches taller. He'd had to stoop as well as turn his body to get into the small compartment and even now could not stand straight.

"Yes Cap'n," his voice was strangely high pitched.

"Have the two guest cabins prepared for these two men if you please," Captain Smith instructed, "and ask the cook to prepare a meal for myself and my guests." Outside the windows of the stern, the night was drawing in. Captain Smith rose and lit the swinging lanterns, the yellow glow enclosing the cabin in a blanket of soft luminescence.

"A glass of Madeira my friends?" it was a request, "you'll find no better afloat believe me." He busied himself pouring the liquid from a galleon shaped decanter placed on a convenient shelf. He sipped his before handing the other glasses to the cabin's occupants, "A truly wonderful wine I'm sure you will agree," he remarked holding out the glasses to Nathaniel and Davenport. The alcohol was the finest that Nathaniel or Davenport had ever tasted and it surpassed anything in Thistlebrough's cellars, which were generally regarded as some of the best in England.

"Now gentlemen," Smith sipped his wine and continued, "you have the run of the ship naturally, but I would ask you to avoid small talk with the crew. They are busy almost constantly, apart from that you can do anything you wish or go anywhere you please. Ah," he exclaimed, "the food, I trust you will enjoy the fare." The cabin boy placed steaming plates before the men and tended them as they ate.

There was small talk and a lot of drinking over the next two hours. Nathaniel was quite exhausted and asked to be excused but his companions seemed set for a long period of supping, and as Nathaniel lay in the bunk of his quarters he could hear muffled laughing sounding through the walls. After a while even that ended and he fell into a deep sleep.

The next several days were spent reading or talking for Nathaniel and his travelling companion. Captain Smith was fully occupied with the running of his ship but every night the three of them met for dinner and the two Captains regaled the party with stories of their exploits. Life aboard ship became mundane for the two voyagers, they had little to occupy themselves with. Sometimes at sunset they would stand at the rail and watch spectacularly coloured skies; red, orange and golden yellow normally but on one evening the sunset brought an angry sky with evil black clouds scudding over the ship. The rain held off but the heavens were no less spectacular for their swollen, forbidding intensity.

One morning the men awoke to the sight of Portugal off the port side. It was a welcome relief for Nathaniel who was looking forward to getting his feet on terra firma once again. The voyage so far had been tedious and he looked forward to meeting new people again.

"Well Nathaniel, are you looking forward to landfall?" Captain Smith called to him from his vantage point by the ship's wheel.

"Yes I am Captain, very much," he smiled up at the mariner. "Have you visited Portugal many times?"

"Too many to mention," replied Smith, "but there is nothing like the first time so enjoy it won't you?"

Davenport appeared through the hatchway leading to the cabins and inhaled deeply, savouring the morning ozone. He tucked his shirt into his breeches and joined Nathaniel by the rail.

"How far to Lisbon?" he enquired of the Captain.

Smith thought for a moment, "We've joined the coastline about half a day from the city so I suspect we will anchor just after midday."

"How long will we be staying?" he queried, still adjusting his dress.

"No time at all I'm afraid," returned the Captain. "We will board our cargo of port and be off again on the evening tide, but it should give you a few hours to explore the city."

The disappointment in Nathaniel's face was difficult to erase. He had expected at least a day in the port and a bed on land for once. Captain Smith hurried away to the stern portion of the Lady Bamburgh.

"Excuse me gentlemen, I have things to attend to," he advised.

The two men eked out the morning talking on deck in the hazy sunshine, watching the crew go about their business. Over the voyage so far, the companions had been impressed with the professionalism of the ship's company. They were as efficient here in the rapidly rising heat as they had been sailing from the cooler climate of Britain. The smell of sweat though was overwhelming, its sickly sweetness tainted the fresh sea air.

As the Captain of the vessel had predicted, the port of Lisbon came into view in the late morning. Several ships were already lying at anchor in the harbour and Smith picked his way judiciously between them until he found a suitable spot in which to settle his vessel. With a great metallic reverberation the anchor chain paid out, the metal pin of the anchor itself plunged through the waves to its resting place on the sea bed below.

When he was satisfied, the Captain called for all sail to be struck and the ship secured from sea duty. At the Captain's orders the longboat was swung out from the side of the ship and a crew of eight selected to man her.

"Will you join me?" the Captain invited Nathaniel and his companion. "Your transport awaits," he indicated the boat bobbing at the side of the ship.

As they wove between vessels, Nathaniel was struck by the size of many of them. They dwarfed the Lady Bamburgh, one French three master was almost twice as high as the Morgan Line craft.

Spanish, French and English merchantmen were all evident in the harbour, their flags billowing in the offshore breeze. The sight was deeply impressive and as the longboat rounded the bow of the French leviathan, Nathaniel spotted two British frigates lying calmly at anchor. Their lines were sleek being built for speed and the open gun ports showed the metal of cannon poking out from the side of the ships.

As the longboat tied up alongside the quay, Nathaniel was staggered by the number of people milling around on the dock. Street sellers plied their trade, dealing in everything from jewellery to prostitutes. Within a few yards of the boat's berth, he had been accosted several times and Captain Smith shooed them away expertly.

The houses along the waterfront were low and sun bleached white, painfully dazzling to the eye. There seemed to be a continual traffic in and out of the buildings and Captain Smith explained that the more popular of them were bordellos, he cautioned Nathaniel to stay out of them, while he and Davenport talked with nostalgia about past visits to similar establishments.

Ebenezer Smith paused outside a dwelling and gestured toward the interior. "This hostelry should afford you a little entertainment in my absence." The Captain seemed anxious to leave. "Excuse me if you will? I need to supervise the loading of my cargo, please return to the ship by nightfall."

The two men watched him stride purposefully down the quay towards some dockside warehouses, before entering the building as the Captain disappeared from sight.

"Smith is a trifle preoccupied today, Nathaniel," advised Davenport who ordered two glasses of port in deference to their location.

"Yes," agreed the boy, "I suppose he has work to do."

Inside the building, the temperature thankfully reduced by a number of degrees. Nathaniel felt relieved, since their arrival he had begun to sweat profusely and he wondered how he would fair in the baking climate and harsh conditions of Africa.

The establishment was certainly upmarket. Its clientele seemed to be exclusively well born ladies and gentlemen, interspersed with naval officers from the varying ships in the harbour. Uniforms of every hue were in this place, the rich royal blue of the British navy well represented. Suddenly a voice boomed out from the centre of the room.

"Nathaniel my boy, is that you?" The overweight man rose from his table, pushing and excusing himself as he fought a way through the customers to the object of his cry.

"My God," laughed Nathaniel, "Mr Armstrong how are you?"

Armstrong fairly beamed at the boy, "I'm well Nathaniel, well, but why are you here, is your father with you?"

"No," the boy answered, "may I introduce Captain Christian Davenport, we are travelling to Africa together."

"Delighted to make your acquaintance Captain Davenport," enthused the man who turned his attention to Nathaniel once more. "Please gentlemen have a drink with me if you would be so kind."

Armstrong steered them to his table, Nathaniel explaining to Davenport that he was a close family friend and one time business associate of his father. On reaching the table the man dismissed his previous companions and proffered the empty seats to the two men.

Nathaniel decided that here was a golden opportunity to send a message to his mother, whom he knew would be anxious of his whereabouts and well being. The drinks arrived and the men engaged in small talk for a few minutes until the boy questioned Armstrong.

"When are you heading back to England, sir?" he inquired.

"I leave tonight, Nathaniel," the jovial man replied. "I have been here a month and my ship sails imminently."

"Might I ask a favour of you. Could you pass on a message to my mother?" he begged.

"Yes of course I can Nathaniel," responded Armstrong. The boy briefly outlined his communication, simply telling his mother not to worry, that he would be home one day, fortune made and that he loved her very much. He, Davenport and the man spent an hour together.

"Well," his friend added, "I must take leave of you, the Captain of the Belinda wants to sail at the earliest convenience, but do not concern yourself my boy. Your mother will receive your message directly when I reach England," the man turned to Nathaniel's companion. "Captain Davenport," he held out his hand to Christian.

"Mr. Armstrong," Davenport enthused, "I wish you bon voyage." Armstrong rose, located his companions and left the building.

"A good friend," Davenport pointed out, "there seems little to occupy us here but alcohol Nathaniel, what say we return to the ship and a little rest?" The thought had also crossed Nathaniel's mind but he was loathe to voice it in case the ex-army Captain was enjoying his visit. The two men left the hostelry and sought out a boat for hire to row them back to their vessel.

When they climbed on board the men noticed the cargo hatches were unfastened. They could see the barrels of port stashed neatly and lashed tightly to prevent movement. A number of small boats had been ferrying the casks from shore, the last one approaching the ship's starboard side, ready to offload its consignment.

This final vessel carried Captain Smith, who had personally satisfied himself with the transfer of the load, his long black locks were wafting in the wind, and he stood in the centre of the boat directing operations. As the small craft clunked against the planking he expertly negotiated the rope ladder to the deck where he spied Nathaniel and his colleague intently watching the transfer of the goods.

"So gentlemen," Smith called. "The delights of Lisbon were not to your taste for long."

"We missed your scintillating company," quipped Davenport, "and we can sup just as well aboard the Lady Bamburgh, the quality of your liquor is comparable to anything we could find ashore."

"Then allow me to conclude my loading and we will crack a bottle in my cabin. Till then gentlemen," the Captain began supervising the last kegs into their positions into the spacious hold.

One hour later, the three men were nursing glasses in the seaman's quarters.

"We head directly to Cape Town," advised Smith, "I trust that will be a convenient place for you to disembark?"

"That will be perfect," announced Nathaniel, who took the initiative for the two men and continued. "And may I say that the voyage has been most pleasant and the company very fine indeed." He was beginning to feel the after effects of the drink and he was slurring his words. A monumental thirst overwhelmed him and he downed the carafe of water on the Captain's table in one. Smith called for his cabin boy, who hurried in with an even larger container of Adams ale.

The men talked as the evening began to creep over the ship. Lady Bamburgh swayed with the movement of the waves as the twilight tide gathered in strength. Eventually, Ebenezer judged the burgeoning swell sufficient for weighing anchor and excused himself from his guests, instructing them to continue drinking if they so wished.

The lapping of the waves against the planking of the ship's side set up a relaxing rhythm, so peaceful it lulled Nathaniel into a contented sleep.

CHAPTER 5

The voyage from Lisbon to their present position midway to Cape Town, had been a carbon copy of the first stage from Newcastle to the Portuguese city. Nathaniel thought he would go mad with the tedium at times, his desire to get off the ship becoming obsessional.

Davenport was equally bored, his good humour had deserted him days before and for the first time he and the boy had squabbled over something trivial, thankfully for them both, it had blown over almost as soon as it started.

This evening was balmy, the scant breeze afforded little relief for the companions as they sat on deck before turning in.

Overhead the sky was crystalline clear, millions of stars sparkled down, the full moon beating a shimmering pathway across the inky water.

Nathaniel looked back over the stern, expecting to see a continuation of the peaceful scene, instead he was perturbed to make out ominous clouds chasing the vessel down from that direction.

Ebenezer Smith stood next to the helmsman, a frown spreading across his handsome features as he watched the scene unfolding, experience told him a very dangerous storm was approaching. He judged it was perhaps half an hour away but it was closing relentlessly fast.

The watch crew saw it too, sending a shudder through the most sea hardened of them. Forks of lightning tore through the angry clouds, the intensity of the flashes staggering. Like a volley of cannon, thunder rumbled ominously across the sky.

Smith barked some orders to his men and called for a muster of the whole company. The hatches were battened down and the Lady Bamburgh prepared as best she could for the coming assault.

Sails were struck in record time by men climbing like crazed monkeys through the rigging, although Captain Smith left some canvas in place for manoeuvring purposes. Every seaman was back on the deck in fifteen minutes, stowing anything on board that could move and fastening themselves with rope to the sturdiest parts of the ship.

The first buffeting was mild enough but presently grew steadily in force, wildly flapping canvas covering some of the secured equipment.

"Captain," yelled Davenport, "is there anything we can do?"

Smith was trying to do several things at once, "Gentlemen please find some rope and lash yourself to the ship," he advised, "I fear this will be dreadful."

"Would it not be better to be below, Ebenezer?" questioned Nathaniel.

"Absolutely not," Smith yelled back, "stay on deck. You do not want to be trapped below, trust me on that."

Suddenly the full force of the howling fury was upon them, the crashing of the first real wind, scudding the ship over the angry sea. A truly awesome crash of thunder exploded overhead, ringing the ears. It was followed by an enormous jagged zig zag of lightning which bathed the ship in an eerie luminosity.

Rolling waves of thirty feet of more started crashing over the decks, smashing timbers as they hit. Nathaniel looked toward the helmsman, lashed to the wheel, struggling to keep course, his knuckles white with the effort.

With an ear rupturing din the stern rail shattered. A three foot section flew through the air and pierced the helmsman through the back, its jagged point exited the man's chest and lodged in the spokes of the ship's wheel. His body slumped over but stayed upright, held by the lashings to the steering device. His chin rested between the handles of the wheel, the gargoyle face staring blankly into space.

Two seaman rushed to the position and unhooked the man from the wooden circle. One of them replaced him and began fighting with it, trying to avoid the viscous blood, hands slipping constantly on the liquid.

In spite of the bindings, all manner of item loosened and flew dangerously around the decks, water kegs dashed against the rails and disappeared over the side, gone forever into the seething sea. It was a scene from hell thought Nathaniel, the devil had visited the ship and was wreaking havoc.

He believed he would die on the deck of the Lady Bamburgh, all he could think of as he watched the scene played out before him was Thistlebrough and Sally. The two things he held most dear in his heart. He judged that he might never see either one again.

Despite his prayers to the contrary, the storm was building to a new level of fierceness. Waves of fifty feet or more, whipped up by hurricane force winds, battered remorselessly into the ship. His clothes were saturated from the crashing surf, as well as the ceaseless rain which had begun just after the first crack of thunder, shivering he cowered down to avoid further soaking.

The display on deck was being played out in slow motion before Nathaniel, men were dashed around like rag dolls, dancing to the bidding of nature. As he looked on, a wave lifted one man up, propelled him across the deck straight into a taut rope slung across the beam of the vessel. There was a sickening crack, audible over the clamour as the man's neck crashed into the strand, ripping his head back and shattering the vertebrae. He died instantly, falling back to the planking in a jumble of lifeless limbs.

Captain Smith stood erect by the wheel. If he was perturbed it didn't show in his face. Amidst the carnage around him he directed operations with cool authority. He was bleeding profusely from a gash on his temple, caused by some flying object and still he carried on regardless.

Self-preservation was the order of the day, the men possessed supreme confidence in the master of their ship, knowing their best chance of survival lay in listening to and obeying the orders of their Captain.

A wave of awesome magnitude swept over the deck, caught up Nathaniel and pitched him over the side rail. He fell flailing overboard, hitting the frothy sea and disappearing below the waves, until the rope lashing arrested his descent.

With no time to catch his breath he ingested water, the prospect of drowning a real threat. Fighting for survival, he realised he didn't know in which direction the surface lay. In the black depths he had tumbled over and over until he was disorientated. Now would come death, he mused and a curious calm descended on him.

A pain shot through Nathaniel's midriff, the rope tightening about his body, he realised he was being dragged up by the lashing. Thankfully he exited the sea and gasped a huge breath into his lungs.

As the rope began to drag him back to the ship, it pummelled him into the Vessel's flank, bruising him in the process. It was a small inconvenience for the gift of life. His hands fought to grasp hold on the wet planking. Inexorably Nathaniel was hauled back to the rail where he saw the face of Davenport, furrowed from his exertions, pulling for all he was worth to save his companion. With one huge effort he jerked the boy aboard, the two men floundering in the cold grey water still flooding the deck.

"Are you alright, Nathaniel," croaked his friend, doubled over with exhaustion. The boy flung his arms around his saviour,

"Thank you Christian, thank you for my life." Davenport grinned back at him.

"My pleasure," he was panting hard. "Anyway we made a pact to be together in Africa so it wasn't practical to let you drown."

It took more than two hours for the storm to abate. In that time the vessel had almost foundered several times, canting at such angles that it was a miracle that she could possibly right herself, thought Nathaniel.

There had been one more death aboard, the first mate who Nathaniel and Christian had met early in the voyage. The life had been crushed out of him by two rogue kegs dashing him into the ship's side, pulverising the body against the wood into a bloody mass. One of his ribs had pierced the heart and the man died without uttering a word. A valiant man, he had saved many souls by his quick thinking actions during the height of the storm, he would be acutely missed.

A number of other seamen had received injuries, some seriously, some superficial wounds. As soon as the conditions moderated, Captain Smith ordered that the men should be attended to. The overwhelmed ship's surgeon appealed to Nathaniel and Davenport for assistance and although neither had medical experience, they pitched in as best they could.

In the surgeon's dingy quarters a man lay on the table, one of his legs crushed beyond repair, the doctor was preparing to amputate the limb while the terrified individual swallowed huge amounts of rum.

Nathaniel looked at the surgeon's saw and shuddered, he couldn't grasp the pain this man was about to feel, despite the copious levels of alcohol. The man's eyes betrayed abject fear. At a nod of the surgeon's head, Nathaniel, Davenport and two of the ship's company grabbed the man, holding him in vice like grip as the doctor approached with the knife to slice through the thigh tissue. He worked rapidly and skilfully, having performed the procedure on many naval men during his time with the senior service.

As he cut through the main artery, a plume of steaming blood gushed into the air. From a nearby brazier a seaman handed a glowing iron and the surgeon cauterised the artery quickly to prevent more blood loss. The victim's screams were frightful, thankfully he passed out and the doctor could work without the inconvenience of the jerking form. Nathaniel gagged at the smell of the cauterisation smoke. It was the smell of sweet pork, making his stomach heave and he vomited copiously on the deck. No one took notice.

As the saw grated noisily on the bone, the casualty moaned in his unconscious state but did not come round. The room was becoming intolerably hot, its small, cramped confines filled to capacity by the six men.

Fifteen minutes later the operation was complete, the newly sewn flesh bound and the man returned to his hammock. The next few days would determine if he survived or not, infection was the surgeon's enemy and he would inspect his handiwork every hour for a week, looking for the signs of tissue decay which would indicate the onset of gangrene. At first light the crew assembled on deck ready to witness the burial of their three shipmates. It was a beautiful sunrise, in marked contrast to the cataclysmic conditions of the night before.

Through the night, canvas shrouds had been rapidly constructed for the bodies which now lay on the deck. Inside the sail cloth, spare anchor chain had been placed to weigh down the covers, sufficient links to ensure a quick descent to the seabed.

The crew were exhausted from their exertions but every one of them stood ready for the service. Captain Smith looked particularly drained, moving to the side of the bodies, handsome looks degraded by his night's work. Holding the ship's Bible open at the relevant passages and called the men to order. It was a moving service, thought Nathaniel, who stood at the back of the throng along with Davenport, each anxious to show camaraderie with the company and to show respect to the brave souls who had given their lives in the securing of the ship. Their efforts had been much appreciated by everyone.

"We commend their souls to the deep," drawled Smith, "in the sure and certain hope of their resurrection to God's holy grace." The man's face demonstrated his despondency at the loss of his crew members. With a nod to the burial party they lifted the shrouds onto greased planks, placing them on the ship's rail. At a given signal the wooden boards were angled high and the canvas body bags slipped silently over the side, hitting the calm water at the same time.

For a few minutes the ship's company milled around, lost in thought about their comrades, before moving away to take up their duties.

Nathaniel moved to the Captain's side, he was peering down at the sea, the loss seemed to be affecting him greatly and for a few seconds the boy seemed to be reluctant to break into the man's reverie.

"Captain," he eventually said, "may I offer you condolences on the loss of your crew. Brave men and I'm sure they will be sadly missed."

"Thank you Nathaniel," he retorted as Davenport came to join them. "And may I thank you both for your efforts in ministering to my crew. It was something that was beyond your duty." He seemed to be thinking about something and then went on. "Gentlemen because of your service to the ship I am returning your passage money, it's little enough to do for you after your endeavours."

It was a magnificent gesture thought Nathaniel, "But Captain it was in our interest to save ourselves," he returned.

"Nevertheless my mind is made up," the ship's master continued, "much of what you did was horrific, particularly in the surgeon's cabin and you deserve some reward for that alone."

Several days were spent in restoring the ship to a seaworthy state, the ship's carpenter the busiest man aboard, repairing the wooden fabric that had been so degraded by the storm. Just as the Lady Bamburgh seemed to be renewed to something like its original state, Cape Town appeared before her, set out in magnificent splendour under the fierce sun.

The sight of Table Mountain rising grandly from the centre of the city impressed everyone on board who had never witnessed the spectacle, including Nathaniel. To him it looked like God had deposited the mass purposefully in the middle of the conurbation. He was amazed at the horizontal plateau, the evenness of which looked as if some giant knife had sliced the peak clean off.

Golden sand stretched away along the beach in the foreground, unique flora completed a scene of staggering loveliness. Captain Smith pointed out the Supreme Court building to the travelling companions, its impressive façade with arched windows in the upper tier and square in the lower, silhouetted against the backdrop of the mountain. It was a curious mustard colour but complimented the buildings surrounding it perfectly.

"My God," exclaimed Nathaniel. "It's so beautiful."

"Yes," agreed Smith, "but like all cities the world over it has its dark side; still if one remains vigilant there is no reason to worry."

Davenport gazed on the scene equally inspired, "I have seen many sights during my army career but nothing to rival this, nothing even comes close."

Smith wandered away from the two men to his duties, the friends remaining at the rail, drinking in the scene before their eyes.

Half an hour later the Lady Bamburgh was anchored offshore, gently bobbing in the swell. The longboat was launched, clattering gently against the side planking at her mooring. In their cabins, Nathaniel and Christian gathered their belongings, heading up on deck presently to board the transport to shore.

The sights on land only added to the men's appreciation of the city, most striking of which was the stone walled Castle of Good Hope, along with the Lodge de Goede Hoop, built by the Freemasons sixteen years earlier in 1804.

From his books at home in Thistlebrough Hall, Nathaniel knew that magnificent beasts roamed the dense forests of the cape, he looked forward to seeing these animals in their natural state. Hippo, lion and elephant vied for ascendancy in the fynbos.

Sweltering heat made Nathaniel sweat profusely, he began to feel dizzy and disorientated and his thirst was monumental. Spotting a drinking fountain in a nearby street, he rushed over and drank deeply of the fresh, cold liquid.

"I suppose we better find some accommodation my friend, you're looking a bit unwell," Davenport advised, looking concerned. He guided the boy away solicitously in the direction of a nearby hotel.

As they crossed the street, Nathaniel noticed inky black slaves hurrying behind their masters and mistresses. In this part of the globe the number of blacks an individual possessed enhanced their standing. Two was the minimum. More than ten was a positive feather in the cap.

Women twirling parasols, looking serene and cool in the blistering heat, strolled along the thoroughfare, talking between themselves of inconsequential matters.

It was a scene familiar to any city in the civilised world, people going about their business, the highborn and slave alike, only their personal circumstances differed.

Davenport shepherded the boy into the foyer of the Star hotel, the dehydration in Nathaniel acute. The captain sat him in a plush lobby chair while he sought out the hotel's manager. The interior of the entrance hall was mercifully cool but the heat exhaustion had already taken a heavy toll on the young man, who slumped over in his seated position, delirium setting in.

Davenport returned, having secured rooms for themselves. His money was depleting fast, he knew that somehow they would have to find more soon. It worried him greatly but his friend's well-being took precedence.

Two burly porters assisted him in hauling Nathaniel to bed and there he collapsed in a fitful sleep but only after his companion had forced as much water down his throat as he could take.

CHAPTER 6

The boy awoke to warm sunshine streaming through the room's enormous window, he had no idea where he was or how he got there. A pounding headache thumped remorselessly in his cranium, like some demented pixie attacking the brain with the point of an ice axe incessantly.

"Good morning," called his companion who had opened the door to his friend's chamber, "how are you feeling, Nathaniel?"

"Not well, Christian," moaned the invalid, pouring and drinking a glass of water from a jug on the bedside table, "my head feels as if it might explode."

Davenport pulled a seat to the boy's bedside and sat down, the greyness in Nathaniel's face concerned the Captain acutely.

"I have some news which might improve your spirits," Davenport smiled. "Last night I dined at a sort of gentleman's club along with Captain Smith." The information intrigued the bedridden man, he couldn't understand who Davenport would know anywhere in a city he had never visited. "I met a man there called Willem Devries who is one of the wealthiest men in Cape Town," continued the Captain, peering out of the window at the Lady Bamburgh bobbing gently at anchor in the millpond harbour.

Nathaniel was feeling nauseous. "Why is he important to us Christian?" enquired the youngster.

Davenport vacated the chair and crossed to the window, looking down on the activity in the street. Horse drawn carriages trundled up and down the dusty roadway carrying men to work. "The Cape Transit Trading Company is the leading supplier of ivory to the world," he advised, waving at Captain Smith who was passing below the window. "Devries is its Managing Director and he has put a proposition to me, which may be to our mutual advantage."

The boy in the bed raised himself on one arm, his mood brightening, "Go on Christian," he prompted.

The Captain retook his seat. "We have been offered employment by Mr Devries, tracking elephant for his company and gathering ivory for his business to convert into expensive gifts. It will mean long periods hunting in the bush but the money is substantial and will tide us over until we decide what to do for ourselves." The news seemed too good to be true to the youth, who shared Davenport's concern about the men's prospects.

By early evening Nathaniel had recovered to a great extent, he'd managed some weak soup in the mid afternoon and now his hunger had reached voracious proportions. Large amounts of water had been drunk by the boy too, who was taking salt, to deal with the losses caused by dehydration. Periods of deep sleep had helped him improve, he almost felt like his old self, despite a general weakness brought about by his condition.

Christian Davenport looked in on him periodically throughout the day, thankful to see gradual progress in the boy.

It was 6.00pm and Davenport was with him, having stayed since his last wakening just after 5.00pm. They had talked about the Captain's exploits in the army and Nathaniel's early life at Thistlebrough.

Davenport weighed up the situation with the boy before speaking, "Nathaniel, if you feel up to it we have been invited to dinner by Mr Devries at his home this evening," he ventured.

"Absolutely," answered the youth, "I could eat a horse." He began to rise from the bed, steadying himself on the mattress until he felt balanced. He began to dress, Davenport handing him his attire from the chair where it lay.

"The carriage will be here at 7.30," informed the Captain, "Devries wishes to tie up our involvement as soon as possible." As he dressed, Nathaniel's face took on a look of concern.

"I'm worried about this Christian," he voiced his apprehension, "we have no experience of the ivory trade."

"I know that," replied the Captain, "but this man is willing to take a chance on us until we find our feet and besides we will have native guides and bearers who will be able to assist us in the short term."

"Why should he take such a chance Christian, when there are experienced ivory hunters out there?" questioned the boy.

"I can't go into that at the moment," said Davenport, "just accept the man's good auspices for the time being."

Nathaniel was unsure about the explanation but Davenport had been a staunch friend, there was no reason to distrust him so he accepted it and determined to make the man worthy of his trust. He finished dressing. It was as plush a carriage as the men had ever seen, the deep red material luxurious enough for royalty, the upholstery well padded offering a smooth journey. Two magnificent beasts pulled the vehicle along at brisk speed, scattering people and other modes of transport before them.

Nathaniel glanced out of the side of the coach. They were heading out of the built up area of Cape Town into a more sedate district. Houses of prestige appeared, growing ever larger, their substantial exteriors becoming grander as the journey wore on.

With a drag on the right rein, the coachman guided the horses through an imposing gateway along a gravelled drive. Standing to attention on either side of the roadway, thick trees hid the dwelling from view until the very last minute.

As the carriage emerged from the driveway, the full splendour of the structure was laid before them in the twilight. The darkness was fast approaching, although enough light lingered to see the vast, white, two storey edifice, rising out of acres of lush verdant lawns.

Peacocks and peahens wandered regally about the grounds, their shrill calls eerily echoing in the half-light. Dotted here and there and rising from the grass, shrubs of various varieties, lovingly groomed, rose impressively. It was a scene of unimaginable elegance.

The house itself was completely lit up inside, streams of golden illumination seeking escape through the countless windows, made iridescent pools of light on nearby grass.

Nathaniel and Davenport exited the coach in front of an enormous entrance. Twelve foot high, solid oak doors decorated with ornate carving stretched up towards the sky.

As they climbed the steps to the entrance, one of the doors swung wide and a small individual emerged into the half-light. He was completely bald and ostentatiously attired. Nathaniel thought the man looked comical but there was something in the face which hinted at determination and even ruthlessness.

"Christian," the voice was high pitched but strong with a marked Dutch accent. "Good to see you again my friend," he turned his attention to the captain's companion. "And you must be Nathaniel, I trust you have recovered from your heat exhaustion?" Almost as an afterthought he introduced himself, holding out his palm to the boy, "Willem Devries, at your service." Nathaniel noticed the firm grip, surprising given the man's slight proportions. Devries smiled at the boy expansively.

Devries ushered them into a marble floored entrance hall, decorated with many forms of art, which Nathaniel later discovered the owner had collected over many years. A courteous host, he described the masterpieces in some detail as they swept down the chamber.

Following the men, a negro butler dressed in the British tradition tottered after them, finally scurrying past to open a door to the householder's study.

Once inside, the liveried servant poured three very large whiskies from an antique crystal decanter, the amber fluid of the finest Scottish malt. Davenport realised how high the quality of the whisky was, as the velvety smoothness of the liquid slid down his throat without the hint of harshness associated with its cheaper counterparts.

The men sat in high backed chairs facing one another around a highly polished walnut table, Devries puffing on a fat cigar. Christian and Nathaniel had declined the offer of a smoke when invited, preferring to stick to the whisky.

"Well Christian," began the little man, "have you appraised Nathaniel of my offer?"

"I have and I am afraid he is a little sceptical," stated the Captain. Nathaniel looked uncomfortable at this divulgence of his doubt.

Devries seemed unperturbed, "Why are you concerned my boy?" he queried between puffs.

"We have been in Cape Town for a very short time, Mr Devries, and within a few hours the Captain here tells me he has secured excellent positions for us with a very rich man he has never met before," he paused. "Surely that in itself is very unusual. Don't I have a right to doubt it?" Davenport and Devries exchanged conspiratorial glances, the philanthropist allowing the Captain the opportunity to answer.

"Nathaniel," he was choosing his words carefully. "Remember that I told you I had attended a gentleman's club last evening. Well the organisation we belong to is dedicated to helping its fellow members, and our benefactor here came to my aid when he discovered our predicament," Davenport chose his words carefully. "And that is as much as we can tell you about that, save to say that Mr Devries is a man who can be totally trusted and will honour everything he says."

Willem Devries rose from his seat anxious to end the conversation, "Gentlemen, now we will eat and eat well. My cook is excellent, I'm sure you will enjoy the fare."

Over dinner, Devries outlined his plans for the two men. He would supply all equipment and personnel to Nathaniel and the Captain necessary to perform their duties, two trained bearers would coach the inexperienced pair in tracking and killing techniques until the men were proficient in the job. It would be gruelling work he advised but he was confident in their ability to learn fast and do a good job.

The repast was sensational, each of the four courses as perfect as the one before. Nathaniel marvelled at the presentation of the food, the wine complimented each course to perfection.

Devries was the perfect host, a man used to entertaining the very highest in society. His dining room, large and well appointed was dominated by the imposing dining table, which could seat fifty easily. This evening the three men sat at one end of the phenomenal structure, built out of mahogany. As they sipped a delectable Madeira, they talked long into the night. By midnight they had agreed to work for Devries and would start immediately.

A different carriage from Devries' stables took the drunken men back to their hotel, the night cool and silent. Nathaniel dropped off to sleep in the coach, only waking up as it pulled up to the hotel entrance.

They sought out their rooms and in his drunken state Nathaniel fell into a deep slumber in his clothes, his thoughts on Sally back in England in the moments before he lapsed into a contented unconsciousness.

CHAPTER 7

Nathaniel lay on his cot in the tent, listening to the sounds from the surrounding countryside, the calls of the Namaqua Dove and the Karoo Korhaan mingling with sounds of armoured crickets. The occasional growl from a large cat completed the scene. Could it be only five years since that first meeting with Devries, he pondered? It had taken him and Christian more than a year of intense instruction by the native bearers to become proficient in the hunting techniques required but now they were skilled as any in the trading organisation.

The man was falling off to sleep when he detected a growl much closer than the others, its low rumbling utterance caused him consternation. It was clearly in the vicinity of the camp and his hand caressed the stock of the double barrelled muzzleloader underneath the cot, ready for any eventuality.

A scream rent the air. Nathaniel leapt to his feet, the gun already in hand and primed in advance. In a second he was out of the tent, crashing by the pole as he rushed to the aid of the bearers sleeping in the area of the camp fire.

Outside utter confusion reigned, he could see at least four lions prowling the encampment. Bearers panicked and ran chaotically, trying to escape the jaws of the beasts but one was being attacked where he had been sleeping, caught unawares. Nathaniel watched a huge male close its teeth around the bearer's skull and with a horrendous popping sound the bone shattered and the animal ripped off the head in a spray of steaming blood, which soaked the animal's pelt and mane in a crimson gush. Furiously, Nathaniel lifted the weapon to his shoulder and fired, striking the animal in the midriff, catapulting its carcass into the night air.

Davenport yelled from his rear, "Nathaniel behind you, behind you." He came face to face with a lioness already charging and almost upon him. He crashed the stock of the rifle into the animal's mouth as it sprang, shattering teeth in the gaping aperture. The smell of the lioness's breath overwhelmed him.

As the attacking creature hit the ground in a cloud of dust, Davenport fired his own weapon hitting it through the head and killing it stone dead. The other lions dashed from the area in a mass of confused flesh, crashing into each other in their haste to escape. One large male stopped at the beginning of some nearby undergrowth and roared a defiant call before turning and padding away into the bush.

With the demise of the lions, bearers who had fled the camp returned within a few minutes from their positions, hiding in nearby scrub. Saul, the slave who lost his life in the attack, was disfigured in death beyond recognition. The head lay on the earth some way from the body, a bloody mess of white cranium and mass of exposed brain.

For the rest of the night, no one in the camp slept. There was a chance the beasts would return, so everyone kept a vigil until light dawned.

Veins of vivid orange punctuated fluffy clouds in the heavens as the sun worked its way up the sky, dispelling early morning coldness and evaporating the dew. Saul remained where he had fallen, covered with a tarpaulin for respect. The bearers were subdued at the loss of their comrade who had constantly smiled while carrying out his work, exposing brilliant white, tombstone teeth.

Over a scant breakfast, Nathaniel tackled Davenport about Saul, "The question is Christian, do we bury the man here or take him back at the end of the hunt?" he asked.

Christian finished eating. "I think we should ask the bearers that question," he replied, calling over Abraham, the head of the native contingent. The man ambled over to the two men, he looked inconsolable, Saul's death had hit the native porters hard.

"Abraham, Mr Davidson and I have been discussing what to do with Saul's remains but we wanted the opinion of his comrades first," Davenport questioned the man tactfully. "The options are to take him back at the end of the hunt or bury him here, we would like to know the feelings of the other men, will you put it to them?"

Nathaniel interjected, "Of course if we bury him here, Abraham, it will be done with due respect," informed the young man.

Abraham acknowledged the suggestions, "Of course," he said in his curiously lilting tone, "I will ask them now." He wandered off unhurriedly to his colleagues and called them together in a circle around him, returning to inform Christian and Davidson the men thought it best if their friend be buried where he lay. Nathaniel was impressed by the unity of the bearers, having noticed throughout the years that, no matter how many times the personnel changed, they formed a strong bond of mutual respect and friendship. Many western men could learn a lesson or two from the teamwork of these proud individuals.

Before the searing heat of the day could build to its exhaustive climax, the men had sunk a grave for their fallen comrade gathering around the now occupied pit, waiting for the service that Davenport had promised earlier in the morning.

He and Nathaniel came to the spot at the head of the grave, the Captain carrying the large Bible he always carried on safari. The man had chosen to keep it brief but dignified beginning.

"The Lord is my shepherd, I shall not want." As he drawled on with the 23rd psalm, his friend looked around at the faces of the bearers, to a man there were tears falling, genuine expressions of grief at the loss of a good friend. Sitting near their tents following the burial, Nathaniel and his friend ate a hastily prepared meal, the hunt was almost complete, the men had already decided the following day's tracking would be the last.

"Nathaniel," opened the Captain, "how do you feel about ending the hunt now, there is really no stomach for it among the natives now and in any case it's been the most successful expedition we've ever done?" The young man was delighted at the suggestion, for some reason this expedition hadn't been a happy one for him.

Normally he loved being in the bush but this time he had felt downcast much of the time.

"I think you're right Christian, it's certainly been a successful trip. Let's just close it now and go home."

Decision made, Nathaniel and the Captain informed the bearers of their intentions and supervised the dismantling of the camp. Davenport checked the wagon and made sure the tusks were secured before harnessing the horses, the milky white ivory shone in the fierce sunlight and spelt a good remuneration for the two men when they returned to Cape Town.

It would take many days to return to the metropolis from their position near Augrabies Falls, hot trekking through the bush with all its attendant dangers.

Three hundred and fifty miles of South Africa lay before them until they would see the city once more, it would take more than a month to arrive.

Near the impressive Hantam mountains the expedition wound its way around the foothills, moving slowly in the heat of the scorching day. As they crested a small mound they spotted a dwelling in the distance placed incongruously among the Cape's rugged territory. It was European in style, giving it an air of absurdity in its wild location, nearby were several low stable buildings. The whole scene shimmered in the heat haze of the day.

In front of the house a large corral was fenced off, containing numerous horses grazing around the confines. Even from a distance the animals were obviously thoroughbred, their sleek lines testimony to a splendid bloodline.

As the men stared at the scene below them, several black tribesmen dashed from the rear of the house, pulling a slave along by his arms and throwing him down in the dirt, where they speared him to death with their short weapons. It was a grizzly scene. Suddenly a white woman raced from the house, making for the corral, long skirt hampering her progress. She had almost reached her objective when a huge tribesman dragged her to earth and began rustling up her skirts. The woman fought like a demon, scratching the man deeply on his face, desperately trying to keep her thighs together but the native was winning, his strength overwhelming.

Nathaniel and Christian kicked their horses into action at the first sight of the horror taking place, bearing down on the tussle as fast as their animals could cover the powdery dirt.

As Davenport rode to the aid of the victim, Nathaniel sped on towards the house to deal with the attackers assailants, firing his saddle rifle into the throng as he rounded the rear of the domicile. The jolting of the galloping horse meant he couldn't hope to fire with any accuracy, his bullets missing their targets by large margins. The sound of gunfire and the daring rider bearing down on them was enough to impel the natives to flight, they scattered in disarray toward the nearby scrub, seeking shelter from the manic horseman.

With the tribesmen gone, Nathaniel trotted his horse back to the scene of the potential rape. Dead on the ground, the body of the woman's attacker rested in a puddle of scarlet with the throat cut wide open. Standing close by, Davenport clasped the sobbing woman to his body, her intense crying making the pair shake uncontrollably.

"The others have gone, Christian," informed Nathaniel. The woman controlled her weeping lifting her head from Davenport's chest and looked directly into Nathaniel's eyes. This was a woman of extraordinary beauty, the skin a smooth tan from the African sun. The raven hair hung past the shoulders, tied back with a blue ribbon, its sheen glinting in the sunlight, full lips of a perfect shape looked astoundingly kissable to the young man and in an instant his heart was given over to the vision before him.

"This is Mary Berhardien, Nathaniel," declared Christian, "she owns the horse ranch here."

"Mrs Behardien, I hope you are not hurt," it was all he could think to say to the beautiful woman before him.

"Your friend saved me Nathaniel," she spoke his name in a lilting fashion, which weakened him inside. "If you hadn't arrived when you did I probably would be dead now and I thank you both for your timely appearance."

The voice was English, there could be no doubt about that. She couldn't be more than twenty-two years old, her bearing showed sophistication, Nathaniel wondering what she was doing here in the austere countryside of the Cape.

"Gentlemen," the singing voice staggered Nathaniel. "Please join me in the house, you will stay to dinner," it was a statement rather than a question.

"We would be delighted, Mrs Behardian," replied Davenport who was looking on in amused fashion at the gaping jaw of his colleague.

Inside, the house was cool. The European furniture, looking brand new, was plentiful but not overstated or excessive. A few frightened slaves stood around as they entered, still apprehensive after the recent attack and the woman busied herself calming them with quiet reassurance. They responded well, eventually going about their tasks in an easier frame of mind. She invited the men to sit and Nathaniel noticed outside that their bearer contingent had arrived and were being tended by other members of the household servants. After the rigours of their journey, the two men sank back in the easy chairs, enjoying a little taste of comfort for the first time in weeks.

Mary excused herself, leaving the two men with a full decanter of whisky from the ornate sideboard. The horses needed tending she informed them, she would be back in an hour or so.

As they sipped the intoxicating liquor in the relaxing sedateness of the house, Nathaniel and Davenport reflected on an eventful expedition, before drifting off into slumber, the whisky had exerted its soporific effect.

It was late evening when the younger of the two men woke with a start. Nathaniel could not understand what had dragged him from his slumber, he looked around the room, now softly lit and noiseless. Christian sat opposite, still lost in deep dozing. His mouth drooped open and the empty whisky tumbler had fallen to the floor. A striking of metal echoed from the kitchen area, a single blow but enough to persuade him that someone was preparing a meal, reinforced by the wonderful aroma of roast pork. In the kitchen,

Mary Behardien and a girl slave busied themselves with food, attempting to make it as quietly as possible. The white woman looked around as Nathaniel entered the room.

"Nathaniel," she beamed, "you're awake, how are you feeling?"

"I think our expedition took more out of us than we thought," he exclaimed. "And the whisky was the last straw. Christian is still asleep."

She sat down at the simple wooden table in the centre of the room. He joined her, sitting alongside and smelling a wonderful perfume from her proximity. The native girl continued to potter around the room avoiding them as she peeled vegetables and checked progress of the meat.

Nathaniel gazed into Mary's eyes until he realised that it could be discomforting for her and he shifted the focus of attention elsewhere.

"What are you doing in this part of the Cape, Mary?" he questioned.

"I married Paul Behardien three years ago, he was much older than me, I was nineteen and he forty-four." She poured them both a glass of milk from a jug in the centre of the pine table. "He wanted to breed thoroughbred horses," the woman explained, "so we purchased some high class blood stock in Cape Town and settled here." There was an uncomfortable pause. "About a year ago, Paul decided to break in a stallion we had reared from foal," she looked tearful as she continued. "At first it seemed to be going fine, the horse seemed really calm, taking to his first ride well but as he neared the corral fence the animal went berserk, Paul was thrown off and his head struck a fence pole," the catching in her throat was worsening and she choked. "It took him two days to die, Nathaniel." As he looked at her bowed head, a feeling of crushing pity flooded his soul. He wanted to hold her to his chest and tell her it would be alright.

Mary's teardrops splashed on the surface of the pine table, leaving areas of deepening discolouration in the wood. No words were spoken for several minutes, he just let her sob, allowed her to grieve for her loss. It was evident that she had never broken down in this fashion before.

Eventually the woman drew herself up and composed herself, drying her eyes on a nearby towel.

"I'm sorry Nathaniel, I didn't mean to do that," she rose from the table, pacing around the kitchen now the maid had left. "You and Christian are the first white people I've seen since Paul died. I think I just needed a friendly face and someone to let me get it all out."

"It must have been truly awful for you Mary," Nathaniel sympathised, "I'm just pleased I could be here for you." A glance passed between them, the man thought it held more than mere gratitude, it seemed to disclose deep affection but he dismissed the thought as an imaginary aspiration on his part.

"Perhaps you should join Christian, dinner will be a little while yet," she informed him.

Nathaniel suspected that the outpouring of emotion had made her intensely uncomfortable, that she needed some time to recover from the discomfiture, he returned to his companion who had woken from his slumber.

It was past nine o'clock when dinner was finally complete, the men and their host moved out onto the verandah and sat in the cool of the night, listening to the noises of the cape, eerily echoing with the sound of beasts. They talked well into the night, Mary describing how she and her parents had moved from their home in England and come to South Africa, how she had met Paul Behardien and fallen in love with the dashing man. As she talked with great fondness about him, Nathaniel felt twinges of jealousy as he looked on her lovable face, showing intense warmth at the memories of her husband. The young man felt mortified at his unjust attitude. At midnight, they retired to their rooms and in the darkness Nathaniel thought of her for a long time until he fell into a disturbed sleep.

CHAPTER 8

Morning dawned majestically, streaks of scarlet radiance punctuating the small amounts of grey cloud in the heavens. Christian Davenport entered his friend's room,

"Good morning," he chortled, "a fine morning, Nathaniel, are you ready for breakfast?"

"Lead me to it," replied the man, feeling as cheerful as his companion looked. It was amazing he reflected, how one night in a comfortable bed, could restore the soul.

In the dining room, silver serving trays were arranged with military precision on the sideboard, they contained all manner of breakfast fare, bacon, eggs, sausage, tomatoes and kidneys. A wonderful hunger inducing aroma emanated from the metal dishes, the two men selected their favourites and sat down to eat in respectful silence, breakfast was a time for contemplation rather than conversation.

Several minutes later, Mary swept into the dining room, she looked radiant thought Nathaniel, who by now was hopelessly besotted with her. No hint of the previous day's ordeal seemed in evidence and her smile lit up the room.

"Nathaniel, Christian," enthused the woman, " I hope you slept well?"

"Admirably," replied Christian, a forkful of bacon and tomato hovering between his plate and lips. "When you've spent the best part of six weeks lying in restrictive cots in a tent, your comfortable beds are a godsend."

"It was the best sleep I've had since we left Cape Town," agreed Davenport's compatriot, "a truly restful night."

"I'm so pleased you were comfortable," she exclaimed, choosing her breakfast from the dishes and joining them for the leisurely meal.

After the early breakfast, Davenport excused himself, saying that he wanted to walk alone in the nearby scrub for a while. It pleased Nathaniel who knew he would have a little while alone with Mary. They chose to sit on the verandah once more, watching Christian set out on his long stroll. He disappeared around the side of the house, the trademark rolling gait always a source of amusement for Nathaniel.

"What are your plans when you return to Cape Town?" inquired the woman, "will you be returning this way in the future?"

It gladdened him to think she would like to see him again, "I think I can safely guarantee that you will see us once more," he smiled at her and in return she beamed back at him.

They talked for almost an hour, two people sparring with the first social niceties of love. Although neither of them spoke candidly of their feelings, both aware of the burgeoning emotion but Mary was appalled at the feelings so soon after the loss of her husband.

The reverie was broken by the yelping of a slave as he tore towards the house.

"What is it, Jeremiah?" demanded Mary.

"It's the other gentleman," the man panted, "out there in the scrub," he pointed a bony finger at the low lying bushes.

In a second, Nathaniel was racing across the ground to the place indicated, Mary followed with equal haste. They realised the severity of the situation without having to be told of its exact nature.

Davenport was lying on his back, breathing laboured, eyes glazed. As the two people bent to his aid, Nathaniel noted his friend was becoming delirious from his incoherent mumblings.

Jeremiah arrived at the scene, indicating a slithering mass disappearing into the scrub, its greeny grey body propelling it as if by magic.

Christian's mouth opened and closed as if he was trying to say something but no words poured from the stirring orifice.

Black Mamba venom was one of the most toxic poisons in South Africa and Nathaniel knew it meant almost certain death for his friend, probably within a few hours.

"Help me, Jeremiah," he demanded, as he slid his hands under Christian's arms. The slave took the feet and they edged slowly out of the bushes, Davenport's body, limp and heavy, made the journey to the house arduous.

They dropped the man unceremoniously on the bed, pleased to be rid of the weight, and Mary dismissed the pair so she could administer to Christian's needs.

In truth, she was painfully aware there was little she could do for him but keep him warm and try and feed him, if he could stomach that. He would perspire excessively one minute and shiver violently the next.

It took a few minutes to remove his clothes and get him between the sheets, he moaned incoherently as the toxic liquid coursed through his veins. Once she had gotten him comfortable, she called Nathaniel back, a look of concern agonisingly etched in his boyish features.

Davenport's face had drained of colour and a dirty grey sheen began to occupy his features.

For the next two hours, Nathaniel and Mary wiped the man's perspiring face as he thrashed about beneath the bed covers, he became coherent but only briefly.

"Nathaniel," he croaked through parched lips, "I've had some ideas about how we can start our own business."

"Don't speak Christian," advised his friend. "Save your strength until you recover, we'll talk about it then."

After a few minutes of general talk, Davenport lapsed back into confusion, the flailing started once more, only this time it was considerably more violent.

Several hours passed, the man's respiratory functions becoming weaker, more laboured and Nathaniel knew his friend's time was near. He and Mary fought for him but in the end there was nothing they could do to save him.

In the cooler conditions of the evening, Christian Davenport passed over to his maker, the actual death peaceful and dignified. After the violent threshing he died like a man, slipping away quietly.

"I'm so sorry Nathaniel," wept Mary as she lifted the blanket to cover the man's face, "I'll leave you alone with him."

She left the room, glancing back at the man who stood, shoulders slumped, looking like a wizened old stick of a man.

Looking down at his friend's corpse, he began to cry. In five years Christian had become a friend without equal, someone he had come to trust and rely on implicitly. The grief he was feeling attacked his soul voraciously. How long he stayed with the corpse he wasn't sure but night had invaded the heavens and the room was in darkness, only faintly lit by beams of the full moon, streaming in at the window.

He felt a hand on his shoulder, the angelic face of Mary gazed down on him compassionately. She eased him towards the door and downstairs to the kitchen.

Mary prepared some soup for him, it would be the first food he'd eaten since breakfast but he found it difficult to eat. Nathaniel played around with the liquid in the bowl, the woman cajoling him to sip it. It took half an hour to get him to finish it, there was no resolve to consume it. He had no idea of the flavour and he left the roll she had put out on a side plate.

"He died knowing you were his friend, Nathaniel, there is much comfort in that," the woman stated.

The words were banal, giving little relief to him but he knew she was trying to soothe him in his time of grief. It was typical of her to be there to succour him, he knew she was right but somehow it was scant consolation.

"Will you take him back to Cape Town or would you like to bury him here?" she continued.

Something about the word bury stressed the finality to him and he broke down once more, Mary rising and coming to stand behind his chair. She wrapped her arms around him, allowing him the necessary period of his anguish. With that simple illustration of kindness, Nathaniel knew he could never be without the woman again.

CHAPTER 9

Christian Davenport's funeral was a simple affair. Mary had suggested a spot to Nathaniel beneath a Transvaal Gardenia tree at the edge of the scrubland, it was a peaceful site and there he'd taken her advice with just a nod of his head.

The bearers dug the grave at first light, the last act of respect for a man they liked and esteemed. Now they stood, heads bowed, genuine grief etched on their features.

Nathaniel walked along the line accompanied by Mary, stopping at the bearer called Abraham, whose features were wreathed in smiles.

"What the hell are you smiling about Abraham?" he exploded.

"Mr. Nathaniel," replied the slave in his rich deep voice. "The others feel sorrow and so do I but I also feel that Mr. Davenport lived a full life and I think would he would not want us to grieve for his soul but rejoice in his existence." He stared directly into Nathaniel's eyes, "I think he would want the latter don't you?"

It shook Nathaniel who, up to this minute had only wanted to mourn. As the man spoke he realised that he was right, Christian was the type of man who would want people to remember him as he was in life. Nathaniel touched Abraham gently on the shoulder, his eyes showing appreciation to the bearer.

At that moment the sadness lifted from his soul and Nathaniel viewed the funeral in a different light, while it was still a solemn occasion, it could be viewed as a celebration and for the sake of his friend, the man determined to be positive. When the coffin had been laid in the earth, the bearers looked to him to say some words. He gathered himself.

"Christian Davenport was my friend," he began falteringly. "He was a man who loved life and was as loyal as the day is true. I was only privileged to know him for a painfully short time and over that period, he was steadfast in his friendship to me and I will miss him greatly." Mary looked on with pride at the man she knew she had fallen deeply in love with, the handsome face lined from past sorrow but what she loved about him most was his compassion. Not even Paul had made her feel like this young man did, it scared and excited her at the same time. Nathaniel talked directly at the body in the coffin.

"Christian, the time we spent together was the most wonderful of my life, I pray to God that He grants you the peace you richly deserve. Goodbye my friend." Picking up some dusty earth, he cast it into the hole. With a resigned shrug he walked away from the grave, into the scrub to be with his thoughts for a while. The woman watched him go, realising company was the last thing he needed but it didn't stop her from feeling distressed for him.

By the time he returned to the house night had fallen, its cloak all encompassing. An impenetrable cover of cloud hid the moon and the first huge droplets of rain splashed into the dirt, its commencement cooling the night further. The globules of liquid tossing dirt upwards and outwards from their points of impact, like a series of tiny meteors impacting the earth.

Mary stood in the hallway as he entered, he could tell she had been crying. There was an electricity between them now, its power too much for the pair to overlook anymore. She rushed to him and fell into his arms.

"I was so worried about you Nathaniel, you've been gone hours." Her breath caught between sobs.

He pulled her to him with desperation. " I love you Mary." It was a simple statement and came from the realisation he must tell her how he felt and take the consequences if the feeling wasn't reciprocated.

The lips held up for him to kiss dispelled any doubts he may have had, for several minutes they revelled in the touch of each other, frenzy of first passion vanquishing any uncertainty.

Through the developing storm, the two lovers entwined, no heed was paid to the enormous claps of thunder or the flashing forks of lightning. Afterwards they lay quietly watching the scene out of the window. It seemed no words were necessary, they were lost in the magnificence of the emotion. Mary fell asleep and he watched her for hours until he too succumbed to morpheus' bidding.

Voices dragged him from slumber. It was morning, he looked down but Mary had gone. He felt a pang of disappointment inside, wanting to kiss her again, he rose dressing quickly. As he donned his apparel he identified her voice outside the window along with a man's he didn't recognise.

Philip Brent was a powerful and handsome individual. Mary introduced him as the overseer of the farm, he'd been delivering horses for transit at the recently formed city of Port Elizabeth. Despite his recent arrival after a long journey and his dusty appearance, the man carried an air of refinement, he addressed Nathaniel warmly following the introductions.

"It appears Mary has a lot to thank you for Nathaniel," commended Brent. "She has told me of the loss of your friend, I'm very sorry for you, she says he was a good man." It was opening a raw wound to talk about Christian.

"Yes," Nathaniel replied. "The best," he changed the subject. "Have you had a successful trip, Mr. Brent?"

"The horses we breed here are the best you can find in Africa, Nathaniel, we are fortunate to always have them well accepted."

"Mary," Brent excused himself, "I need to clean up and check on the horses; till later Nathaniel." He walked off to his quarters at the edge of the compound, lifting his hat to Mary as he went.

At breakfast she tackled Nathaniel about his plans. The last thing he wanted to do was leave having found her but he had a responsibility to Devries to deliver his consignment.

"I must deliver the ivory to Cape Town, Mary," he explained.

"Then I will come too," stated the woman.

He had hoped she'd say so but his face displayed concern. "You have your horses to consider and you are running a business here

Mary," he knew he was right but it pained him to try and put her off.

The woman set her jaw, "Now that Philip has returned I can leave the running of the place in his capable hands, Paul had full confidence in his ability and so have I," she advised. "Unless of course you don't want me to join you."

Accepting the situation gladly, he suggested they leave that day. Outside he assembled the bearers, instructing them to make ready for the trip. Singing as they worked, they were happy to be going on once again, the smiles showed that.

In the house, Mary gathered her things together for the journey, Nathaniel advising her to travel light. By early afternoon the party was organised, Brent had been given instructions by his employer and he watched as the ivory cart and its horses made their way slowly out of the confines of the house grounds and into the surrounding bush. A gaggle of accompanying bearers followed on foot, Abraham the cheerful porter at the head of the pack. Since his conversation to Nathaniel at Davenport's interment he had become the ivory tracker favourite, a good and intelligent man whose infectious humour kept the workers morale high.

CHAPTER 10

It took four weeks of incessant travel to reach the outskirts of the city of Cape Town, days of mind deadening boredom, punctuated by nights of unbelievable pleasure at Mary's cot.

Finally they rode into the enclosure of the Cape Transit Trading Company, a mountain of ivory heaped in the centre of the complex, natives with glistening ebony torsos, moving it piece by piece into the nearby workshops for fashioning into statuettes and other products.

Devries stood at the centre of the activity, directing operations, his familiar features cracked into a wide grin when he saw Nathaniel and the party ride in. As he dismounted, Devries took Nathaniel by the hand.

"Good to see you back, my boy," he looked towards the gates of the company, expecting to see Davenport bringing up the rear. "How is Christian?" he enquired.

Nathaniel's face clouded, "I'm afraid he's dead, Willem."

Devries was shell shocked, his crestfallen face showed a great magnitude of grief. "My God, how?" he stammered. The man's desolation pained Nathaniel, the depths of his despair acute.

"Snake bite, Willem," the young man informed him, "a Black Mamba bit him as he walked in the bush." Mary had now dismounted and was standing next to him. "I'd like you to meet Mary Behardien, Willem." Despite the shock, the Dutchman composed himself to acknowledge the beautiful woman before him.

"It's a great pleasure to meet you my dear," the words were uttered honestly but there was little enthusiasm in them. "Come to my office Nathaniel, there are a number of things we must discuss." Willem's face seemed strangely persistent, "Mary can take tea in the boardroom while we talk, if that is acceptable." She nodded, all three making their way into the cool of the company buildings. Devries assigned his secretary to look after the lady visitor and led Nathaniel along the familiar route to his office.

They entered, Willem offering his employee a chair, he moved to the drinks cabinet while Nathaniel sat. The older man passed a drink to him as he ensconced himself behind the huge monster of a desk.

"Nathaniel, you remember how Christian informed you of his success in gaining employment here for you both five years ago?" began Willem.

"Of course," replied the man.

"Well he probably didn't tell you the whole story," continued Devries. "It may not mean much to you but Christian and I were brother Freemasons and on the night you arrived in our beautiful city, he and Captain Smith, another of our brotherhood, attended my lodge here in the city." Nathaniel was ignorant of the organisation Willem described but allowed the man to continue without interruption.

Devries rose, staring out of the window, gazing at the scene in the yard before beginning again.

"The Freemasons are a fraternity dedicated to the brotherhood of mankind is all I can say; Christian and I talked on the evening of your arrival; it was through that conversation that I offered you both employment with my company. I knew him to be a man of the highest character and anyone travelling with him to be equally dependable."

"We were fortunate to be given the opportunity," said Nathaniel, who knew there was more to come.

"Christian asked me to do something for him at the start of your association with me," Devries poured himself another whisky and re-seated himself. "He asked me to look after his affairs in the event of his death and it appears I will have to carry out those wishes, although it pains me to realise we won't see him again."

"He must have placed great trust in you, Willem," asserted Nathaniel.

"My boy, I think you better prepare yourself for a shock," the employer cautioned before continuing, "I know you are unaware of much of Christian Davenport's past but he was a very wealthy man; the fact of the matter is that Christian had no surviving relatives and has left his entire estate to you, it amounts to some £20,000."

The announcement stunned Nathaniel. It took him several seconds to recover. "I had no idea Christian was well off," he declared, "although I suspected he must have a little means at his disposal; we never went without anything prior to joining the company." The man was struggling to come to terms with the news. Following his discussion with Devries, Nathaniel sought Mary out, briefly explaining his windfall to her.

"That's wonderful news," she gushed, delighted he was set for the rest of his life by Davenport's generosity.

Nathaniel made up his mind instantly, "I love you beyond words Mary. Will you marry me?" They had discussed the possibility on the arduous journey from her home, no decisions had been made, the woman concerned about marrying so quickly after her husband's passing.

The new circumstances seemed to dispel her reservations, she knew she was in love with him, more deeply than she had been with Paul.

"Yes if you want me Nathaniel, I'm yours."

They fell against each other, grasping each other's bodies like a starving man clutches at food, mouths fastening in a passionate hysteria of kissing, desperate in intensity.

"My God," he breathed, "I love you so much Mary, I'll make you the happiest woman in the world or I'll die in the attempt."

"Just love me, my darling, that's all I need; just be there for me and never leave me, that's all I ever want." It was said with such conviction that, in that moment, he knew the depths of her feelings undeniably.

In the courtyard, Abraham supervised the unloading of the ivory as Nathaniel and Mary arrived at the scene of sweating labour. A huge, milky tusk was in the process of being offloaded, taking three bearers to lift it from its propped up position against the side wall of the cart. It was a magnificent specimen, probably the best the two men had ever come across and Nathaniel thought back on the regal bull elephant who'd provided it. He had become used to culling the creatures, although this animal's death had pained him when he saw it sink to its knees and collapse on the ground, its steely grey hide was peppered with scars from violent battles with other males over the years.

As they watched, the twin tusk was removed from the cart, not quite as large as the predecessor but still imposing in its splendour. Porters transported the ivory directly to the workshops, this quality of product was always given preference by the craftsmen, who could fashion fine artefacts from the ivory's excellence.

"Abraham, finish the unloading of the cart and then take the men for something to eat, tell them to return in the morning and I will pay them then," instructed Nathaniel.

There was a task Nathaniel had to do which he wasn't looking forward to, he had to notify the authorities of his friend's death.

CHAPTER 11

The Governor's residence was another architectural spectacle in Cape Town, surrounded by affluent homes in a quiet residential area. Nathaniel and Mary presented themselves to the British sentry at the gate, imparting the time of their appointment to him. With a snapped salute, the man directed them to the entrance of Government House and continued with his duty.

Inside the building, it was sepulchral in its quietness, the expansive hallway rich in painting and statue art.

They had been shown to chairs positioned along one wall by a Lieutenant who told them that he would inform Major Bryant of their presence. The Major dealt with these matters on behalf of the crown, advised the Lieutenant.

"Mr Davidson, Mrs Behardien, Major Bryant at your service, would you care to join me in my office?" He was small in stature with a ginger moustache that matched his hair, the dress uniform immaculately pressed with razor sharp creases in the trousers and tunic.

As the three seated themselves in the Major's office, Nathaniel came straight to the point, "Major, I have to report the death of a British subject here in South Africa."

The man selected paper from the top of a sheaf and a pen, holding the quill above the sheet in preparation of the information.

"Name, please?" he asked.

"Christian Davenport," responded Nathaniel.

"When and where did this occur?" continued Bryant as he scribbled on the paper.

"Approximately a month ago near the Hantaam mountains, at Mrs Behardien's horse farm," he indicated Mary with a wave of his hand.

"It must have been very distressing for you my dear," sympathised Theodore Bryant, his brow furrowed with feigned concern.

She nodded, "Christian Davenport was a good man," she stated, "of course it was distressing." Mary didn't like Bryant, something upset her about him and she could not identify what it was.

The officer turned his attention back to Nathaniel. "And the circumstance of the death was what exactly?" The young man rose and paced the room, "A Black Mamba bite, he died several hours later from the venom."

Major Bryant completed the formalities, Nathaniel making their excuses, leaving the residence without the proffered refreshments. Theodore Bryant watched them leave, his eyes never leaving the woman's form. He found her a very sensual creature, reluctantly he turned from the window to deal with his correspondence.

Numerous horse drawn carriages negotiated the thoroughfares of the city, to Nathaniel the crackling sound of the wheels over the uneven roads, a reminder of similar sounds from his days in England. The general hubbub was deafening, as he and Mary strode along the busy pathways.

They skirted the harbour, Nathaniel spying the sleek lines of a ship he knew well. Lady Bamburgh rocked at anchor on the tide. He could hardly believe his eyes and he wondered if Smith remained her master.

"Mary, we must sail over to that ship in the harbour," he indicated the craft with his finger, "she's the ship that brought me here five years ago."

A price had been negotiated with one of the port boat keepers at the dock and they were just boarding, when a rich fruity voice hailed Nathaniel.

"Good God, Nathaniel Davidson, how are you my boy?" Ebenezer Smith's face was wreathed in smiles, Nathaniel could see genuine pleasure in the handsome features as the Captain climbed onto the dock from one of his vessel's long boats.

"It's excellent to see you Ebenezer, what brings you to these shores on this occasion?" the man asked.

"Company business as usual," answered the Captain. "And who is this?" he enquired.

"This is Mary Behardien, Ebenezer."

She held out a cool hand which Smith took, bowing slightly.

"Delighted to make your acquaintance, Mary, any friend of Nathaniel's is a special friend of mine."

"We're to be married," Nathaniel proudly informed the Captain.

Smith beamed even more widely, "Then let me congratulate you both, I hope your prospective bride understands what she is taking on," he playfully remarked.

"Only the best man in the world, Ebenezer," she advised, slipping her arm through her fiancés, staring affectionately into his eyes.

A sailor moved up to the party's position, addressing Smith, "Captain, what would you like me to do with the men?"

Ebenezer turned to face Nathaniel once more, "I'm sorry Nathaniel, I need to attend to business, perhaps you and Mary will join me for dinner this evening on board the Lady Bamburgh." The men clasped hands.

"Of course, Ebenezer, we would be delighted to accept," he agreed.

"Until this evening, then," Smith said, joining his crew as they proceeded along the dock.

The afternoon was as warm as any Nathaniel had encountered in South Africa as he and Mary spent a relaxing day seeing the sights of Cape Town, Table Mountain dominated the skyline, rekindling memories for Nathaniel of the day he first observed its flat top. The city had grown up around the base of the mount, spreading ever outwards.

William Devries had made a house available to him and Christian at a modest rent early in their employment with his company, the lovers made their way to the small dwelling and dressed for dinner once they had unpacked their belongings.

A longboat had been despatched to the quay by Smith for their convenience. On board, the Captain waited for them near the rail as the two people climbed onto the deck.

"Good evening, my friends," he welcomed them to the Lady Bamburgh. Looking around the ship, Nathaniel noted some changes and improvements since its near destruction by the storm a few years previously.

Smith's cabin hadn't changed much from his memories of it, the small cot remained the focal point of the room, surprisingly diminutive for the man's size.

Once seated at the table, set impressively for dinner, Ebenezer began talking, "It's so good to see you, Nathaniel, but where is Christian?" he smiled.

Nathaniel and Mary exchanged distressed glances, there was no easy way to break the news, they knew. "Dead, Ebenezer," the words pained him and as he saw shock spread across Smith's face, along with a watery secretion in the Captain's eyes, he pitied him.

Smith rose and turned away from his guests, staring through the cabin windows at the unique mountain in the distance.

"I'm sorry Ebenezer, there was no easy way to say it," sympathised the man, "it happened more than a month ago." The Captain was silent, hardly able to take in the solemn information. For some minutes no words were spoken in the cabin, an uncomfortable period for Nathaniel and Mary as they stared at the broad back of the man at the windows.

In a desperate attempt to break the lull, Nathaniel searched for words, "How have you been, Ebenezer?"

The master of the vessel replied without turning, "Well, Nathaniel, I'm well," he drawled, the voice depressed.

"And still Captain of the Lady Bamburgh," his guest declared.

"Not for much longer," advised Smith, rejoining his visitors. "This may be my last voyage for the company."

Nathaniel was surprised, "Why is that, my friend?" he asked.

The Captain sat down sipping at a glass of sherry. "For some time I have been saving money to purchase my own ship and finally

I have managed to attain it. She is named the Adventuress, presently docked in Portsmouth undergoing refit."

"That's wonderful," exclaimed his friend. "So now you are master of your own fate, I'm so pleased for you."

Dinner proceeded and Smith seemed to have recovered from the news of the tragic demise of Christian Davenport. The evening was pleasant, the food proving delicious, a marked improvement to the fare served on his previous visit to the vessel, reflected Nathaniel.

In the flickering orange light of the cabin lanterns, which cast mysterious shadows on the walls, the mood improved dramatically as the wine flowed. Joyous laughter interspersed the conversation, Mary watched the renewed friendship of the two men flourish as only male friendship could. She excused herself on the pretext of needing fresh air, declining Nathaniel's offer to join her.

"No, you and Ebenezer have some time alone," she said, opening the door and disappearing down the companionway.

"A remarkable woman," said Ebenezer as the door closed. He sought out a bottle of rum and poured stiff measures for him and his guest.

"You must miss Christian enormously?" the Captain's face had clouded once more. Over the next half hour, Nathaniel explained Davenport's phenomenal generosity to him, the Captain not at all surprised at the man's actions toward his companion.

It was well after midnight when Mary returned from her foray onto the deck, cold from the dank sea air. Smith escorted them to the deck for departure.

"Will you come back to Cape Town, Ebenezer?" asked his friend.

Smith smiled, "You can rely on it, my friend, I intend to make this my base of operations with my new ship."

"Perhaps we could retain your services for the transportation of our horses," suggested Mary.

The way she had already begun talking in the context of him and her, gladdened Nathaniel. It showed the commitment she had to them, he squeezed her hand in the moonlight and felt a response in return.

"I would be delighted to be of service to you both," Smith told them.

As they rowed off into the bay, Nathaniel watched the Captain standing at the rail, his hand raised in farewell. It was at that moment that he realised his acute fondness for the seafarer.

CHAPTER 12

Several days later, Nathaniel and Mary were quietly married by the British Governor at his residence, it was a simple ceremony, conducted by special arrangement. The service was rapid and as far as the bride and groom were concerned, it was just how they hoped it would be.

Devries agreed to be best man, turning out in his finery and proving a credit to Nathaniel who knew he would fill the role admirably. Sir Thomas Collins, the crown representative, solemnly carried out the procedure, his best dress white uniform, gleamed in the afternoon sunshine. The Governor's wife Isabella, acted as Matron of Honour, her relaxed deportment a contrast to Mary's edgy behaviour.

The ritual went off without a hitch and afterwards they dined in the grandeur of the residence dining room. Lady Collins had confided in Mary that the Governor was a deeply romantic man, despite, his businesslike exterior. Hors d'oeuvres and champagne were served by immaculate stewards, standing erect and motionless, the silver salvers rigid in gloved hands.

In addition to the bridal party, the Governor, his wife and Devries, Major Bryant and his wife had also been invited to attend along with sundry officers of the Governor's staff. Five couples and two unmarried servicemen joined them at the ornate dining table, their regimental uniforms, elaborately colourful.

The meal was served, its quality could not be equalled by the finest restaurants in the world. As coffee was brought, the Governor rose to his feet, slightly from the after effects of the wine but it fell to him to make the first speech.

"Mr and Mrs Davidson, it has always been my custom to refrain from giving newly married couples advice and I have no intention of starting now," he remarked. "So I will content myself with some general observations about marriage and mine in particular."

Lady Collins whispered something in Nathaniel's ear which the Governor observed.

"I see my wife is already wondering what I am about to say, so we will put her out of her misery. Marriage is a journey of exploration for the participants. There is no map to aid their passage, no manual to guide their actions, it is a completely unknown odyssey," he paused for effect. "The journey may not always go well, there may be obstacles along the way, which seem insurmountable but you will face these together and come through closer people and if you are as fortunate as I've been with my choice of life companion, you will survive the tribulations with a rock steady love and a partner of rare quality."

"Sit down you old fool," Lady Collins was suffering acute embarrassment at the eulogy.

"Ladies and Gentlemen, I give you the bride and groom," it was his last act of defiance to his wife.

The guests rose and drank the health of Mary and Nathaniel, who seemed equally discomfited by it all. In the background Willem Devries looked on fondly, realising it was his turn to speak next.

The speech demonstrated his resolute liking for Nathaniel, much of the address concentrating on the man's unwavering loyalty to him and his company. When he came to talk about the unique relationship between Nathaniel and Christian, the young man's eyes watered. There was a void for Nathaniel, not having his best friend at his marriage, he thought of how the man might have made the best man's speech if he had been alive. At the end of the formalities Lady Collins rose.

"Ladies," she exhorted, "I believe we should retire and prepare the bride for her wedding night; it will give the men a little time for their brandy and cigars." She lead the way to the dining room doors, where a steward swung them wide, the ladies trooped out after the matriarchal figure including Mary, who looked back affectionately at her new husband.

When they had gone, the gentlemen moved to join the Governor at the head of the table.

"It's extraordinarily kind to allow us to spend our wedding night here in the residency, Sir Thomas," thanked Nathaniel.

"Think nothing of it, my boy," retorted the crown representative to South Africa. "Just see that you have a night to remember," he winked.

Two of the assembled officers began conversing with the Governor about political business, the man stopping them in their tracks. "This is hardly the time or the place to be talking of such matters," he advised them, "unless it is urgent kindly save these matters until morning gentlemen."

The men looked suitably chastised by the attitude of the Governor and Devries, who was sitting on his friend's left, placed his hand on Nathaniel's arm, "I have something to say, my boy," the man looked troubled.

"What is it, Willem?"

"I didn't want to bring this up tonight, Nathaniel, but I have no choice. The business has not been going well of late and I am afraid the bank has lost patience and foreclosed."

Devries looked devastated, the man wondering how he had got through the day looking so happy when this pressure was on his shoulders. They were talking in hushed tones, Nathaniel glancing around to ensure no one was listening but the men were laughing and drinking to a man.

Nathaniel struggled to find words to say to his dejected friend. "Is this final?" he questioned, "no chance of a reprieve?"

"I'm afraid not," Devries informed him. "In truth, its been going on for a while; I thought I could turn the business around but the more I continued trading the more I lost, to the point now where I am financially ruined."

A loud guffaw exploded from the other men at the table, in response to a bawdy joke related by a Guard's officer. The others were taking no notice of the men's conversation.

Devries seemed to shrink in stature as he told his friend the news, his slumped figure in the chair looked wretched, Nathaniel feeling for the man.

"What will you do, Willem?" Devries looked at him resignedly,

"Sell the house and any other assets I still have, that should keep the wolf from the door for a while."

"But your Freemasonry friends, couldn't they assist you in some way?" The moment Nathaniel said it he knew it was the wrong thing to utter. Willem was one of the proudest men he had ever known, there would be no way he would request charity and even less chance of him accepting any, should it be offered, Devries chose not to dignify the question with an answer.

Later, as he and Mary sat on the verandah in the rapidly reducing heat of the evening, he recounted Devries' decline to his wife. She was full of pity for his plight but her priority was Nathaniel.

"At least you are independently wealthy now, my love," she said staring into his eyes, the pools of piercing green were his most striking feature and when he gazed lovingly into her own, she dissolved like a giddy schoolgirl. "The horse farm will remain a source of income for us too," she continued.

He sighed before speaking, "Mary, I need a project of my own, something I can take on from scratch and make successful; the fact is, I need to know that I have it in me to succeed by my own efforts," his jaw was set in an act of steely determination.

His wife sympathised, she had come to realise his ambitious nature and his doggedness. He was young, driven by a desire to achieve by his own merits and he needed to fulfil his aspirations as rapidly as possible.

In her family, marriage meant a woman's compliance to her husband's wishes. "Then darling, you will have to follow your heart," she smiled, "and I will be with you in whatever you do."

It was a belief in him few had ever shown before. He felt pride in his new wife, he would never be able to articulate. That one moment demonstrated her love, commitment and belief in her choice of partner which terrified Nathaniel. If he succeeded all well and good but if he failed, how could he live with himself, knowing that he had let her down?

"Do you have something in mind, sweetheart?" she asked him.

"Yes, as a matter of fact I have, Mary." Before he left Willem to his port in the dining room with the other men, Nathaniel discussed the very same ambitions with his friend. Devries recommended that he consider the wine trade, which he said was growing at a phenomenal rate. It was a very important facet of South African trade he had informed him and would continue to be successful, with its established export routes to Britain and the North American continent.

"Devries made a suggestion that I consider the wine trade," he stated. "Apparently it's burgeoning just now and he knows a vineyard owner who is looking to sell because he is retiring."

A look of concern spread over Mary's features. "It's a very specialist business Nathaniel," she cautioned him, "do you have any knowledge of it?"

"Not at the moment, but with my newly acquired wealth, I should be able to employ someone who does," he informed her. "He can deal with the growing aspects of the business and I will deal with the administration of the company until I can learn the rudiments of the trade."

They retired to bed. After they were spent from lovemaking, Nathaniel lay holding his new bride, thinking of new adventures ahead. All he wanted to do was make the woman proud of him and watching her in slumber, he knew that he had found his soulmate.

Without warning, he thought of Sally and smiled. Their brief encounter and his feelings then, were simply the first steps on the ladder of experience in his young life. He knew his emotions for her were infatuation, not love. A curious detachment was how he viewed this important step in his life but as he watched the slumbering form of his wife and her angelic face in sleep, he knew perfectly the difference between infatuation and true love.

Menacing and dismal grey boiling clouds, heralded the morning. As Nathaniel awoke the first drops of rain pattered rhythmically against the window panes. While he looked out on the drab colourless day, the flow of water grew in intensity, battering the glass with a rumbling reverberation.

Mary woke, startled by the noise, she was in the half world between unconsciousness and arousal. For several seconds she was unsure of her whereabouts, until she spotted her husband, staring out of the window at the intensity of the squall, "Good morning, sweetheart," she drawled, her voice thick with the dryness of morning throat.

He left the gloomy scene and crossed to her, bending to gather the woman in his arms, kissing her almost violently, the lips crushing together in passionate fervour.

"Come back to bed," she demanded impishly.

"I would love to, Mary, but I promised to meet Willem and the vineyard owner this morning, I'll have to go soon."

"Don't you think it's a bit premature to be thinking of doing this, my love?" Mary asked.

"It's something I have to do," he reiterated from the night before. With a sigh she accepted his conviction.

"Would you like me to come with you?"

"This is something I need to do on my own, beloved."

The premises of the Cape Transit Trading Company shocked the man as his carriage plunged through the pillared gate posts. In the familiar courtyard, where once ivory had been graded, the assets of the company were laid out. Furniture was dotted everywhere, brought into the open to ease the auctioneer's work. Fortunately the rain had stopped but shimmering pools dotted the enclosure.

The sale started at noon but a crowd of people already milled around, scrutinising the property in advance, opening drawers and examining the upholstery on chairs. It was a sickening sight to Nathaniel who watched Devries' life about to be sold off piece by piece.

Willem was sitting on one of two remaining chairs in his now Spartan office, a portly man of about sixty occupied the other seat. He was sweating profusely, the flushed ruby face a dangerous indication of impending medical difficulties. Devries himself looked lost, the screwed lines on his face showing the extent of his despondency. At Nathaniel's appearance, he made a huge effort to smile.

"Nathaniel, my boy, good day," he exclaimed, greeting his friend with a warm handshake. "May I introduce Mr Lucas Redelighuys, who owns the Redelighuys Wine Company in the Durbanville region." Pendulous jowls characterised the man perfectly, they shook vigorously as he rose to greet the visitor.

"Very pleased to meet you, Mr Davidson," his voice was unnaturally high, "I understand congratulations are in order, Mr Devries has informed me of your marriage yesterday."

Redelighuys was one of those unique individuals that everyone liked on introduction and Nathaniel warmed to him instantly.

"Thank you, Mr Redelighuys," he replied, "it's an honour to meet you sir."

"Please call me Lucas," the man replied, "everyone does."

Willem Devries interjected, "Perhaps we should talk business, gentlemen, I have a busy day ahead," the man advised them.

Reseating his bulky frame, Lucas progressed the dialogue, "Devries tells me that you may be looking to move into the wine business."

"It's true that I am looking for a change in direction certainly, I could be interested in that type of concern," sparred Nathaniel, who was canny enough to know that negotiation started from the very first word.

"As you know," continued the vineyard owner, "I am looking to sell the business I have built up over the last twenty years but perhaps you aren't aware of the reasons why I have to dispose of my company."

Nathaniel said nothing, waiting patiently for the man to continue, the expression on Lucas' face told him he should not interrupt.

"My doctors have advised me, I must give up my present lifestyle as I have a dangerous heart condition." He did not seem unduly upset as he related this to the potential purchaser.

The news did not surprise Nathaniel in the least but he felt sympathy for the man,

"I'm very sorry to hear that, Lucas," he said.

"No matter," Redelighuys returned, "the point is for my own health's sake I need to part company with something I have built up and nurtured by the sweat of my brow."

For the next hour they discussed everything to do with the sale of the Redelighuys Wine Company, Nathaniel learning it was close to the city and the main emphasis was to produce a rich fruity red wine.

Redelighuys said that his vineyard was positioned on a hill slope, cooled by sea breezes and moderate summer heat, with a dry atmosphere and the chances of fungus or disease, small.

"My native workers are of the highest calibre," Lucas assured Nathaniel, "and I would set them against any other vineyard in the country."

"That's very encouraging," Nathaniel declared."

At the end of the meeting, Nathaniel and Redelighuys shook hands on a deal for Nathaniel to purchase the Redelighuys Wine Company, without him actually seeing it. He knew Mary would be dismayed at his rash behaviour.

The men crossed the street outside to the offices of Devries' solicitor where a contract was rapidly drawn up, signed by the seller and the buyer and witnessed by the outgoing Managing Director of the Cape Transit Trading Company. They repaired to a hostelry to seal the bargain in alcohol, Nathaniel escaping an hour later, leaving Devries and the prior owner of the vineyard propping up the bar. He felt Devries might not be in a competent state for the auction, in view of the sadness of the occasion, Nathaniel felt Willem was entitled to try and block out the tragic events of the day.

He was correct about Mary's disappointment at his hasty behaviour, she was despondent when he relayed the news. The woman recovered quickly, not showing him the true nature of her feelings. All she wanted to do was to support her spouse and she began talking in glowing terms about their future life.

In her heart though she suspected the next few years were going to be difficult with considerable hard work the only prospect.

CHAPTER 13

Nathaniel gazed at the house, perched precariously on the hillside, not believing the transformation in two years. Away to his left, above the vineyard slopes, the bottling plant flashed white in the midday sun. Matchstick figures entered and left as they went about their toil. At this distance it looked like a model factory, placed with imprecision amidst a sea of miniature foliage.

From the gates to the house a rider trotted their horse towards him. Mary had performed the ritual of delivering his lunch and eating with him each day since the purchase of the business. They had come to enjoy this part of the day as most of their time was spent in toil, which stretched well into the night. this was a little portion of daytime togetherness they guarded jealously.

The lush vines were beginning to yield better production quotas but it would take five years or more to realise the vineyard's full potential.

Nathaniel recollected that fateful day in Devries' office, when he had shaken hands on the deal for the company with Redelighuys. He and Mary had ridden to the vineyard the following day, finding it overgrown and untended. Lucas had been in trouble for some time but had kept it quiet. By the time Nathaniel and his wife returned to the city, they found Lucas Redelighuys was long gone, the money transferred to his account and no one knew of his whereabouts.

Mary hadn't uttered a word, she neither chastised him or criticised his decision, simply getting on with the job of helping make the company a viable concern. It was an attitude her husband knew, showed the woman's dedication to their marriage.

Tethering her horse close by she walked the few yards into the rows of vines, hair billowing in the breeze. Whenever she joined him for lunch, she dressed like a man in breeches and shirt, accentuating her body, the attire making the horse ride comfortable. The fullness of her breasts strained the cotton material of the shirt, Nathaniel feeling a longing when he saw the vision approach. On several occasions they made love after the meal, wrestling passionately amidst the growing fruit.

"What is it today?" he called to her as she ducked under the vines, carrying the lunch bag.

"Beef," she smiled, planting a huge kiss on his sweat stained lips, the passion had never waned and the man was thankful for it. Desire had quickly abated for many of the couples they knew and they were determined the same would not happen for them.

They sat on the slopes, eating quietly, gazing proudly on their domain. It had been back-breaking work getting the company to its present standard, Nathaniel contemplated. Now they were almost in a position of profit, perhaps soon they would see a return on the investment.

Soon after finishing lunch, Nathaniel lay back on the heated earth, closing his eyes. He had no intention of sleeping, but the warmth of the day and the recent meal conspired to convey him to slumber.

He woke with a start, hearing shouting nearby, coming from a native worker, christened Isiah, by Nathaniel. Like most natives, the man's real name was almost impossible to pronounce, so the vineyard owner followed the custom of dubbing his workers with names from the Bible.

Isiah was close by now, stopping yelling as he negotiated the slope to his employers' position.

"What is it, Isiah?" demanded Mary, "you know we are never to be disturbed at lunch."

"A man to see the boss, Mrs Davidson," Isiah informed her. "He's up at the house and says it's urgent."

"Who is it, Isiah?" asked Nathaniel, rising from his recumbent position.

"No name," the worker declared, "he just said it was urgent and I was to find you immediately."

"Alright, get about your business," instructed the man's employer, "we'll be there directly."

Nathaniel retrieved his horse, grazing peacefully at the entrance to the row of vines he was working, trotting to Mary who was likewise seated on her animal. The pair made their way back to the house.

In the compound at the front of the dwelling, a houseboy took the reins of the animals, the riders easing themselves to the ground. Mary's maid Rachel, stood on the steps of the house awaiting their arrival.

"The gentleman is waiting inside for you," she said, taking the empty lunch bag from her mistress's hands.

Nathaniel made his way to the sitting room, stopping dead in his tracks. Sir Toby Davidson leaned against the fireplace, glass of whisky clutched in hand, face drawn and ashen.

It took Nathaniel several seconds to rally from the shock. In the years since last laying eyes on his father, the ravages of time had decimated the man, the hunched frame and lifeless expression shocked Sir Toby's son.

"Hello, Nathaniel," even the voice was a pale shadow of its former glory, no one in Parliament would have been able to equate the reedy tones with the man who had fired so many debates with his booming rhetoric. "Are you well?" he continued.

Now recovered, Nathaniel introduced his wife who had followed him into the room, "Father, may I present your daughter-in-law, Mary?"

The Parliamentarian walked unsteadily to where she stood, "And a magnificent wife too," he remarked fawningly.

"To what do we owe this visit, Father?" Nathaniel's tone was icy, the visitor couldn't fail to understand his presence was unwelcome.

Nathaniel was to receive the second bombshell of his day, Sir Toby seemed genuinely grief stricken, declaring, "My boy, there is no easy way to say this, I'm afraid your mother is dead."

The man collapsed into a nearby chair, head in hands, weeping uncontrollably. In his haste to escape the clutches of his father, Nathaniel had taken flight in such haste, he now regretted his actions. Now he would never be able to speak to his mother again and tell her what she meant to him. Agonising sobs racked her son's body, Mary coming and crouching before him, clasping his shaking form tightly in her arms.

Nathaniel pulled her to him, needing the warmth and comfort of another human being. Sir Toby stood uneasily over the scene, reluctant to show emotion towards his son. The memory of his behaviour towards him, fresh and graphic in his mind. He had changed since the death of his wife, seeking out his only son to make peace between the pair, but could that be possible he wondered?

"How did she die?" wept Nathaniel.

Sir Toby turned away before answering, "It was heart failure and very quick, Nathaniel," the man was struggling to control his own feelings. "I found out after the event, that your mother had been consulting a specialist for some time, apparently the condition was extremely serious but she never breathed a word to anyone."

An enraged animal cry escaped Nathaniel's lips, he leapt to his feet, knocking Mary unceremoniously to the floor. Anything which came to hand he began to throw, furniture, ornaments, whatever was around was directed at the walls or windows.

Sir Toby grabbed him in a bear hug and held the riotous body firm before his son could hurt himself or damage the property further.

Seconds later the men were hugging in a different manner, weeping in concert for a woman they adored. It was the closest Nathaniel had ever been to his father but somehow he found sufficient compassion to sympathise with his father's plight.

Mary looked on benevolently, feeling an overwhelming sadness for them both. It was a moment that would change the relationship between father and son forever. Knowing the history of their background from her husband, the reconciliation was a welcome development.

While his wife picked up the shattered pieces of ornament from the floor, Nathaniel and Sir Toby sat facing one another on the porch.

"I'm so sorry," his father began, "if I could have saved you that, I gladly would have."

"How long is it since she passed away?" enquired the man's son.

"Over three months now. I had to attend to the arrangements before I could find you to let you know."

"Is she buried at Thistlebrough?"

"In the family vault as all of us eventually are," confided Sir Toby.

A long silence ensued, uncomfortable in the extreme for Sir Toby. Nathaniel conjured up the picture of the cold stone mausoleum, he'd never liked its ostentatious size and grey bird spotted exterior, he consoled himself with the thought though that his mother wouldn't have wanted to be buried anywhere but Thistlebrough's grounds.

The tomb was located in an overgrown copse at the rear of the hall. He recalled playing there with friends, telling terrifying ghost stories at ten years old. It was a lifetime away now.

Nathaniel looked at the pitiable state of his father in the chair opposite, surprised to feel concern for the parent, who had spent years abusing him physically and mentally.

Sir Toby was encouraged to retire by his son and daughter-in-law. It was plain to see the man was exhausted, and when he had complied, husband and wife returned to the sitting room.

"Tell me about your mother, Nathaniel?" Mary begged. "You've told me about the problems with your father but next to nothing about her."

His eyes filled with tears again, thinking of the woman's angelic face. " She was a saint, Mary… I know everyone says that about their mother, but in this case the expression scarcely tells the truth about her."

The man peered through the window as he spoke, the vines of the estate were bearing the first signs of fruit, ripening in the hazy sunshine. On the slopes, workers tended the plants, indistinct and ghost like through his watery vision. It was a scene he was proud of and would have liked to have shown to his mother.

"The way she stoically put up with my father's attitude was a lesson in humility, she saved me from countless beatings," he warmed to the conversation, Mary allowing him the freedom to continue. "Everyone liked her from the highest born to the estate workers, she had the capacity to engender admiration from anyone she came into contact with." He sat down looking directly into the pools of his wife's eyes. "When I was a child, my father wanted me to be brought up under the tutelage of a nanny, but she would have none of it, it was the only time she defied her husband's wishes, the one decision she made that he realised was better not to argue with."

Mary crossed to the sideboard, pouring her husband a whisky, handing it to him before reseating herself, continuing the conversation continued.

As evening drew on inexorably, the vineyard workers were making their way down the slopes, encrusted with dirt and singing as they always did at the end of the day. Nathaniel and Mary continued to talk about the merits of his mother. It was helping him to get his feelings out, sometimes there was tears, sometimes laughter but always an unconditional love from the man to the woman who had borne him.

Around seven o'clock, Sir Toby appeared, refreshed and looking more like the man his son remembered. He had shaved the stubble from his chin and dressed in a fresh shirt, it was a transformation of astounding extent.

Dinner was a strained affair, the new found respect between the two men had perversely caused distance between them, neither knowing how to react to the new situation and the conversation was no more than cordial between father and son.

As the wine flowed, the situation began to improve, Sir Toby questioning his son on his life since leaving England.

"You have done superbly well, my boy, you must be very satisfied with your achievements." There was no hint of envy in his father's comments, only genuine admiration, thought Nathaniel.

"It seems to be going well," agreed Sir Toby's son, "but we have a long way to go with the vineyard, it may take as much as five years to get it to full production."

Sir Toby gave the impression of having something else to say and his son waited patiently for him to confide what was on his mind. The maid cleared away the dishes from the table and placed coffee cups before the diners.

Eventually, Nathaniel's father opened his thoughts, "Nathaniel, I'm bankrupt," he blurted out. "I'm afraid I've had to sell Thistelbrough, in addition to that I have resigned my parliamentary seat."

It was news that pained Nathaniel greatly. "When did this happen, Father?" he questioned him.

"I have been living on borrowed time for a while now," Sir Toby appraised him. "For the last five years I have been gambling heavily and run up substantial debts. The debts were eventually called in, the only way I could settle was to sell the hall." He looked worried as he relayed the story.

"Even then," the man continued, "there wasn't enough to cover my commitments and the people I was responsible to, were threatening to expose me to the Prime Minister. I felt my only option was to resign from the government and save them any embarrassment."

Nathaniel glanced at Mary who sat quietly, taking in the information and looking with commiseration at her father-in-law, opposite. Sir Toby's eyes were minutely examining the pattern on the table cloth, "I'm ruined Nathaniel," he disclosed.

There was silence in the room, which seemed like hours to Nathaniel but in reality was mere seconds. He didn't have any idea of what he could say to mollify the man, eventually mumbling unconvincingly, "It will be alright, father."

"You can stay with us as long as you wish," said Mary.

As he looked up, Sir Toby Davidson's eyes glistened. "I need to say something, Nathaniel," he began, "something I should have said long ago," he sipped at a glass of port also brought by the maid with the coffee, trying to find solace in the rich ruby liquid. "All those years I treated you so abysmally, it was because I was under pressure with my personal life. It's no excuse but I want you to know that deep down it wasn't really me, I was drinking heavily all the time and you were an easy target."

The admission was staggering and hugely embarrassing to Nathaniel, who had never known his father be so forthright before and the subject evoked memories he had long since banished from his mind. He was seeing the human face of a man he had always regarded as a monster and it disturbed him.

"There really isn't anything to apologise for now," Nathaniel's words were full of emotion. "It's passed and we go on from here," he smiled at his father.

Sir Toby stretched out a bony hand across the table and grasped his son's in a gesture of gratefulness, which almost dissolved the elder man to tears. Nathaniel knew how much that signal had taken to perform.

As Mary lay in his arms later in their four-poster bed, they discussed Sir Toby's predicament.

"What can we do for him, sweetheart?" said his wife.

"I really don't know," he replied. "In the short term I suppose he could help us run the vineyard here."

Mary shifted her position so that she was looking down on her husband. "The way things have worked out for him, he would see that as charity and he is too proud to accept that," she asserted. "May I make a suggestion, sweetheart?"

"Of course," he replied, reaching up to kiss her in passing.

"Philip Brent is looking after the horse farm pro tem, why don't we send your father out there with responsibility to administer it, give him the opportunity to manage it without interference?" suggested his wife.

99

It was a wonderful idea, just what the man needed to get back in the swing of things, thought Nathaniel; he was worried at the same time though, saying: "Mary, I know we are married now, but the farm was yours and Paul's and I have never interfered with what goes on there, it's really yours, not ours."

She smiled in a mischievous way. "Then I can do as I please," laughed the woman,

"And I would like Sir Toby Davidson to take control of my farm." His wife never failed to surprise Nathaniel and he pulled her to him and lost himself in the world of her embrace.

CHAPTER 14

In the striking first light of the day, the vineyard owner and his father mounted horses setting off to tour the vineyard's confines, it was Nathaniel's suggestion to show his father the extent of his estate, the older delighted to accompany his son. It was another step on the road to reconciliation.

Sir Toby couldn't fail to be impressed, especially when his son recounted the story of Redieighuys' deception. For a man of his son's delicate years, he realised that his business acumen was outstanding. As they trotted around the estate, the extent of the further potential was glaringly obvious to Sir Toby.

Long rows of vines were untended, the native manpower of the vineyard didn't have the time or numbers to begin working on them.

Nathaniel picked the lunch break to broach Mary's offer to his father. It was a delicate matter which required much thought and he agonised about the best way to approach it. His wife was right, Sir Toby was a proud man and would never accept charity, if he thought for a second it was being offered, Nathaniel suspected he would turn the offer down.

"Father, I have a problem," Nathaniel confided between mouthfuls, "Mary and I own a horse farm some way from here and though we have someone to oversee it in our absence, we feel that it needs someone closer to us to administer it on our behalf." He searched the man's face for signs of doubt but couldn't detect any, he continued, "It would be an opportunity for you to pick up the pieces of your life and more importantly it would give Mary and I peace of mind knowing you were running it, so we could concentrate on the vineyard here."

Sir Toby gazed into the distance, lost in thought, "This wouldn't be charity, my boy, would it?" he exclaimed.

"Absolutely not, Father," replied the son, "our present overseer Philip Brent has done a fine job but he isn't family and however good he is, the man is not kin, we need someone who we can trust implicitly, blood is thicker than water where the development of business is concerned."

The word trust clinched the argument in Sir Toby's mind.

"Then I accept, Nathaniel."

"Thank you, Father," answered the man's son, astonished at the ease of the situation, "I'm sure the arrangement will suit everyone."

They spent an hour over lunch, sipping glasses of the vineyard's ruby wine, which Mary had thoughtfully packed in the hamper. In that short period, the men learned things about each other which a few years before, they would never have dreamed of confiding in each other. Sir Toby talked about his life in politics, a fascinating insight into the times Nathaniel hadn't seen his father, due to his commitments in the capital. He always felt government business would be dry as sticks but the way his father talked about the cut and thrust of the everyday machinations, was a revelation, the man seemed to come alive as he talked and it showed a different facet of his character.

The son gave a description of his life since leaving England and an emotional account of his friendship with Christian Davenport, who remained a constant miss in his life. He talked in glowing terms about his friend, Sir Toby detecting a loyalty and admiration in his son which he had never seen before, maturity had given the boy the very best of manly attributes.

Finishing the food, father and son remounted their horses, continuing their excursion of the estate. A one storey, whitewashed building stood gleaming in the sun at the far side of the vineyard, well away from Nathaniel's house. Father and son tethered their mounts, crossing to the structure and entering the cool interior.

A dormitory style building, the edifice housed over forty beds, Sir Toby was struck by the absolute cleanliness of the living quarters.

"I take it this is your workers' accommodation, Nathaniel?" It was an enquiry rather than a statement.

Nathaniel examined the building minutely, ensuring everything was as it should be. "Yes, Father, we try to provide them with good living conditions, it serves to make them work harder if they have somewhere reasonable to live."

The building had been positioned precariously on the slopes, the direction of the positioning would ensure the sun would be less fierce in the afternoon. Attention to small details like that made the vineyard owner a popular man among his workers.

It was mid afternoon, the building empty, its occupants toiling on the creeping vines, their possessions neatly stacked by their mattresses in the accommodation awaiting their return.

When Nathaniel was satisfied with the condition of the building, he and his father returned to their horses, setting off for the house, arriving tired and dusty from the day's endeavours.

Sir Toby elected to bathe, heading for his room, while his son and daughter-in-law sipped cool water on the porch.

"He accepted the offer of managing the holding, Mary," he informed her.

The woman's eyes crinkled at the edges as she smiled, "I'm so pleased, sweetheart, I'm sure it will be a good thing for all of us, but particularly for him."

"I hope so," he answered, "despite all I've been through with him, I realise he needs some stability in his life now."

Over the next two days, Nathaniel and his father prepared for the trip to the Hantam hills region. Mary had declined to accompany the men, knowing someone had to manage the business in her husband's absence. Nathaniel would be away some weeks, it was to be the first parting since their marriage, the prospect making her intensely upset.

As she packed for him, she became tearful, "I'll miss you so much my darling," she sobbed to her husband, who watched her stow the items into a large portmanteau. He pulled her to him, her head resting on his broad chest, arms snaking around him, tightening as if she would never let him escape.

"It won't be long," he soothed, "and just think of the welcome when I get home."

Nathaniel's words did not placate his wife in the least, she trembled with the violence of her emotion. "Please come back soon, sweetheart, I need you so much." The terrible prospect of leaving Mary began to dawn on the man. Up to this moment he had been caught up in preparations for the trip but now as the warm body of his wife enveloped him, doubts crept into his mind. Could he endure being away from her for so long he wondered? It took great willpower to dismiss the disturbing notion, especially as the woman was breaking her heart, but he held firm, "It's for the best my angel, I'll get father established there, then I promise you we will never be apart again."

At the front of the house, Sir Toby sat erect on his horse. It was an overcast day, disordered clouds scurrying, menacingly grey across the heavens.

Nathaniel eased himself into his saddle, leaning down to kiss his wife gently. They had said their true goodbyes in the room before coming down.

"Look after my husband, Toby," the woman demanded.

"Never fear, Mary," replied her father-in-law, "he'll return safely to you, that I promise."

Standing, hand raised in farewell as the two men cantered out of the courtyard, she remained until they had disappeared from sight, tears clouding her eyes as she turned forlornly towards the house.

An hour later, rain began drenching the men, pouring from the sky as they rode through the first leg of the journey.

"Reminds me of Northumberland," commented Sir Toby, examining the agitated sky. "Remember the rain there, Nathaniel?"

Some of the downpours at Thistelbrough were truly awesome, mused his son. "What I remember most was the freshness of the air after the rain ceased," reminisced Nathaniel. "That and the vividly changing colours of the landscape following a downpour; the lush green hills and rich brown turned earth of the ploughed fields."

He hadn't thought of Northumberland in a long while, by talking of it he realised how much he missed the staggering beauty of the county and emotion swamped him as he harked back to his childhood there.

"I wonder if I'll ever see it again?" he asked his father.

"I'm sure you will," replied Sir Toby.

At the outset of the journey, Nathaniel had visited the native workers' accommodation and selected four of the men there to act as bearers, they trailed in their masters' wake now, carrying the necessary paraphernalia for the trip.

By mid morning, it was as though the rain had never existed, hazy clouds of evaporating moisture billowed up from the earth and foliage, heated by the ferocious sun, intensely beating down during its inexorable path across the sky.

The white men suffered greatly in the unceasing, soaring temperature, their intake of water prodigious as the day wore on. Even the native porters were struggling, so Nathaniel called a halt to the expedition just before noon, finding a spot below some trees where they could sit out the hottest part of the day.

It was after three before the men continued on their way. Even at that time the heat was phenomenal, it was the hottest day Nathaniel had known since his arrival on the continent. Thankfully by early evening the temperature began to abate, Nathaniel keeping the party moving for an hour longer than planned, to compensate for the earlier delay.

As the natives pitched the small tents, Sir Toby extracted a flask of brandy from his pocket.

"Would you care for a drink?" he asked his son. Nathaniel accepted the liquid gratefully.

"I think we've made reasonable time, despite everything," he informed his father. Sir Toby swigged at the container, which his son had returned to him.

"I've never known heat like that, my boy, I feel completely drained," the older man confided, "I hope tomorrow will be cooler."

Lanterns were strung on nearby trees, ostensibly to keep animals at bay rather than give off meaningful illumination. A large fire was set in the centre of the camp, the wood crackling and spluttering spasmodically in the darkness, sending occasional torrents of sparks into the night sky.

The men sat at the edge of the blaze, staring intently into the licking flames. For a while they were lost in thought until Sir Toby shifted his position.

"Do you and Mary plan on children, Nathaniel?" he asked without warning.

"We've never seriously talked about it," replied Nathaniel, "but I'm sure we want them."

His father looked uncomfortable, "Then don't make the same horrendous mistakes I did when bringing you up, Nathaniel, promise me that," he pleaded. Look of regret in his father's eyes disturbed the son.

"Yes Father, I will promise you that," he affirmed.

"I've learned many things over the last few months," Sir Toby continued, "and the harshest lesson I have had to learn is my shocking behaviour toward my only son; that's a lesson I never want you to have to discover, Nathaniel." He looked genuinely contrite, "I hope you give me grandchildren soon."

"I'll certainly try, Father," he smiled, trying to lighten the mood.

For the rest of the evening the men reminisced of England, before collapsing exhausted into their cots.

Chapter 15

Nothing had changed at the horse farm as Nathaniel's party rounded the hills and saw the estate extended before them.

Several horses stooped their heads in the corral, tearing at tufts of grass while others cavorted around in the sunshine.

Winding their way down to the farm, Nathaniel took in the scene in detail, noticing that the corral had been extended. There was more than fifty horses in its confines, Mary had told him she never managed to have more than twenty at a time. There was no doubt the manager had enhanced the business, mused Nathaniel.

"What a wonderful setting," enthused Sir Toby, "a treasure amongst the bush."

They walked the horses on, passing the limits of the estate and up towards the house. Native workers regarded them as they passed, some of whom Nathaniel could remember, others clearly recruited since their departure.

A new coat of white paint revitalised the residence, making the building stand out prominently against the earthy colours of the surrounding terrain. Nathaniel looked to the left, at the spot where Christian had received the fatal bite from the snake, the memories flooding back of that fateful day when his friend had passed away. A huge hand seemed to squeeze the heart in his chest to pulp.

Sir Toby noticed his son's pained expression, "What is it?" the peer asked. Nathaniel pointed out the area and explained where and how Davenport had met his fate, heading to the location with his father following. He stood looking down at the earth where he had tended his friend before carrying him to the house.

An uncomfortable silence descended on the scene, Sir Toby shifted in the saddle, feeling for his son in his distress. "At least he had a good friend in you," his father ventured, "there is that to consider, Nathaniel." Dismounting, Nathaniel crouched where the man had lain, tears filling his eyes as he touched the pebble dotted earth, for a moment he thought he saw the supine body lying there once more.

"I didn't think it would affect me quite so much," announced the man, "he is a huge miss in my life." Sir Toby's features displayed concern as he gazed down at the disconsolate figure of his son, giving him a few minutes with his thoughts, then cleared his throat, to try and bring the man out of his reverie.

Reluctantly, Nathaniel stood up and remounted, wheeling away towards the house. The spectre of his friend's death exorcised, he knew he could put Christian's death behind him but he would never forget him.

Inside the house it was as though he and Mary had never left, it was immaculately clean, Brent hadn't changed one aspect of the décor or the fabric of the dwelling. Familiar smells pervaded his nostrils. Aromas of cooking and house plants mingled in an evocative cloud of recollection.

Philip was conspicuous by his absence, Nathaniel learning from a new houseboy that Mr Brent would be back the following day.

Following their unpacking the men enjoyed a light meal, prepared by Mary's old maid, Rachel, after which they retired to their rooms for some much needed sleep. The first time in many days the men slept in proper beds, the slumber deep and undisturbed.

Over breakfast, the men discussed the work of the farm, Nathaniel explaining to his father the history of it and Mary's first husband's creation of the business.

"We breed thoroughbred horses here, Father, animals which are much sought after throughout the continent and abroad," he appraised him. "The farm has an enviable reputation for the best animals and we need to keep that esteem in the business. Many other horse farms are springing up but our history of the provision of quality creatures should ensure we still have a head start over the others in the field."

"Your horses are certainly some of the best I've ever seen," Sir Toby commented. "Quite magnificent animals."

The men pored over the accounts for an hour after the morning meal. At ten o'clock they heard muffled voices outside the window, peering out to see Philip Brent and two native workers dropping down from their horses. Brent gripped a riding crop, swishing it against his leg as he spoke to Rachel, who was informing him of Nathaniel's arrival. They watched him hurry into the house, less than a minute later he was standing before them,

"Mister Davidson, we didn't expect your arrival," the voice was deeper than Nathaniel remembered. "Have you been attended to?"

Something about Brent's manner had always disturbed Nathaniel, though he could never put his finger on what it was.

"Yes thank you, Philip, may I speak to you alone for a minute?" he turned to his introduce the manager to Sir Toby, "Father, may I present Philip Brent." The men shook hands as Nathaniel continued, "I wonder if you would excuse us for a few minutes, Father."

Sir Toby swept out of the room, his son proffering a chair to the manager who sat opposite Nathaniel, lighting a cheroot, smoke drifting lazily upwards.

"First of all Philip, I want to say that Mary and I have been delighted with your management of the business here, you've done a first class job for us," he said. "My father has now joined the business with Mary and I and she wishes him to have control of our interests here." Brent's face was darkening but Nathaniel ignored it and carried on, "You of course will retain control of the workers and the development of the horses but my father will make all commercial decisions in relation to the business and be responsible for the accounts."

"You bastard!" Brent's vehemence shocked Nathaniel.

"There's no need to take that attitude, Brent," he declared, "I have told you of our gratefulness for what you have done here but the decision to run the farm is my wife's and it will be obeyed."

"Then it will be obeyed without me," said Brent rising and striking Nathaniel across the face with the crop still grasped in his fist.

Blood trickled from the wound in Nathaniel's cheek, the liquid warm and sticky. Launching himself at the farm manager, the pair crashed to the floor, knocking over several chairs as they grappled.

Sir Toby plunged into the room, alerted by the commotion and dragged his son off Brent.

"I think you had better get out of here," the older man shouted at the farm manager.

"With pleasure," spat Brent, he turned to Nathaniel. "But, understand this Davidson, you haven't heard the last of me yet," storming to the door of the room he turned, "I'll make you pay for this."

"What was all that about?" demanded Nathaniel's father. Nathaniel dabbed at the laceration on his face.

"It appears he wasn't happy about you taking over the farm, Father."

The man's parent pondered for a moment, "Has he ever been like this before?" he asked.

"We've always had an excellent working relationship," advised his son, "but there was something about him which always made me suspicious of him."

"Then I think there is a lot more to this than meets the eye," remarked Sir Toby.

The suggestion was there in his father's comments, nefarious activity had been undertaken in the farm's business affairs or the possibility of it but Nathaniel expressed reservations.

"If you are suggesting that Brent has defrauded us, I find that difficult to believe, Father," said the younger man, "we've always been satisfied with the way he has run the business."

Nathaniel's father took a seat. "When a man acts out of character, there is usually a sinister reason behind it, I'd better look over the accounts, my boy."

While Nathaniel checked on the workers and the general well-being of the horses, Sir Toby sat in the house, perusing the accounts minutely. Several hours had passed when he rose from the ledgers and stretched to alleviate his aching back.

Nathaniel found his father drinking a glass of wine, relaxing after his marathon examination of the estate books.

"Well, Father?" the young man enquired, taking a seat.

Sir Toby poured another glass of the rich, red fluid, setting it before his son.

"Brent has embezzled more than £5,000 from you and Mary, and it could have been a lot worse but for the fact we arrived when we did."

If there had been one person in life, who Nathaniel would never have believed would defraud Mary, it was Brent. His mouth fell open, the look of surprise evident to his father.

"Where money is concerned, my boy, I learned long ago never to trust anyone, however honourable they may be. Money is a mistress that few can resist when they have control of it," Sir Toby continued. "In fact the more trustworthy they appear seems to indicate a good chance that they will let you down."

"Are you absolutely sure about this, Father?"

"I am, but the question now is, what do you intend to do about it?" pressed Sir Toby.

There was no easy answer in Nathaniel's mind, "I need to sleep on it," he informed his father.

"You must take it to the authorities, son, he has to be brought to book," Sir Toby insisted. "To do anything else would be foolish."

"I said I will sleep on it," the statement from Nathaniel left no ambiguity in his father's mind who was in control, realising his son was adamant, he approached him no more about it.

The next day, Nathaniel showed his father around the farm, the man was even more astonished by the quality of the animals on closer inspection. Sir Toby had much experience of the horse, though he had never seen so many excellent specimens in one place before.

111

Sun flashed from the expertly groomed coats of the creatures, grazing calmly in the paddock. Sir Toby could tell why the farm had built such an excellent renown in its stock, any horse enthusiast would have been astonished at the sleek lines and noble heads on display.

Native workers groomed a few animals in the stalls of the stable block as the men entered. One huge, ebony individual rhythmically pumped a bellows to the furnace, the coals bursting into flame as the oxygen penetrated the centre of the fire. When the man was satisfied with the fiery glow of the raw metal, snuggled in the glowing embers, he extracted the horseshoe he was producing, clanging down the hammer on the radiant material, positioned on the anvil head, fashioning the final shape he required.

"My God," exclaimed Sir Toby, "the heat in here is enormous, how do they cope with it?"

Nathaniel looked about him, "I suppose they just get used to it, Father."

Various tools used for attending to the horses were hung around the walls of the block. To the untrained eye they may have resembled mediaeval instruments of torture, rather than objects of horse welfare.

The men's efficiency impressed Nathaniel's father, getting on with the job expertly in an atmosphere of cheerfulness which Sir Toby concluded, would have been there in spite of the attendance of their management.

They spent the morning introducing themselves. Nathaniel presented the native workers he already knew to his father, in turn they introduced the new employees to the management.

He ran through the procedures for managing the farm with Sir Toby, who picked up everything quickly, absorbing it like a sponge.

One thing stood out to the new manager of the horse farm, the absolute serenity of the domain.

"As far as hiring and firing goes, Father, you will have complete autonomy, one of the senior workers will advise you about our main customers and any new clients who have expressed an interest in the stock," advised Nathaniel.

"You have established routes and clients, who purchase the horses on a regular basis then?" his father questioned.

"Mainly on the eastern seaboard, for some reason we do quite well there and of course in Cape Town where a lot of the animals are shipped abroad, the USA and Britain being our two main export areas," the younger man stated.

He looked at his father, who had puffed up with pride, genuinely pleased with the confidence his son had placed in him.

It had been a long day as they watched the sky, tinted vividly red in the sunset, the pair leaned against the wooden fence posts of the corral, eyeing the farm stock grazing serenely in the field.

CHAPTER 16

Nathaniel awoke, unsure of why or what time it was, his room was bathed in moonlight. The indistinct shapes of the furniture items seemed unreal. He heard the sound of galloping hooves outside and the panic stricken shrieks of men.

The man leaped out of bed, running to the window. Horses were scattering away from the compound, blindly bolting for the surrounding hills with men chasing and harrying them.

As Nathaniel watched, he saw a figure sitting astride a horse at the gate to the corral. There was no mistaking the physique. Philip Brent gazed straight back into his eyes, the moonlight scarcely hid the expression of satisfaction on the features of the man in the flickering torchlight.

The owner of the horse farm threw on his breeches and boots, bounding down stairs two at a time, out into the shadows of the night, aware that Sir Toby was close on his heels, dragging his clothes on too.

By the time they reached the corral, the horses had been stampeded away, all save five and the two men crashed the gate closed to prevent the remainder escaping too. None of the attackers were in evidence, having spirited away beneath the cloak of darkness.

Nathaniel's native contingent appeared, wiping the vestiges of sleep from their eyes, some of them chased after creatures who had stopped bolting just outside the confines of the farm, eventually leading six of the stock back to the security of the paddock.

The chances were that Brent and his henchmen wouldn't try another attack on the estate the same night but Nathaniel took no chances, detailing three of the workers to stand guard for the remaining hours of darkness.

Despite the safeguards, he could not sleep at all, sitting up with a gun cradled in his lap.

He considered the Brent situation, wondering how they could have been so spectacularly wrong about the man. In the chair opposite, Sir Toby slept fitfully, fully clothed, should another attack occur. Looking vulnerable in the state of slumber, his son felt pity for the man who had lost the woman he loved so cruelly.

Mary filled his thoughts, knowing she would be sleeping, the warm welcoming temple of her body invaded his thoughts and he shook himself to be rid of the disturbing images. As first light broke over the land, he wandered outside and passed some words with the guards, the men struggling to stay awake. Nathaniel sent one of them back to the accommodation to rouse three replacements, sending the first watch back for some well earned rest as their successors arrived.

Having organised the men, he returned to the house and breakfasted with Sir Toby.

"You really must inform the authorities about Brent now," pleaded his father. The situation had become personal for Nathaniel, his only intention to deal with the former employee himself.

"No, Father, I have no plans to involve anyone else in this."

Sir Toby's face showed concern, the look of pure hatred on his son's features disturbed him. Nathaniel exhibited an uncharacteristic air of violence as he talked, his father knowing that his son may well have been charged with murder if Brent were there at this precise moment.

"Do nothing reckless, my boy, I can see how your blood is running," he cautioned. "There will be a time when you will be able to pay this man back without resorting to bloodshed."

Nathaniel stomped away from his father, an air of pure menace clouded him, a welling up of vehemence which was foreign to the young man's nature and he knew he had to find a quiet spot in which to calm his feelings. Throughout the day, workers continued to search the surrounding bush for more livestock finding two more animals, quietly tearing up grass, some distance from the farm.

The farm owner stayed out until nightfall. In his absence the workers naturally gravitated towards Sir Toby for instructions, which he organised with military precision.

Nathaniel returned to the house, his feelings toward the former farm manager had not diminished one iota. The first priority was to keep the farm running, following which he had made up his mind to seek out the aggressor and teach him a lesson he would never forget.

For the next few days, he and his father established a routine of working in which each slipped into the roles they were best suited to, meeting once a day to discuss the security of the farm.

On a sweltering afternoon they sat wearily on the porch, debating the best way to protect their asset.

"We've established a system of guards, Father," began Nathaniel, "but all they can do at the moment is call us if there is an attack, perhaps we should arm the watch and teach them to shoot."

"Do you think it's wise to arm the native workers, Nathaniel?" replied his father, "it would be a mistake if they decided to turn on us."

Nathaniel stood up, pacing the limits of the porch thinking, "But if there was another attack, it may be too late to repel it, if we are sleeping in the house," he pressed. "No, I've made up my mind that the guards will be armed, Father. Would you see to it?"

The workers assembled in a field behind the house the next morning, where Sir Toby had erected a rudimentary range for the tests. As the day wore on, each worker tried his hand at firing. Many were surprisingly good shots. Sir Toby recorded the most efficient in order to set up a rota of guards.

"How are they coming along, Father?" Nathaniel questioned, after the contingent of workers had completed the examination.

"Two in particular are gifted marksmen, considering they have never held a weapon before," advised his father. "I think we should use them as the leaders of the guards."

"Very well, if that is your recommendation, Father, I will go along with that."

Over the next few days, the horse farm returned to a semblance of normality. Another two horses were discovered and Nathaniel and his father set about the task of putting the mares out for impregnation by the stallions. It would be sometime before the stock was replenished to the levels before the attack, but the seed had to be sown immediately. It was fortuitous that the incursion had happened when the mares were in season. Blistering heat and powerful sunlight turned the white men a walnut brown as they continued to labour with the horses in the open, needing frequent rest to restore their levels of energy, sleeping two hours every afternoon.

A month after the men had arrived in the Hantaam mountain region, Nathaniel was working in the corral, tending an animal which had gone lame. As he stood, easing his back from the examination of the chestnut mare, he noticed a rider approaching the farm in the hazy sunshine. The man was tall in the saddle but from the distance Nathaniel could make out no features. It would take the horseman twenty minutes to reach his position, so he bent to his work again, periodically glancing in the traveller's direction.

Long, dark, flowing locks were the first distinctive things he noted about the person on the horse as he closed on the farm owner's position; for a moment, Nathaniel thought he recognised him, then dismissed the notion from his mind. It couldn't be, he thought but the next time he peered in the direction of the man he was sure he was right.

Leaving the corral, he sprinted towards the rider. "Ebenezer," he called from distance. "What the hell are you doing here?"

Captain Smith dismounted and led the animal towards his friend, "I thought I'd track you down and allow you to buy me a drink," he laughed as the two men clasped hands. "My ship is in dry dock, being repaired."

"My God, it's good to see you," shouted Nathaniel, "let's go up to the house, I'm sure I can find you that drink."

They chatted animatedly as they made the short walk to the dwelling.

"How did you find me?" probed Nathaniel.

"It wasn't difficult, I merely called on your wife and she told me where you were," said Smith. "Oh and I have a message from your wife," continued the Captain.

"What is it?" asked the farm owner.

"She asked me to tell you," he paused for effect. "That she is pregnant, congratulations Nathaniel." Nathaniel stood, his mouth agape, stopped dead in his tracks. "What about that drink, my friend, we have something to celebrate now, don't we?" chortled Ebenezer, dragging his companion into the coolness of the house.

Sir Toby was delighted by the news, pouring three enormous whiskies.

"To you and your wife, Nathaniel," he toasted, "and to the birth of my first grandchild." His face split into an enormous toothy smile.

The potential father could still not believe the information. It was everything he wanted but he was sad to think his wife had not had the opportunity to tell him personally. Nathaniel knew that Mary would be upset about that, he wished he could hold her now and tell her everything that was in his heart about the momentous news.

Nathaniel was gratified to see how Sir Toby and Ebenezer warmed instantly to each other, and though they had just met, it seemed as though the men were long lost friends. News of Mary's pregnancy had brought a jubilant mood to the men, the alcohol further enhancing the good humour. All three were bordering on drunk an hour later, though fortunately they concluded the libations before they eventually reached that sorry state.

"I am master of the Adventuress now, Nathaniel," Ebenezer slurred. "She is anchored at Cape Town, being my base of operations from now on."

"That's wonderful news, Ebenezer," exclaimed the man's friend tipsily.

"There's more, Mary has retained me to transport your horses when they are exported and for the wine carriage too, so I'm working for you now and I have to say I'm delighted with the arrangement." He reached into his pocket and extracted a letter. "It's all here for you Nathaniel."

He grabbed the letter greedily, leaving the room to the grins of his father and friend, seeking out a tree near the house to read the missive from his wife. It was a communication of pure love for the most part and some information about her retention of Smith as transporter of all their business assets. Nathaniel read and reread the wonderful tracts of loving terms, missing his wife immensely.

After a discreet length of time, Ebenezer joined his companion, sitting down under the tree without speaking. The shade suited the men, who were lost in their own thoughts until Nathaniel broke the silence.

"I don't believe that I'm going to be a father, Ebenezer," he said.

"It couldn't happen to two better people than you and Mary," replied the sea Captain.

"The problem is that we don't have a lot of stock just now, Ebenezer, one of our former employees took it into his head to raid the farm and stampede the animals," Nathaniel related the full story to his friend. "It may be some time before the horse farm is back to its former glory."

"That's fine, Nathaniel," Ebenezer stated. "If it's alright with you, I will transport your wine and if I need extra income I will elicit further business with other companies but the moment you need me to be with you full-time, I will be available. Shall we shake on it?"

The contract was sealed with the grasp, the men knowing the gesture was far more important than any piece of paper. Nathaniel looked at his friend who was heading back to the house and knew he could trust this man with his life. Ebenezer had become a friend of the same consequence as Christian Davenport. Nathaniel knew he was more than fortunate to have a second companion of such importance. Most people didn't get one friend as noteworthy in their lives, so he considered himself the richest man where friends were concerned.

CHAPTER 17

Ebenezer Smith returned to Cape Town seven days after his arrival at the farm. Nathaniel lamented seeing him leave but the Captain insisted he had much work to oversee on the Adventuress.

Under the crimson glow of a magnificent sunrise, Nathaniel and his father watched Smith ride off, disappearing from sight.

One of the workers, Mathew, approached his employers, the head of the native contingent, Nathaniel made him up to the position when the Davidsons first arrived. Demonstrating leadership and resourcefulness, the owner had no hesitation in placing him in command of the workers.

Mathew stood patiently to the rear of the men waiting for their attention.

"What is it, Mathew?" Nathaniel eventually asked when his friend had disappeared from view.

"Please, Mr Davidson, I'd like a word with you," stammered the overseer.

"Very well, what can I do for you? Nathaniel asked.

"Please, sir," the man seemed uncomfortable, "I'd like permission to marry."

Sir Toby moved off toward the house, leaving his son to deal with the domestic matter.

"Who is the lucky girl, Mathew?"

"Miriam, boss," he used the woman's biblical name given her by the owner of the horse farm, their native names continuing to be too difficult to pronounce for Nathaniel and his wife.

Nathaniel thought about the situation, realising the lovers had been constantly in each other's company while they worked.

"I'd like to marry today, boss, if that is alright with you," continued the man. His English was improving daily, thought

Nathaniel. Some of the phraseology disjointed but his intonation and word usage were excellent now.

"It's very short notice," announced the employer, "but I suppose it will be alright." Mathew didn't move, "is there something else?" queried Nathaniel. The man's features cracked in a broad grin, displaying a mouth full of gleaming tombstone teeth.

"Yes, boss, could the workers have permission to come?" Mathew was a likeable rogue, one of those rare people in life who could get away with anything just by smiling, the way most individuals could never do.

The situation appealed to Nathaniel's sensitive nature, recent news of Mary's pregnancy filling him with goodwill.

"Yes, yes, alright, Mathew, tell the workers they may have today as a holiday to celebrate your marriage," he smiled, "but inform them, this is the only marriage where this will happen, I don't want them coming to me on a daily basis to get married."

The man galloped off in the direction of the workers' accommodation to break the good news to his comrades, his feet kicking clouds of dust into the air as he sprinted away.

It was something which would be good for the workers, who had toiled ceaselessly since the Brent incident, mused Nathaniel.

Preparations for the wedding of Mathew and Miriam were begun, natives singing tribal ritual as they readied the ceremony. The colours of the native dress were striking and a complete contrast to the drab garb they wore for work.

Rhythmic chanting was taken up by the tribal women, its eerie cadence slicing the air to reach Nathaniel and Sir Toby's ears. Wonderful beefy aromas of basting meat drifted invitingly around the dwelling, carried by the gentle breezes of the calm day, wafting from the direction of the low slung workers' bunk block.

The ceremony took place in the afternoon, the white men were invited to attend, Nathaniel declining on their behalf, knowing tribal ceremonies were traditional and very personal to the native peoples.

Instead he and his father gazed over the scene from the interior of the house, marvelling at the splendid sight before them. If anyone knew how to put on ceremony, it was the tribes people, the celebrations continuing long into the night and were finally coming to a close when Philip Brent and his henchmen returned.

This time Nathaniel and his father were awake and dressed, the guards attending the wedding ceremony had kept their weapons close at hand.

Brent's men swept in as the sentries fired, killing four of his native supporters in the saddle. At least twenty more rode into the scene of the happy event, riding down any workers in their path.

The Davidsons dashed from the house, guns clutched in hand, speeding to the scene of the havoc.

"Brent's mine, Father," panted Nathaniel. "If he's here I want him," instructed Sir Toby's son.

They neared the utter confusion of the attack, when an assailant broke off from the rest of his comrades, galloping towards Nathaniel, who immediately dropped to one knee, aiming and firing as the knee joint crashed into the dirt.

The shot caught the man full in the centre of his face, mangling the features into a bloody confusion of skin, blood and bone. Rushing past his son, Sir Toby entered the fray, becoming lost in the mass of bodies and horses, calling instructions to his men as he went.

Noticing that three of the men lay dead, the violence in Nathaniel's soul rose to mammoth proportion, all he wanted now was to find Brent and kill the man. No compassion was left in his soul, just fervent detestation of the individual.

The fight was coming to a close when he finally located him, seated on a white horse, watching the unfolding display. Without hesitation Nathaniel fired at him, missing him by inches, close enough though to disturb the man who picked out Nathaniel among the fracas.

Spurring his mount into action, Brent galloped directly for the owner of the farm, closing on the man before he had the opportunity to reload.

Nathaniel tossed his weapon to the floor and faced the charging creature, saliva spewing from its mouth from the exertion. It looked like the Devil's own conveyance, with its snarling bared teeth and sweating flanks.

Horse and rider seemed as one entity as they thundered down on Nathaniel's position, Brent's drawn back lips an emulation of the horse's expression.

They had reached his location, ready to trample him when he neatly sidestepped at the last second, grasping the leather rein as the horse attempted to stop, forward momentum carrying it on despite the best efforts of the rider to slow its progress.

The animal was off balance, hooves grappling with the ground, the impetus sliding the horse in Nathaniel's direction. With an almighty heave on the leather strap, he helped the creature's movement towards him and it crashed to the floor in a flail of legs, throwing Brent clear.

In one movement he hit the floor rising at a run, hell bent on crushing the object of his hatred. Head bowed, he pummelled into Nathaniel's midriff, driving the breath out of him.

They hit the floor as a tangled mass, clouds of dust enveloping them. Brent had the upper hand, his bulkier frame too much weight for his opponent to contend with. The man's knees trapped Nathaniel's chest to the dirt, no amount of pitching could dislodge the mass.

Grasping Nathaniel's throat with one hand, Brent laid into the man's face with his fist, bloodying the features with the force of the blows. The farm owner was beginning to lose consciousness as the blows rained in.

Suddenly the attacker collapsed onto Nathaniel, a large hole emerged in the chest, and blood spattered over his face as the shot plunged through the torso.

With a massive heave, he threw the inert form of Brent from himself, seeing Sir Toby still at the aim twenty feet away. His father slowly lowered the gun to his side.

"Are you alright, my boy?" he asked. Nathaniel clambered up, sliding his sleeve across his face, removing some of the blood.

"Thank you, Father," wheezed the man, "if you hadn't interceded I suspect I may be the one lying there."

Surveying the scene of the battle, they counted eight bodies, including Philip Brent. They couldn't hide the fact the men had been killed but the closest authority rested with the British Governor back in Cape Town.

Sir Thomas Collins would understand the situation, Nathaniel was sure. From the day of his wedding at the residency they had become firm friends. In the meantime there was the question of what to do with the fallen. The heat of the day meant there was no possibility of leaving the cadavers above ground, so Nathaniel detailed a party of his natives to inter them, burying them with as much reverence as they could.

Under a brilliant, glowing orb of a clear moon, an eerie burial ceremony took place, attended by the Englishmen and a gaggle of natives.

As the writing on the wall became evident, Brent's surviving attackers had vanished into the surrounding bush. It was past midnight when an exhausted Nathaniel Davidson and his father crossed the threshold of the house, between them they cleaned up the wounds inflicted by the former farm employee. One deep cut needed more stringent medical attention but it not being available, Sir Toby pressured the wound for an hour until the oozing blood finally stopped and he could dress it.

Nathaniel collapsed into bed and fell into a fitful sleep, in which grotesque apparitions of Brent attacked him again and again, only in this scenario the attacker had become the victor and Nathaniel lay dead on the reddened earth of the farm.

CHAPTER 18

The vineyard lay before Nathaniel, verdant on the familiar slopes. He could see the house in the distance. Within days of the attack on the horse farm he had left Sir Toby in post, managing its day-to-day operations while he returned to Mary and then to report Brent's death to the authorities in Cape Town.

He watched the workers tending the vines from his vantage point on the hill. They were moving like ants among the foliage, going about their duties.

As he covered the last few yards up to the house, he was feeling as excited as a schoolboy, knowing he was about to see his precious wife again.

On the journey home, his mind had gone over the meeting time and time again, how he would walk into the house, she would see him and they would subside in each other's arms.

As Mary rushed from their home, that picture was destroyed, running toward him, her face wreathed in smiles. Dropping from the horse in time he caught the excited woman in his arms, their mouths meeting in furious embrace, months of pent up frustration and yearning lost in the welcome.

They kissed, not daring to let each other go. She was laughing and crying at the same time, Nathaniel fearing the excitement might harm his unborn child.

"Calm yourself, sweetheart," he urged her. "Think of the baby."

"My God, Nathaniel, I've missed you so much," she told him. "Are you happy about the baby?" His face told her everything she needed to know.

"Of course I am, my darling," he enlightened her. Nathaniel lovingly touched the dome of her stomach, it wasn't huge but unmistakably apparent.

The young couple walked to the house, clinging desperately to each other, terrified if they left hold of the other, they might lose them forever.

Inside Nathaniel led his wife directly to the bedroom, though he voiced his concern as they closed the door, "Mary, I need you desperately," he breathed hard. "But will it be alright, my love?" She took his hand and placed it on her breast, the burgeoning nipple hard to his touch.

"Yes," she murmured, "take me now, sweetheart."

Fervour enveloped them, but the man still held back as much as he could, anxious about the baby's welfare. Mary threw herself into the lovemaking with a desire fermented over the weeks. After they were spent, sleep overcame them, enfolded in each other's arms as Morpheus exerted his influence.

He was confused about his surroundings when he woke, having spent some weeks away, the topography of the bedroom was unfamiliar as he opened his eyes.

Looking down at the sleeping form of his wife, a radiance clearly associated with her condition, pervaded the beautiful features, the skin seemed to glow with vitality. She stirred her arm, snaking it around his body as she shifted to a more comfortable position. Mary's eyelids separated, looking straight into his eyes, a devastating smile playing around the full lips.

For a long time they lay together, Mary telling him about progress in the vineyard since his departure and the visit of his friend Ebenezer Smith.

"I'm delighted you've retained him to transport the stock, my darling," murmured Nathaniel, between stolen kisses.

"It seemed the logical thing to do, him being our friend and someone we can trust," replied his wife.

Reluctantly she exited the bed and dressed, Nathaniel watching the spectacle with longing in his eyes. Mary was a magnificent woman and in her pregnant state he found her as desirable as ever.

The morning after his arrival was overcast, dismal clouds heaped up in the sky with vivid tumult, it was a portent of coming rain.

In the breezy coolness a worker waited, tending two horses in the traces of a carriage, waiting for his employers to enter. As they embarked, he closed the vehicle's door behind them, climbing into the driver's position.

Sir Thomas Collins' residency was some distance away but the coachman made good time, coaxing excellent speed from the animals.

The Governor entered his office, where the two visitors had been seated by a member of the residency staff. He looked every inch the royal representative in the land.

"My friends, this is a great pleasure, how are you both?" enquired Sir Thomas.

"Well," returned Nathaniel. "Very well. As you can see Mary is with our first child."

"How wonderful for you both, I wish you the best of everything," continued Collins taking Mary's hand, bending to brush it with his lips.

"I'm afraid we have some important news to impart to you in your official capacity, Governor," began the man.

Over the next ten minutes, Nathaniel explained the account of Philip Brent's attacks on the horse farm and his subsequent killing by Sir Toby.

Collins listened intently, his face demonstrating more and more concern.

"What action needs to be taken, Sir Thomas?" asked Mary.

"I'm afraid, my dear, that Sir Toby will have to be taken into custody and charged with the murder of this Philip Brent."

The shock to Mary and her husband was profound.

"Surely my father was within his rights, in view of the fact the man was attempting to kill me," pleaded Nathaniel.

"Brent was a British subject and a full investigation will have to take place," Collins advised the pair. "Your father will need to stand trial."

Major Bryant was summoned to the room, greeting the Davidsons warmly before being briefed by the Governor.

"Major Bryant, you will issue orders for the arrest of Sir Toby Davidson on the charge of the murder of Mr Philip Brent, a British subject, living here in South Africa," commanded the royal representative.

It seemed like an unpleasant dream to Nathaniel, wishing he would awake from the horrendous implications of the Governor's actions.

"Governor, surely there is some way to avoid this?" appealed Sir Toby's son.

"I'm afraid the law is the law and procedures must be adhered to, Nathaniel. It is my responsibility to ensure that we uphold the legal process here in South Africa."

On returning to the vineyard, Nathaniel was profoundly quiet, Mary allowing him his thoughts during the journey. The coach trundled along, shaking the occupants from the unevenness of the ground.

Staring out at the magnificent splendour of Table Mountain, bathed in sunshine, Mary reflected on the day's events. She was equally concerned for his father.

"We will just have to brief the best lawyer we can find, Nathaniel," she said grasping his hand.

Her husband squeezed the cool palm gently, his reverie broken, "That's the least I can do," he advised her. "But it will be some time before they bring him back to Cape Town."

"Let's go back to the city tomorrow and brief our lawyer then," Mary decided.

Silence became their associate for the remainder of the trip. They reached the vineyard as night was falling, coolness of the evening air enveloping the man and woman in a cloying embrace.

Dinner proceeded in silence, no enthusiasm for the food could be generated by either Nathaniel or his wife. It tasted bland, the two of them propelling the items around their plates absentmindedly.

"He will be alright, sweetheart," ventured the woman. Nathaniel gazed at her, realising how much his wife meant to him.

"I'm not so sure, Mary," voiced her husband. "Supposing they find him guilty of murder and he is sentenced to death."

Rising and standing behind the man, she hugged him to her, bending to kiss his neck.

"I'm sure it will all work out, my angel," it was a statement she didn't truly believe, but she wanted to take his hurt away, for her it was a small and necessary deception.

CHAPTER 19

They sat in the outer office of Anderson and Van Leer, waiting for the senior partner and personal lawyer for their interests, the man and woman lost in their thoughts of Sir Toby.

A huge, overweight individual swept into the company, clutching legal briefs and a myriad of other papers.

George Anderson was a larger than life man, who loved the excesses of good living, generally regarded as the foremost gourmet and wine expert in Cape Town and consequently, he was invited and attended all the fashionable parties. He was an exceptional lawyer too.

Nathaniel rose to meet his legal representative. The man dragged his obese frame across to his clients, shaking hands warmly with a perspiring palm.

"How are you, my friends?"

An attentive clerk approached, reminding Anderson of a coming appointment in half an hour. The lawyer dismissed him with a gesture of the hand, his business with the Davidsons had proved lucrative over the short time he had acted for them and they took precedence over any of his other clients. Nathaniel was amazed each time he saw the interior of Anderson's office. It was the most cluttered place he had ever seen. Scattered haphazardly over every inch of desk and chair space were legal documents, vying with open legal textbooks, a court wig and several empty glasses of red wine, the dregs of which almost certainly originated in the Davidsons vineyard.

It appeared the last legal chambers one would ever visit a second time but Nathaniel and Mary had learned quickly the man lived expertly on chaos.

Anderson's chair creaked alarmingly as he lowered himself into it, protesting at the weight.

"And what can I do for you today, Nathaniel?" he questioned, motioning him to remove some papers from two chairs so they could sit down.

"My father is being arrested on a charge of murder, George," the man appraised him.

The story of Brent's attacks on the farm and the circumstances of his murder took twenty minutes to relay, at the end of which he looked imploringly at his lawyer.

"So tell me, George, does he have a chance of acquittal?"

"There are a number of issues to be considered," Anderson began. "Firstly, it isn't a case of self-defence as your father wasn't being attacked personally and secondly the prosecution is bound to bring up the fact that Brent was not armed and more than reasonable force was employed to subdue him, I fear they may have a case." To Nathaniel and Mary it sounded bleak. Despite his usual bullish attitude to hopeless cases, the way Anderson was acting was a worry.

"His followers killed several of my workers, George, surely that counts for something doesn't it?" pleaded Sir Toby's offspring.

Anderson rose and moved through a sea of scattered paper until he was standing at the front of his desk, looking at his visitors.

"You see," he explained, "Brent was clever, he never actually attacked anyone till you, Nathaniel, and he certainly didn't maim or murder anyone, so the prosecution could argue he had no control over his associates and didn't incite them to violence by his own actions."

The statement was sound to Nathaniel, put that way Sir Toby was up against it.

"There's at least a little time while they bring your father into custody," advised Anderson, "I will need you to dictate a statement to my clerk so that I have the full facts on paper, our defence will need to be constructed as soon as possible."

The Clerk was a tiny man in contrast to his employer, with a flaky skin condition around the mouth which Mary found abhorrent. Instructing Nathaniel to begin, he reiterated the facts to the official. This time the farm owner was much more thorough with the aspects of the case, itemising the smallest detail which he knew might have a vital bearing on the outcome.

George Anderson rose to dismiss his clients, conscious of the fact his appointment had been waiting some time.

"I won't deceive you, Nathaniel," he informed the man. "We have our work cut out with this case."

"All I can ask is that you do your best, George, and pray to the Almighty for some divine intervention."

"I fear he will need it," Anderson muttered, as he returned to the sanctuary of his office.

Mary visited a small exclusive shop before they left the city, purchasing a dress which she had seen in the window on a previous visit. She wanted her husband's opinion but his mind was elsewhere, thinking over the ghastly consequences of a guilty verdict. His answers were clipped, the perfunctory remarks of no help to Mary.

Nathaniel spent the days working in the vineyard, all the while contemplating how best to help Sir Toby, the days drifting by, each one much the same as the previous. He had lost weight, Mary growing increasingly concerned for his health.

It was a day of contrast when the representative of the Governor rode up to the house, the morning had been dull and cool but early afternoon was a dramatic change, grey clouds scudding away to leave a striking cloudless, blue sky, the yellow disc of the sun beating down mercilessly on the landscape.

Lieutenant Rhys informed Nathaniel that his father had arrived in the city and was being held in the Castle Of Good Hope. He knew the fortification but had never visited it, the oldest structure in South Africa, its pentagonal shape unique in the city. Nathaniel travelled back with the army officer, heading directly for the castle.

An impressive gateway stood at the entrance to the formidable edifice, leading into a courtyard where the men dismounted. A bleak, dreary place, thought Sir Toby's son, who shivered despite the heat of the day.

A limping jailer guided them to the cells below ground, the dank air heavy with foist. Shivers here came from cold, not fear. Opening the door to the chamber, Nathaniel saw his father for the first time in weeks, looking anxious, but otherwise well and in good health.

"This is a pretty state of affairs, my boy," the man attempted humorously, "and I don't regret my actions in the slightest."

"George Anderson is our lawyer Father, he's been briefed to defend you and will be coming to see you in a day or two to discuss the case." Peering around the bleak cell, the stone grey, lichen covered walls were depressingly chilling to the visitor and would be intolerable for the occupant. Flagstones of the same hue covered the floors, cracked, eroded and filthy from years of neglect.

A wooden bed stood in one corner of the cell, with one blanket and a filthy pillow perched on the shabby mattress. High up in the wall, a small barred window looked out at courtyard level, allowing in pitiful light and in inclement weather, unwanted, dirty rainwater.

Nathaniel stayed for half an hour until told by the jailer his visiting time was over. Father and son said their farewells, the young man exiting, promising to return soon.

As the door banged into place, Nathaniel turned to the keeper of the cells, "Who is in charge here?" he demanded offhandedly.

"I am," spat the jailer.

"I mean, who is your superior?" snarled Sir Toby's son, tiring of the minion.

"Perhaps you should think twice before you adopt that tone with me," snorted the guard, "I have the power to make your father's life even more hell than it already is in this place."

Nathaniel moved his nose to within an inch of the other man's, "And maybe you should think twice before you say that kind of thing to a friend of the Governor."

Squinting, the jailer weighed up the validity of Nathaniel's statement, eventually deciding discretion was the better part of valour.

"Captain Keen," the man expounded, rattling the enormous metal disc containing the cell keys. In the stone passage the sound reverberated around the walls.

"And where would I find him?" requested Nathaniel.

"Follow me," the man instructed.

In the labyrinthine passages, Nathaniel could hear pitiful moaning sounds of prisoners in their cells. Rounding a corner where the locked chambers ended, a series of administration offices appeared, the jailer halting at a dark wood door where he tapped briskly on the surface.

"Come in," called a voice and the guard entered, Nathaniel following closely on his heels.

"Captain Keen, this is Nathaniel Davidson, son of Sir Toby Davidson," he indicated the visitor with disdain after their spat. "He wishes to talk to you."

"What can I do for you, Mr Davidson?" the man asked, comfortably seated behind his ornate desk. "You can go, Thompson," he added before Nathaniel spoke.

"I would like to know why my father is being held in such abominable conditions," Nathaniel demanded. "His cell is not fit for human habitation."

Shuffling some papers on his desk, the officer extracted a buff coloured sheet, scanning it with interest for several seconds.

"Your father has been detained on a charge of murder, Mr Davidson and as such he is incarcerated on orders of the Governor while awaiting trial," Captain Keen enlightened his visitor. "Sir Toby is held in this place quite legally and properly," he ended.

Nathaniel grasped the back of a chair facing the Captain's desk, "May I sit?" he enquired.

"Please do," responded Keen resignedly, realising his opening statement was not getting rid of the man.

Sitting down, Nathaniel weighed up the officer. His military bearing and forthright manner told him that remonstrating angrily would only serve to antagonise the official, making him intransigent, so he adopted a more conciliatory tone.

"Captain, I realise the seriousness of the charges levelled against my father but at this stage he has been found guilty of nothing." The officer was looking intensely bored with the whole business as the visitor continued. "I ask you, is there not a way his time could be made more comfortable, he is, after all, a man of advanced years?"

Icy blue eyes stared directly into Nathaniel's pupils and the man leaned forward, "Mr Davidson, most of the people here are awaiting trial on some charge or other and they are all innocent until proven guilty, this is the designated place of imprisonment here in Cape Town," he leaned back once more. "Your father is detained in the appropriate conditions."

"He is a gentleman, Captain, and a former minister of the crown, surely there is a more appropriate place to retain such a man," Nathaniel implored.

Captain Keen measured his response carefully, "You think that your father should be cosseted because he has a title, is that it?" his temper was fast deteriorating. "Why should he receive preferential treatment because of his rank?" This wasn't going as Nathaniel planned, realising he had seriously miscalculated the man.

"I merely meant," he began but the Captain raised his hand to cut him off in mid flow.

"You merely meant to intimidate me, Mr Davidson, and I do not take kindly to that kind of behaviour; I run this prison strictly and fairly, your father will remain precisely where he is and that is my final decision."

Sir Toby's offspring bridled, "Then I will approach the Governor personally, Captain Keen, as I am not satisfied with your treatment of my father," he advised. The officer's features did not change.

"That, of course, is your prerogative, Mr Davidson, but I warn you that his reaction will almost certainly be the same as my own, this meeting is now at an end." His eyes drifted down to the papers on his desk.

Storming out of the office and the castle, Nathaniel sought his mount in the courtyard, riding directly to the Governor's residence, seeking an audience with Sir Thomas.

Half an hour of waiting ensued, until the Governor entered the chamber, greeting his visitor with a smile. "Nathaniel, this is an unexpected pleasure, I'm sorry I took so long but there are some political figures from London here and I had to greet them in my official capacity."

"I need to talk to you about Sir Toby," he started. "I have just visited him in the cells of the Castle Of Good Hope and he is living in appalling conditions there," he paused. "A Captain Keen is in charge of the jail and I have made representation to him that my father should be housed in more appropriate conditions, commensurate with his status and he has refused, therefore I have come to ask if you can intercede on my behalf?"

"And what did Captain Keen say to you, Nathaniel?" asked the official.

The younger man recounted his meeting with the officer verbatim, Sir Thomas listening to the account carefully.

"This is a very difficult thing for me to have to tell you, my friend, but Captain Keen is absolutely correct in his actions. Your father is being held on a charge of murder and is held in the appropriate manner and Nathaniel," he fixed his gaze on the man, "Do not attempt to browbeat my officials in this land again, they carry out my orders and I will not tolerate them being intimidated in this fashion." Nathaniel looked despondent and Sir Thomas continued sympathetically, "I count you as a friend, but I will not allow anyone to circumvent the law here in my jurisdiction, do you understand?"

Nathaniel headed for home, feeling as dejected as he had in a long time. He wanted to help his father but the Governor had let it be known in the strongest possible terms that Sir Toby would remain imprisoned where he was and the trial was set for one month hence.

within 21 days of purchase and be in
perfect condition.

Shop online at Waterstones.com
Free UK delivery to store

Waterstone's

Exchange and refund policy

Waterstone's is happy to exchange or
refund your items on presentation of a
valid receipt. Goods must be returned
within 21 days of purchase and be in
perfect condition.

Shop online at Waterstones.com
Free UK delivery to store

Waterstone's

Exchange and refund policy

Waterstone's is happy to exchange or
refund your items on presentation of a
valid receipt. Goods must be returned
within 21 days of purchase and be in
perfect condition.

Shop online at Waterstones.com
Free UK delivery to store

Halting his mount on the picturesque slopes above the vineyard, he dismounted, allowing the horse to graze, as he sat down on the warm earth and contemplated his life.

For such a tender age much had happened to him, lots of it sad with the occasional burst of happiness thrown in. Mary was the constant joy to him and the baby would no doubt be his pride and joy, but the worry of his father at this time was overwhelming him.

He watched the horse grazing peacefully before him, wishing he had the same tranquil existence. It seemed life for everyone else was continuing as it always had but he was empty inside, scared and thoroughly powerless to help his father in his terrible predicament. Tears of frustration poured down his face leaving glistening trails down the cheeks; he roared with frustration, an animal utterance, violent and deafening. Nathaniel had lost one parent and now faced the loss of the other, simply because Sir Toby had protected him as any father would. He questioned the ordained path that God was directing in his life, wondering whether he could keep faith with a supreme being that heaped so much misery on his shoulders.

Over the next hour he wrestled with his conscience. If God was truly beneficent, he would help Sir Toby now, it was the divine entity's final chance to retain his soul; if his father was sentenced to death and swung, he would no longer be dutiful to God.

Mary was waiting for him at the door to the house, she had seen the horse from a distance, coming out to meet her husband. He looked tired and forlorn as he slid down from the saddle, they kissed passionately, Mary sensing his utter dejection.

"How is your father, my love?" she inquired.

The man held firmly onto his wife. "It doesn't look good, Mary, they have him locked away in terrible conditions; he doesn't deserve that."

"And the Governor, what did he say?" she pressed him, knowing full well that he would have made representations in that direction.

"Sir Thomas says that the due process of law must take its course and my father will remain in that awful place."

They entered the house, Mary instructing her maid to prepare food for him. He ate but showed little enthusiasm for the fare and her concern grew with each passing second.

Life went on as normally as it could, Mary and Nathaniel visiting his father whenever the work on the vineyard allowed. Sir Toby was becoming increasingly resigned to a guilty verdict and the death penalty. It proved almost impossible to alter his outlook, despite his son and daughter-in-law's assertions to the contrary.

Anderson had worked to construct the best defence possible, his efforts hampered by the distance to the horse farm from Cape Town. All the while he forewarned his clients about the likely outcome. The case would not be easy but he would do his best, he said. It didn't fill Nathaniel with unqualified confidence.

Six weeks to the day of Sir Toby's imprisonment, they were informed that the trial would take place fourteen days later at the main city courthouse. In that period, Nathaniel went through many changes of mood, one minute feeling elation at knowing his father would be acquitted to sheer black attitude of certain execution. It was stretching his sanity to the limit.

CHAPTER 20

As if to reflect Nathaniel's fears and state of mind, the day of his father's hearing dawned, cold and thoroughly depressing. The rain was holding off but it was debatable how long it would last.

He and Mary arrived at the court chambers an hour prior to the trial beginning at 10.00am. At that stage, they were the only people in the courtroom, its reverential quietness offering them the chance to muse over the outcome for the thousandth time.

Grasping his arm, Mary looked directly into the eyes she loved so much. "Whatever happens, my love, I want you to know that I adore you and I will be here for you always," she said.

By 9.45am a smattering of people had occupied the public seating, most of them regular attendees, this their preferred source of entertainment. From the wealthiest to the poorest they mingled, looking forward to the juicy prospect of a murder trial involving an ex-MP of the British establishment.

The polished oak wood fabric of the courthouse gleamed as the sun struck its surface, where it flooded through the sizeable arched windows. Court officials drifted into the legislative area, gowned and wigged for the coming fray, talking in hushed tones about the proceedings to come.

Anderson took his seat directly in front of the Davidsons, placing a considerable sheaf of legal papers he carried on the table before him. He turned to Nathaniel shaking his hand warmly, Nathaniel speaking first, "Do your best, George," he pleaded.

"Don't I always, Nathaniel?" the man grinned.

The prosecuting attorney bounded into the room, closely pursued by three junior aides. He was tall at six feet two inches and carried himself with an air of haughty arrogance.

Anderson nodded a greeting in the lawyers direction, who returned the gesture curtly before settling himself in his seat at the adjoining table to the defence solicitor.

"That's Bernard Chasen, the crown prosecutor," Anderson told his clients.

At ten precisely the Clerk to the Court rose, announcing in an authoritative but bored voice, "All rise."

The scarlet clad figure of Judge Roger Trevelyan emerged from a door close to the bench, ambling in the direction of his pew. The clerk made the address to the court, asking everyone to sit as the judge took his seat. Nathaniel's prejudiced eye observed the jury as they entered for swearing, convinced it was a hanging jury by the expressions on the faces, in his depressed state he would have decided that, whoever sat in arbitration of his father's fate.

"Mr Chasen, your opening statement if you please?" instructed Trevelyan.

The prosecutor rose slowly and deliberately to his feet, every eye on the imposing figure.

"The facts of the case are simple and damning and are these," the legal brain began. "Sir Toby Davidson, the accused," he indicated the man in the dock, "shot dead an unarmed man, Philip Brent, who posed him no threat, and did it in a cold and calculating manner. He has shown no remorse for the incident either then or now."

Sir Toby was ensconced in the prisoner's box shortly before the proceedings began, two burly escorts sat alongside him, the prisoner looking on quietly and confidently, seemingly indifferent at the outcome of his case.

Outlining the sequence of events on the day in question, Chasen concluded his opening statement saying, "At the end of this hearing, you the jury, will have no difficulty in bringing a guilty verdict in this case, the facts will be irrefutable and only one outcome will be possible."

The prosecutor left the rail in front of the jury, retaking his seat, his juniors fawningly congratulating him on his opening gambit.

Judge Trevelyan turned his attention to George Anderson, "And now the opening statement from the defence, Mr Anderson," he requested.

Rising to face the jury, Anderson had little confidence in anything he could say in mitigation and he cleared his throat.

"Gentlemen of the jury," he started, "I would like you to picture the scene on that fateful day, Philip Brent had ridden to the farm of Nathaniel Davidson with the sole purpose of wreaking havoc and causing as much damage to the property as he could. He brought with him a band of ruffians to achieve his task, attacking the son of my client violently, with the intention of killing him," he allowed the information to sink in with the members.

"Sir Toby Davidson was involved in trying to protect his son's asset when he came upon the attack by Brent on Nathaniel Davidson," a further pause.

"He came upon the attack from behind, Brent having no idea if the man was armed or not and fired at him in the heat of the moment. One thing I would like you to bear in mind in all this is that Brent had threatened Nathaniel Davidson's life when he was told his father would be taking over the running of the farm; not that Brent would lose his job I hasten to add, but the man could not accept this situation and left with a warning to my client's son that he would do him harm." Anderson took a drink of water from a glass and carafe on the table.

"In those circumstances, what other conclusion could Sir Toby Davidson come to in the violent intensity of the situation, doing what most parents would do, he protected his son. Therefore I urge you to return a verdict of not guilty to murder in this case."

The morning was spent in examining the first prosecution witnesses, mainly members of Brent's band of thugs who had since been charged with their part in the raid but whose cases had not yet been heard so they were at liberty to give evidence. Chasen brought the full force of the law to bear in tracking down the individuals, promising that the prosecution in their cases would be fairly lenient to them. As they were not found guilty at this stage, it was in their interest to be coerced and Chasen was famous for sailing close to the wind to get a conviction in any trial.

Anderson did his best to discredit the individuals but his objections to the presiding official were overruled on the grounds that the men were not convicted felons and their testimony was valid.

The morning wore on, the courtroom increasingly hot and sticky as the procedure continued. Several members of the public were dozing lightly in their chairs, the faint sound of snoring rising into the air. At 12.30pm, Trevelyan brought the morning's process to a close, "We will break for lunch now and will reconvene at 2.30 sharp," he commanded, striking his gavel once to indicate the official end of the session. Mary and Nathaniel joined Anderson in a local hostelry for lunch, questioning him on his opinion of the trial so far. He was non committal and they ate in relative silence, the food good and the general clamour in the popular place loud.

"How long is the trial likely to last, George?" asked Nathaniel.

"Not long, I fear," the defence lawyer returned. "Most of my representation will be conjecture rather than fact. I will be appealing to the jury's emotion rather than logic I'm afraid, Chasen has the upper hand where point of law is concerned."

Anderson tucked into a buttered lobster, Nathaniel and Mary ignoring their plates, despite its reputation the food did not appeal to them one bit. They were far too worried about Anderson's lack of conviction and confidence regarding the outcome of the case.

Without warning Nathaniel exploded, his anger directed at the legal representative, whose only enthusiasm so far seemed for the shellfish in front of him,

"For God's sake, George, you're defending my father on a charge of murder, if your previous bills are anything to go by you will be expecting a substantial amount of money for the privilege, so earn your money," he bellowed.

Mary calmed him as best she could but knew he was right, the lawyer seemed to have given up on the case before it had begun. Dragging her husband from the hostelry, she propelled him to a bench outside the courthouse where they sat in silence for a few minutes.

"He can't be found guilty, Mary, he simply can't," pleaded Nathaniel, looking like a little boy lost. For the first time she saw a man who was really vulnerable and her maternal instinct came through. They hugged as if it were the last time they would ever have the opportunity and she soothed him until his upset was under control, by which time it was the appointed hour to go back into court.

The afternoon session paralleled the morning business. Chasen continued to call witnesses of Brent's band of native thugs, Anderson continued to object and the judge continually overruled him each time.

It was close to 6pm when Chasen stood up, "That concludes the case for the prosecution m'lud," he finished.

Judge Trevelyan consulted with the clerk to the court, announcing the court was adjourned until the following morning at ten when the defence would lay out their case. With a loud clack of the gavel on the block the proceedings came to an end.

Anderson hurried from the chamber without talking to Nathaniel and Mary, the contretemps at lunch still fresh in his mind. Sir Toby was taken down and removed to his cell in the penal edifice close by the court location. Only the Davidsons remained in the empty chamber, looking around the majestic structure of the courtroom. Finally they withdrew to make the journey home, once again carried out in silence. Mary realised he wanted no comfort at this stage, he was too angry to accept that.

When they got to bed that night, he was in need of consolation and they wrapped each other up in their arms. Her warm body helping him to forget the situation for a short while.

They lay afterward, kissing and hugging in the darkness, Mary venturing, "Nathaniel, I know you lost your temper with George today but this case can't be easy for him, the way it has been presented by Chasen is essentially what happened," he looked dejected as she continued. "What I'm saying is that you must prepare yourself for the worst, my love, anything else is a bonus."

"I should apologise to Anderson," he replied, "I know I lost my temper but it's because I know in my own mind that it looks bleak for my father, I will seek George out tomorrow and make peace with him, never fear."

Nathaniel waited outside the robing room the next day for the lawyer, who looked perturbed as he approached his sponsor, the memory of the previous day still fresh in Anderson's memory.

"George," began Nathaniel, "may I speak to you?"

"There is nothing to talk about, Mr Davidson, you made it abundantly clear what you thought of my efforts yesterday."

"Please George, is there somewhere we can talk?"

Anderson led him to an office adjoining the dressing room and closed the door behind them.

"I apologise for my behaviour yesterday, George, It was unforgivable," Nathaniel Davidson remarked humbly. "The case has upset me more than I thought possible."

The lawyer's first thought was to reject the apology but as he looked into the man's face, he saw a genuine contriteness.

"Very well, I accept, but I want to impress on you how embarrassing the whole incident was in front of the hostelry's clientele."

They shook hands.

"Now if you don't mind, Nathaniel, I have to get wigged and gowned," Anderson begged.

Sitting next to Mary in the chamber, her husband relayed the account of his meeting with their legal agent.

"I'm sure it was the right thing to do, my angel," her soft tones seemed appropriate for the atmosphere of the building. This particular morning the court public areas filled to capacity. Word had got round that this would be a quick trial with an inevitable guilty verdict, a neck stretching. Laughing and partaking of fruit in their seats, it upset Nathaniel how little they felt for another human being's life, tossing the peel to the floor. To them it was a sideshow, something which would not affect their lives one iota and he was finding it difficult that people could regard a man's life as entertainment.

Trevelyan got the proceedings underway, asking Anderson to call his witnesses. The lawyer trotted out a succession of Nathaniel's employees who testified to a man they witnessed the attack by Brent on their employer and the subsequent shot fired by Sir Toby in the heat of the moment.

Under cross examination by Chasen, however, they admitted Brent carried no weapon, all they had seen take place was a fist fight.

Anderson had exhausted his band of witnesses by mid afternoon and several more who attested to Sir Toby's character. It was going to be one of the swiftest murder trials on record.

At four Trevelyan called on Chasen to make his closing remarks.

"Gentlemen of the jury," commenced the prosecutor. "You have heard the facts in this case, we the prosecution do not deny that Philip Brent went to the Davidson horse farm with the sole purpose of causing havoc and that he took with him a band of men incited to achieve those aims," he halted briefly for effect.

"However, he took no part in the violence or destruction and was murderously attacked by Nathaniel Davidson and a fight broke out between the two men," Chasen pointed to the man in the dock.

"Sir Toby Davidson came across that fracas and fired at Philip Brent with the sole intention of killing him and that is precisely what he did, therefore I demand that you bring in a verdict of guilty against this man; it is the only way to allow Philip Brent to rest peacefully," he looked imploringly at the jury members. "I rely on your good auspices in the sure knowledge that you will do the right thing."

Chasen sat, satisfied with his presentation of the case. He looked at Anderson, almost daring the man to defeat him, a victorious smile commanding the small cruel mouth with its thin lips.

At Judge Trevelyan's bidding, George rose, facing the jurors before him, he had deliberately rejected the idea of preparing his closing statement in advance. All he could do was to bring his advocacy skills to the fore and plead his client's case on a human and emotional basis.

Anderson inhaled sharply, "Gentlemen of the jury," he began. "Picture the scene on the day in question. A band of ruthless thugs attack the livelihood of Nathaniel Davidson and his pregnant wife, Mary," it was a low tactic to mention her condition but all was fair in love, war and the judicial arena.

"This group of men were hell bent on destroying the business of a man, whose only crime was to pass control of his horse farm from Brent to his father; Philip Brent could not accept that but had the opportunity to retain his employment with the Davidsons. However, because of a bitter and arrogant nature, he left them and fermented plans to hurt them as best he could," Anderson cleared his dry throat.

"The way he decided to achieve that, was by breaking the law and causing violence and destruction. As he and Nathaniel Davidson grappled on the ground, my client Sir Toby happened upon them, seeing his son being overcome by this thug he fired his weapon, killing the attacker in the process. He had been involved trying to quell an attack by a murderous group of ruffians and in the heat of battle he had protected his son. How many of us could truly say we would not have done the same thing in those circumstances and remember, at this stage Sir Toby Davidson did not know if Brent was armed or not? Let me say that again, he had no idea if the man attacking his son was armed," Anderson ended with a direct plea to the members of the jury.

"If you understand that to be the case, I ask you, I implore you, to find the defendant not guilty and I hope you will find yourself duty bound to do so."

There was a silence in the court as the heavyweight lawyers completed their cases, finally broken by the scarlet clad judge.

"Members of the jury, you have heard the cases for the prosecution and the defence, it is now your task to deliberate on these proceedings. On the one hand it has been put to you that an unarmed man was shot in cold blood by the defendant in a calculating manner. The defence disputes this and mitigates that Sir Toby Davidson saw Brent attacking his son and was unaware if the man was armed and therefore used reasonable force to subdue him in the context of the attack." Trevelyan leaned back in the ornate throne. "You must now decide which set of circumstances you believe and are to take as long as necessary to come to your decision."

In keeping with the rest of the trial, the jury returned after a mere forty-five minutes of deliberation, their Foreman rose at the behest of the Court Clerk.

"Have you reached a decision on which you are all agreed?" he demanded.

"We have," spoke the slightly statured man.

"Do you find the defendant, Sir Toby Davidson, guilty or not guilty of murder?"

Leaning forward in his seat, Nathaniel grasped the rail before him, knuckles ivory white and his face strained, heart pounding in his chest to such an extent he fancied he could hear it.

The man charged with the administration of the jury paused, it was his moment of glory.

"We, the jury, find the defendant guilty as charged," the voice boomed around inside Nathaniel's head, he was speechless at the decision.

"Is that the decision of you all?" asked the clerk.

"It is."

Judge Trevelyan turned to the jury as the Foreman retook his seat, "My thanks, gentlemen, for your attention in this case, you have carried out your duties diligently and well."

The Foreman rose once more, tentatively this time, "Your Honour," he began. "If it is not out of keeping with these

147

proceedings, may I make representation to you on behalf of my colleagues?"

"Of course, Mr Foreman, please continue."

"While we have found the defendant guilty of the murder of Philip Brent, we do feel there was real provocation in this case on a day of savagery and chaos and we ask that this be taken into account when sentencing is passed," the man concluded and sat down again.

Trevelyan was impressed with the jury's candour.

"Thank you, gentlemen," he addressed the jury in its entirety, "I will of course give due consideration to your petition," he turned his attention to the dock.

"Sir Toby Davidson, please rise." The black cap signifying death had been placed before him by the clerk, the judge making no attempt to place it on his head.

"You have been found guilty by your peers of the murder of Philip Brent; in normal circumstances the sentence of this court would have been death by hanging, however, I am persuaded by the jury that a certain amount of leniency can be exercised in this case and I am therefore commuting your sentence from one of death to penal servitude for life in the crown colony of Australia," he glanced at Sir Toby's chief escort. Take him down," he instructed.

Head in hands, Nathaniel sat, bent forward in his seat, Mary was sobbing quietly, as she watched her father-in-law removed from the dock to the holding cells. The judge granted them leave to visit Sir Toby and they made their way into the bowels of the building, where the cells were located.

Sir Toby was completely shocked, not able to take in the verdict or the sentence. When his son arrived, the men hugged, Nathaniel promising to instruct Anderson to generate an appeal.

Sir Toby looked forlorn. "Anderson has already informed me that appeal might have the sentence changed to hanging if it were unsuccessful and while I consider myself a brave man, where there is life there is hope, so I have told him not to proceed with any application for the case to be re-examined," he informed his son.

An oppressive silence filled the room, Nathaniel could think of nothing to say, nothing to give comfort or succour to his parent, growing steadily angrier at the way his life kept stranding him in a sea of disappointment.

The hush in the room wore on, before a court official arrived, a small man with a piggy face, he looked distinctly uncomfortable in the presence of the Davidson clan.

"Sir Toby Davidson, I have been instructed to inform you that a convict ship, bound for Australia is currently anchored off Cape Town," he seemed to be saying something and nothing with his nondescript tone. "This vessel will sail later this evening and you will board her immediately, for transportation to your place of incarceration."

"This is outrageous," erupted Nathaniel. "Without leave for appeal or the opportunity to form one, is this an example of justice?"

"That is the decision of the judge, escorts will arrive momentarily to convey you to the ship, please be ready to leave." The man hurried off, delighted to have carried out his duty so quickly, and he almost ran from the room.

"Nathaniel," his father stated. "This may well be the last time we will see each other. I want you to listen carefully to what I have to say." He grasped his son's hand. "I want you to know that I am very proud of you, you have achieved so much in your short life, so much in business and you must carry on providing for Mary and my grandchild."

"Please, Father, it's not over yet, I will find a way to reverse this decision," the son counselled.

Sir Toby smiled, it was the resigned action of a man who had come to terms with his lot, "I don't think I will last long in Australia, my boy," he stopped Nathaniel speaking with a firm hand on his son's shoulder. "So you must take on the family name and build a Davidson dynasty that will astonish the world. This is my hope and, Nathaniel," he looked his son in the eye, "buy back Thistlebrough one day, I know it holds a special place in your heart."

The cell door burst open, the escorts striding in purposefully, manacling Sir Toby at the wrist and ankle, roughly pushing him before them down the corridor.

"Remember what I said Nathaniel, make the Davidson name one to be reckoned with," he shouted, rounding a corner, and was gone.

Time seemed to stop for Nathaniel, the moment his father disappeared from sight. Turning to Mary, she noticed his eyes glistening. He buried his head in her breast, weeping like a new born baby. His wife had the good sense to allow him to expel his emotion, saying nothing until he was cried out, then taking his head in her hands, kissing him with every ounce of compassion in her body. He would never get over the events of the last 48 hours but he was her man and she vowed to herself that she would make his life as happy as she could.

CHAPTER 21

A fortnight had passed since his father's transportation. The vineyard and horse farm were performing well. Nathaniel was becoming a very wealthy individual, he and Mary becoming sought after as guests at the most fashionable soirees in Cape Town.

Mary was almost full term and would give birth at any moment. Watching her pottering in the little garden she had created to occupy her mind while she wasn't able to perform the heavy labour of the vineyard, Nathaniel reflected how much she meant to him. She wasn't adept at raising flowers in the same way she was with the vines but the splash of diverse colour the plants exhibited, provided a beautiful vista in the vicinity of the house.

Always at her side was her native maid Rachel, watching her movement closely for any sign her labour had started. Mary suddenly grasped her stomach, bending forward involuntarily. He didn't need the servant to tell him what was happening. Rushing to her, he swept her up in his arms, carrying her to the house and gently placing her in their bed.

"The time is here my darling," she gasped, "perhaps you should fetch the doctor."

Leaping down the stairs three at a time and bolting for the door, his shoulder crashed into the wood surround as he rushed out. It should have caused him great pain, but with the adrenalin rushing he didn't feel a twinge.

Whipping his horse to a frenzy, Nathaniel drove the animal to its utmost as he cut down the miles into the city. Layers of steaming, white sweat poured out of the animal, the rider spurring it on to greater effort.

Situated in the centre of Cape Town, Dr. Angus McLement's surgery was a building of high stature and real distinction, where the surgeon treated patients of quality. The physician was attending a gentleman for gout as the prospective father burst in,

"Angus," he panted, "you must come now, Mary is in labour."

"Nathaniel, you can't burst in here like this," the doctor chastised him, "please wait outside until I am finished here."

"But you don't understand, Angus," continued the man, "she is in labour now."

The doctor excused himself to his patient, propelling Davidson out of the room roughly. "Nathaniel, you are not the only man to have a baby and these things can take time, now sit down and I will be with you presently." With that he disappeared back into his consulting room.

Every second the doctor was absent seemed an eternity to Nathaniel. Ten minutes after he had left him the Doctor returned.

"Now, Nathaniel," he said, "let's go and see to your wife."

Riding to the vineyard they talked generally, Nathaniel not really listening to the man's conversation, spurring on his horse as the estate came into view, the doctor struggling to keep up with his companion.

The horse had barely come to a stop as Nathaniel threw himself from the saddle, dashing into the house, straight for the bedroom. He burst through the door, a sight of pure rapture meeting his gaze.

His wife lay nursing an infant, gazing down devotedly on the babe, her eyes moving to her husband.

"My sweetheart, meet your son," the woman's voice was filled with pride.

Looking down on his child, tears pricked his eyes. The boy was perfect, lying quietly sleeping in his mother's arms. Nathaniel bent to his wife, kissing her passionately.

"Thank you for this, my darling," he sobbed.

Doctor McLements had followed him into the room, "Congratulations Nathaniel, now get out for a few minutes while I check your wife over," the doctor instructed.

"How did you manage without a doctor, my darling?" Nathaniel asked, heading for the door.

"My maid, Rachel," she told him. "She's delivered many children for her tribe, she was magnificent."

The doctor ushered him out of the room. Reluctantly he left hanging around the passageway outside, desperate to see his son again.

Presently the doctor exited the chamber, "The maid did a wonderful job Nathaniel," he informed the father. "Mary is in excellent health but you must wait about six weeks for her to heal before you begin relations again."

"Thank you Angus," Nathaniel declared.

"Nothing to thank me for my friend, it's the maid you should thank, she did a superb job," he advised. "Now I'll get back to my surgery if you don't mind, I will call on Mary again the day after tomorrow to see how she is doing."

Escorting the medical practitioner back to his horse, the vineyard owner waved him goodbye before returning to his wife. She looked radiant and very pleased with herself, the babe remained asleep, Mary cuddling him as though she would never let him go.

Nathaniel lay on the bed next to his family, looking with affection at his first male child, kissing Mary once more. The proudest day of his life, he never wanted it to end. Exhausted he fell into sleep, arm across Mary in a gesture of protection.

Mary was still asleep next to him when he woke, the child dozing in a wooden crib of native design at the foot of the bed. Nathaniel rose and peered into the structure,. His son was strong and beautiful with none of the wrinkles most new born babies tended to possess; his colour a delicate pink, no flushing indicating a difficult birth.

They christened the boy Toby after Nathaniel's father. It seemed an appropriate gesture and from the very first moment, Nathaniel and his wife doted on their first born. The man had no intention of letting Toby go through the type of abusive childhood he himself had endured, making a pact with himself to give the boy the best education that money could buy.

Although the native maid watched the child at night, he was a well-behaved infant from the start, never crying during the dark hours. He slept all the hours of darkness from the day of his birth.

A few days after the birth, Nathaniel had business to attend to in the city, riding away from his son for the first time reluctantly, albeit for a few hours only. In the heat of the day he plodded along. For the first time his life seemed to be falling into place with a beautiful wife, new born son and two highly successful businesses. Nathaniel had almost been able to forget the plight of his father but occasionally it came back to haunt him. It was strange, he thought, how time could make one forget even the blackest of things, at least for a while.

Cape Town languished under the protective shadow of its famous Mountain. The flat topped mound never failed to astonish him with its beautiful slopes. The sea was calm as a mill pond as he headed toward the harbour. He had grown to love ships, taking the time to peer out into the bay, admiring the cosmopolitan styles. A usual mix of military and cargo vessels nestled together bobbing gently at anchor.

A ship was making its way slowly into the area, the lack of wind slowing its progress. As it approached the shelter of the bay, the shape was indistinct, distance and hazy sunshine combining to hide its features.

As it grew recognisable Nathaniel couldn't believe his eyes, he was sure it was the Adventuress. Of all the days for it to arrive it was too coincidental that it should berth today, the first time he had ventured into the city since Toby's birth.

Desperate to see his old friend, Ebenezer, he galloped to the harbour in preparation to meet the Captain.

It took the best part of three quarters of an hour for the ship to inch its way to a mooring, Nathaniel sat on the wooden staithes watching the slow progress impatiently. With a splashing sound clearly audible from where he sat, the anchor chain paid out, its great metal pin, splashing down into the water, sending a spume of seawater into the air. The ship drifted backwards slightly as the anchor dragged back into the silt, holding at the extreme length of the chain.

Sailors aboard busied themselves, securing the ship from sea duty, easily spotted from shore but Nathaniel could not see anyone who looked like Smith. Sails were furled, the men waiting anxiously for their first steps on dry land in some weeks.

Ebenezer appeared from the bowels of the ship, his flowing locks the trademark of the man, along with his confident bearing and sure stride.

An hour of waiting by, Nathaniel elapsed waiting to see if the Captain was coming ashore. The ship's boat launched, Smith climbing nimbly into it, the half dozen sailors rowing expertly over the flat calm sea to the quay. The vineyard owner got to his feet, making his way to the point where the vessel was heading. Smith paid little attention to the scene on shore, bored from a tedious voyage. All he wanted was to get his feet on dry land as much as his crew did.

Nathaniel loitered at the top of the jetty steps as Smith climbed them, head down. Eventually he raised his face, mouth extending in a wide grin.

"My God, Nathaniel," erupted the sea dog, "what are you doing here?"

"Waiting for you of course," grinned the Captain's friend. "Where the hell have you been?"

They embraced, slapping each other energetically on the back. "I was coming into Cape Town on business and saw the sensual lines of the Adventuress making for harbour," advised Nathaniel, I thought you might welcome a friendly face."

"How are you, my friend?" inquired the Captain as they walked along the bustling harbour, so familiar to them both.

"I'm a father, Ebenezer, I have a son called Toby," Nathaniel informed him.

"Didn't your father explain what would happen if you did things like that with women?" the Captain laughed heartily.

They picked their way among the crowds at the quay, some waiting to board ships for foreign lands, others to purchase wares from cargoes recently landed.

"There's something else to tell you Ebenezer," disclosed Nathaniel, "my father has been found guilty of murder since your last visit and is transported."

Smith dragged his companion inside an inn close by, ordering wine, "Tell me about it my friend," he urged.

The Captain listened while his friend recounted the events leading to his father's incarceration, allowing him to speak without interruption, knowing Nathaniel had been waiting for their close friendship to pour out his anger and hurt to.

At the end of the explanation, Nathaniel was feeling better than he had done in a long time. He blamed himself for his father's predicament but now he knew that if the roles had been reversed, he would have done the same for his parent.

The Captain rose, "And now," he said, downing his drink in one, "I will allow you to introduce me to your son." It was an instruction and one the father was delighted to comply with. His business in the city could wait.

Hiring a horse for the visitor, they made their way out of the city. On the journey to the vineyard, Nathaniel enthused about the infant to the amusement of Smith, who smiled at the infectious zeal. It was as though the infant was the only one ever to be born.

CHAPTER 22

Ebenezer looked into the crib, realising why his friend was so proud.

"Nathaniel, I have a surprise for you too," Smith said, "I would be delighted if you and Mary would join me for dinner aboard the Adventuress this evening."

"What is it, Ebenezer, what is your news?" Nathaniel's curiosity was aroused.

"Until tonight, shall we say 7.30, my friends?" and with that the Captain took his leave of them.

Nathaniel pondered Smith's secret for the rest of the day. It vexed him the man was making him wait. By 5 o'clock, he was anxious to dress for the coming meal, performing his toilet in rapid time, which seemed to tick by agonisingly slowly.

Mary was humming as she attired, smiling at her husband, whose inquisitive nature was driving him to distraction.

As they rowed out to the vessel, he continued to question her about the possible news, fidgeting constantly.

"My darling," she said, "you've only a short time left before you will discover everything, just wait," the smile on her face was radiant.

Ebenezer met them at the ship's rail, grinning like the proverbial Cheshire cat.

"Well," demanded the ship master's guest, "what is this great secret you have to impart, my friend?"

"Oh I'm sure you can wait just a few more minutes," the Captain teased his friend mischievously, "please accompany me to my cabin."

Nearing the cabin door, Ebenezer stopped, palm resting on the handle.

"On my last return to London I met a young woman with whom I fell in love, we married immediately. May I present my wife?" he cracked the door.

Nathaniel drew breath at the sight which greeted him, his head began to spin. Sally stood before them looking joyful and happy. He was concerned that the woman might betray their liaison to Mary but as Ebenezer introduced them, she reacted as any stranger would when being presented to someone for the first time.

"Nathaniel, I'm delighted to meet you, Ebenezer has bored me silly for a whole voyage with stories of you," her cool hand slipped into his. She hugged Mary, "I hope we will be good friends, Mary, I need someone to rescue me from Ebenezer and his crew from time to time," she pleaded.

"I know just how you feel, these men don't understand we delicate creatures," she smiled in the men's direction.

The women moved off to talk conspiratorially, Ebenezer drawing his friend to the deck, telling his wife they were going to take some air.

In the cool atmosphere, Ebenezer turned to his friend, "I know about you and Sally," the words were expressed frankly. "She's had a rough time since her experiences at Thistlebrough, now she's my wife and I intend to make her as happy as I can for the rest of her life."

Nathaniel didn't know where to start, he had so many questions to ask of the Captain.

"Where did you find her?" he finally blurted.

"When your father discovered that you and she had been so close shall we say, he expelled her from his household. I found her destitute and working the streets in London. She had no idea I knew you and we only discovered the fact by accident." The Captain placed his hands on the rail and gazed out into the enveloping darkness listening to the water lapping at the side of the vessel. "There's one more thing, Nathaniel, and you must prepare yourself for a shock."

The captain's friend didn't think he could take many more surprises for one evening, "What is it?"

"Sally has a son, Nathaniel, a nine year old, do I really have to spell the rest out for you?"

Nathaniel stood, mouth agape, the implication almost too much to accept, "You are saying he is my son?" his voice faltered as the realisation burned itself into his brain.

"Yes Nathaniel, he's your son," confirmed Smith. "His name is Jonathan and he is unmistakably yours my friend."

Nathaniel's eyes brimmed with tears at the news. It was an eternity since that day in the stable block with Sally. A fond memory which invaded his thoughts from time to time, always tender and never something which transcended his love for Mary. It was just a pleasant interlude in his life, now he was informed that there was fruit from the union. It pained him greatly to know that he had missed nine years of the boy's life.

"Understand me well here, Nathaniel," commanded Ebenezer. "As far as I'm concerned this boy is my own son and I love Sally with every fibre in me; I ask you as a friend, not to disturb the stability of our marriage," he implored his friend. "I know how you must feel but I beg you to allow me to bring up the boy as my own with no interference, he must never know the true identity of his father."

"Where is he?" croaked the Captain's guest.

Smith turned to him, "He is sleeping in a cabin below, would you care to see him?" the Captain asked.

"Before we go down Ebenezer, I need to tell you something." He cleared his throat. "Although it will pain me greatly, I will obey your wishes, the boy is your son and he is fortunate to have such a magnificent father."

The unspoken respect between them had been strengthened enormously by the agreement reached on Jonathan. Their friendship was staunch, each could be relied on to protect the other. It was a bond women would find difficult to understand but which men searched all their lives to find.

Trimmed lanterns lit the companionway, swinging rhythmically at their stations, casting eerie shadows around the lower deck.

Stopping at a latticed door, Smith quietly opened the portal. Passing inside, the darkness was almost complete save for a ray of moonlight streaming through the porthole and straight across a cot where the young boy lay.

Nathaniel's eyes grew accustomed to the half-light, the boy's features becoming plain, a shock of black hair surmounted the strong face. He was a fine looking specimen of youth and Nathaniel hoped the future years would be kind to him. Sitting at dinner, his mind wandered to the image of the boy several times, making him lose the thread of conversation and Mary had to jerk him out of his reverie constantly, prompting him regarding a question put to him by the Captain or his wife.

Sally had blossomed with age and motherhood, he was glad that Ebenezer and she had found each other. The way she hung on Smith's every word demonstrated amply her love for the man.

Despite his joy at being with his friend again, Nathaniel was pleased when the night finally concluded. In the boat heading back to the shore he was silent with his thoughts as Mary dozed with her head on his chest under a star laden heaven.

She had invited Smith and his family to lunch at the vineyard the next day, Nathaniel wondering how he would cope talking to the boy who was his natural son.

Ebenezer, Sally and Jonathan arrived at the estate around noon, the hired carriage driven by a native slave of Smith's from the ship.

"Nathaniel may I introduce Jonathan," Ebenezer said helping the boy down from the vehicle.

In daylight, the boy was even more striking, piercing green eyes the lad's most prominent feature. He looked directly at his host, "I'm delighted to meet you, Mr Davidson," the voice strong and clear.

"As I am to meet you, Jonathan," replied Nathaniel. The manners of the child were impeccable, a testament to his upbringing.

Sally may have fallen on hard times but it was clear she had brought the youngster up splendidly. Lunch was a happy affair, much laughter circulated around the table, the women and Jonathan listened intently as the men recounted events in their lives. Despite long absences between them, the bond of friendship was as strong as ever.

Suddenly Smith posed a question to Nathaniel, "My friend, have you ever considered returning to England?" he enquired. Nathaniel had thought about it much in the last years but it hadn't crossed his mind in a long while. The table fell silent as he considered his answer.

"It's not something I have thought of recently, Ebenezer, but it's something I would like to do one day," he said.

"I ask for a reason, my friend," the Captain continued, taking a swig from his wine glass. "Before we left England I discovered your old estate is up for sale."

The news rocked Davidson. It had been his ambition for so long to return as master of Thistlebrough, never dreaming it would actually be possible. A flashback of the conversation with his father on the fateful day of his transportation, flooded into his mind and Sir Toby's advice to buy back the estate if it all possible.

Mary looked at him, "Is it something you would like to do, sweetheart?" she questioned him, noticing the excitement in his eyes at the news. Nathaniel thought hard about the prospect, the more he thought, the more the idea appealed to him.

"We'll see, Mary," he stated. "There's much to consider."

"Well don't ponder too long, Nathaniel, I can't see a property of that stature being ignored for long. If you want it, now is the time to grab it," advised the Captain, "it might already have been snapped up."

The Davidsons sat in the parlour following their guest's departure, Mary sewing and Nathaniel sitting pondering Smith's news. His wife looked up from her task.

"It's something you want to do, isn't it, Nathaniel?" The man rose and paced the room.

161

"I can't deny it's something that appeals to me," he replied, "I haven't thought of England for a long time but since Ebenezer's news of Thistlebrough's availability, perhaps it's time to return to the north-east and attempt to purchase it."

She put down her sewing, "Then the question isn't do we leave, it's *when* do we leave?" her forthrightness was something he had always loved about her.

"Are you sure my darling?" ventured her husband, "we have the two businesses here to run."

She stood, gently brushing away some imaginary fluff from his lapel. "The businesses will be fine, we'll find a good quality manager to run them. I want you to be happy, so we will go to England and you must do your best to buy the old estate if it is still available," she lifted her face for a kiss.

Happy to oblige he pulled her to him, their mouths meeting in frenzied passion. How could he have been so fortunate with this woman he thought, she was his rock and his life? As they broke from the embrace, he looked down into her eyes, "You're a wonderful woman," he told her.

The Adventuress was loading supplies when Nathaniel approached her side in a hired boat the following day, its cargo had been disembarked the previous afternoon while Nathaniel and his guests were lunching, now she bobbed much higher in the water.

Captain Smith waved an acknowledgement from his place near the ship's wheel as the longboat neared his ship. Climbing aboard the vessel, Nathaniel strode to where Smith stood. Well drilled seamen dashed around the deck, fulfilling their tasks in a cheery manner. It was something indigenous to a Smith company of men, a happy ship was an efficient ship, the Captain's motto. This was clearly a happy vessel.

"Good morning, my friend," the Captain hailed, watching the actions of his crew intently, "I trust you slept well."

Nathaniel climbed the stairs to the upper deck, "Perfectly, thank you, Ebenezer, and you?"

"When you retire aboard a ship bobbing at anchor, sleep comes easily," he laughed.

"May we talk somewhere privately, Ebenezer?" the visitor asked, eyeing the seaman manning the steering device.

Smith beckoned his guest to follow him, "My day cabin will do nicely," advised his friend, mumbling some instructions to the helmsman and leading his friend below.

Ensconced in the chamber, Nathaniel came immediately to the point, "I've considered what you said yesterday very long and hard; Mary and I have decided we will travel to England to purchase my father's old estate."

The Captain looked delighted, "Then I trust you will use the Adventuress as your method of transport, we sail for the British Isles in ten days; Sally and I would be overjoyed to have your company," grinned the Captain.

Ten days did not seem long enough to get their affairs in order.

"Could you delay your departure by a week, Ebenezer?" pleaded his friend, "I will gladly pay for any loss of trade you might experience." Smith wouldn't hear of it, telling his friend that a week was little enough delay for the pleasure of them travelling on board.

Mary met her husband at the quay as prearranged. She stood beneath a colourful parasol, guarding against the fierce heat, looking simply divine he thought. Standing idly around, the sailors looked upon her lasciviously, dreaming of a night with such a woman of quality and beauty, Nathaniel was proud to know that she only had eyes for him.

"We have some work ahead, my angel," he greeted her. "Ebenezer is sailing in seventeen days and I have arranged passage with him."

"It isn't much time to find someone suitable to run our businesses," she cautioned.

"Or to get our other affairs in order," he agreed. "But we will manage," her husband remarked.

They had everything completed in fourteen days as it turned out, with the help of Anderson, the lawyer, regarding their financial arrangements and the new Manager for their commercial interests.

Jan Van Linden was a personal friend of George, recently arrived in the Cape from his native Holland. He had experience of rearing horses and a first class business acumen, advised the lawyer. Van Linden was pleasant. Nathaniel and Mary knew instantly that he was a man they could trust, an excellent acquisition to oversee their interests.

With everything in order, the Davidsons boarded the Adventuress with their belongings on the day of departure.

Not old enough to realise what was happening, Toby simply gurgled with contentment in his mother's arms as the longboat bobbed along, transporting the family to the Adventuress.

"Welcome aboard, my friends," Ebenezer approached them as they climbed on to the deck. "We sail within the hour." Slipping into the role of efficient ship's master, Nathaniel saw a glimpse of the officer who had brought him to South Africa some years previously.

Mary and her husband watched their possessions unloaded from two other longboats and stowed in the ship's hold, before locating the cabin set aside for them by the ship's First Officer.

They sat in silence for the next half hour, varying degrees of emotion occupying their minds. Sadness was the prevalent feeling for them both. To be leaving the country which had brought them together, brought pain of enormous proportion.

A tap sounded on the cabin door and a boy stood in the passageway smiling angelically as Nathaniel drew open the door.

"The Captain's compliments, Mr Davidson but he asks if you and your wife would care to come on deck, we are weighing anchor for departure."

The anchor was already withdrawn from the harbour silt as the travellers reached the deck. Guidance sail set, the Adventuress crept slowly away from her position, picking her way gingerly between the other vessels moored in the harbour.

Nathaniel and Mary made their way to a position at the rail, sadness bringing tears to the woman's eyes, Nathaniel putting his arm around her shoulder sympathetically.

Table Mountain lay in contrasting weather. For the most part the strong sun baked the earth, but directly above the summit, an accumulation of boiling grey clouds hung menacingly, threatening rain. At distance, the city looked like a clutch of models, freshly painted for some giant child to play with. The ocean was displaying a greenish tinge, adding its own magic to a scene which the Davidsons knew they would never forget.

The scene faded with time. Ebenezer Smith approached them at the rail, "You are feeling despondent, my friends?" ventured the man.

"We are," advised Nathaniel, "it's a great wrench to be leaving South Africa, but we have made up our mind to return to England, so we must make the best of it." He held onto Mary around the shoulders feeling her tremble with sentiment beneath his touch.

Ebenezer sympathised with his friend but reminded him of the potential purchase of his childhood home. "Surely that is something to look forward to for you and Mary?"

Nathaniel hoped so. It would be good to see his home country again. All he wanted was Mary to get over the anguish of leaving the Cape behind.

CHAPTER 23

Several weeks later, the British Isles appeared through the mist of the Channel, a squall brewing. Growing wind whipped the wave tops into white horses, the undulations of the sea growing in magnitude, tossing the ship around like a cork.

Smith bellowed orders to his men, reducing full sale to manoeuvre cloth only. Icy sea spray covered everyone on deck as the waves crashed against the prow, soaking anyone exposed to the elements.

Over the course of the voyage, Nathaniel had become content with their decision to return. Mary was in the cabin nursing Toby, who had become ill in the closing hours of the voyage.

Standing at the rail watching Portsmouth emerging through the grey mist, Nathaniel counted twenty main masts in the port, the height of some timbers astonished him.

Captain Smith eased The Adventuress into port delicately, with consummate skill. Several of his fellow Captains waved to him as he moved his ship to anchor.

Finally the ship came to rest in the security of the harbour.

"What do you intend to do first Nathaniel?" queried the ship's Captain, who had come up on the man quietly from behind.

"Who knows, my friend, I suppose find somewhere to stay for a day or two and then head for Thistlebrough."

"Well I hope you manage to secure the estate," continued Smith.

Mary and Sally approached the two men, Toby asleep in his mothers arms, Jonathan following the women on deck.

Nathaniel shook his friend's hand, "Thank you for a pleasant voyage, Ebenezer, I'll send word when we have lodgings and tell you where to send our belongings."

The wives hugged, their husbands looking on. Nathaniel was pleased the ladies had become firm friends. For a second he looked at Jonathan, the boy seemed to show embarrassment at the sentiment displayed by the ladies.

"It has been a great pleasure to meet you my boy," Nathaniel said, "I hope we see each other again soon."

"I do too sir," the boy intoned.

Smith helped Mary to board the boat for shore, Sally holding on to her baby, before passing him down into the grateful arms of his mother. Nathaniel followed his wife and the vessel slipped from the ship's side, Smith and his family peering after them, hands raised in a farewell salute.

Portsmouth was a typical nautical port, sailors wandering her narrow streets, some in a state of intoxication, others sober and looking for more physical pleasures. Prostitutes plied their trade on street corners. From Nathaniel's observation, the worlds oldest profession was flourishing on these thoroughfares, although the girls were at best plain, at worst downright ugly.

Mary observed the lively scene from a carriage window as the vehicle clattered its way along the uneven, cobbled streets, shaking the occupants violently.

Having hailed the cab driver, Nathaniel requested they be conveyed to the best hostelry in the town offering accommodation.

Its name was the Seraphim, a large structure on the outskirts of the town. From the outside it did not look particularly inviting, peeling paintwork and small, dirty windows inspired no confidence along with a creeping green lichen growing steadily up the exterior walls.

Inside, was the antithesis of the exterior, its plush fabric surprised the Davidsons. It was one of the cosiest inns Nathaniel had ever seen, cheerful dancing flames of a roaring log fire, dispelled the depression of the filthy day outside.

A man in spotless white apron approached them, "Can I help you?" he boomed.

"We would like a room, if that is possible?" asked Nathaniel.

The man's face clouded, "I'm afraid we're full, but I do have someone leaving in an hour or so, if you would care to wait."

Nathaniel agreed, leading his family to a seat by the roaring blaze.

"Can I get you some breakfast?" the owner suggested. It turned out to be a fine English repast and Nathaniel and his spouse sat back replete.

They were shown into a comfortable room an hour later, its décor tastefully chosen, with a large four-poster dominating the chamber.

Over the next two days they got used to being in England once again and the idiosyncrasies of the people, mostly they needed to adapt to the dank conditions of the colder climate. The shock to the system the weather posed, was profound, coupled with the drab housing and greyness of an English town.

Mary was particularly despondent with the new surroundings, her mood deteriorating rapidly.

"Nathaniel, do you think we've done the right thing?" she inquired.

Similar pangs of doubt had enveloped him but he couldn't let his wife know that. As far as she was concerned, he needed to impress on her that the move from South Africa was in their best interests,

"Yes, sweetheart, I do, and I know that when we settle in Thistlebrough or wherever, you will see we were right to come to England, believe me the estate is one of the finest in the country."

The baby developed a severe cough which wasn't getting any better, despite his father calling in a doctor, Toby was not improving. They were assured it was nothing serious, Nathaniel deciding the time was right to take their leave of the inn and the naval town.

Their initial destination was London. They would then head north to Newcastle but as the main offices of the house agents were located in the capital, that would be their first port of call.

The succeeding day dawned bright, early morning sun boiling away the wetness of the morning. It had ceased raining only an hour before and the cobbles were drying by the second.

It was after nine when the coach pulled into the inn's spacious yard, the driver and escort clambering down from their seated position high up at the front of the carriage. Bending to the task of loading baggage at the rear, strapping it into position with leather harness.

Eight travellers were waiting to mount the conveyance. Nathaniel had purchased the most expensive seats inside the coach, Toby riding free on his mother's lap. A man and woman climbed in behind the Davidsons, each around fifty-five and well-heeled.

As the coachman whipped the horses into action, the woman began to make fuss of the baby, stroking his cheek with Mary's permission. The boy murmured and smiled at the attention he was receiving, the lady began talking in the childish words and phrases that infants learn so much from.

Four men on the roof of the coach, who had boarded at the inn, broke out in song as the carriage trundled along at a rate Nathaniel felt uncomfortable with.

"Joshua Merryweather at your service, sir," the man extended his hand in greeting. The suddenness of the introduction surprised him as the man had studiously avoided contact previously, "This is my wife Edith," he said.

The woman looked over for an instant, leaving her attention of Toby and smiled in his direction.

"Nathaniel Davidson, my wife Mary and our son Toby," he indicated with a glance.

"A fine looking chap," stated Merryweather, "a credit to you both."

"You are heading for London, sir?" asked Nathaniel.

The sweating, puffy face cracked in a smile, "Yes, I am Member of Parliament for Portsmouth and I go to sit in the chamber following our recent recess."

169

"You wouldn't by any chance, know Sir Toby Davidson?" inquired Nathaniel.

"Why yes; yes I do very well," the man stated, and with realisation. "Of course, I should have made the connection when you said your surname and the Christian name of your son, how is the old buffer, we miss his knock about style in politics these days?"

Nathaniel drew breath, "He's languishing in the penal colony of Australia, he has been found guilty of murder."

Merryweather was genuinely shocked, "My God, how did that happen?" he questioned his colleagues son.

Nathaniel spent a good portion of the next hour describing the circumstances leading to his father's arrest. The women played with Toby now fully awake and enjoying himself tremendously.

The town faded in the distance, green hills dominated the countryside, Nathaniel staring blankly out of the coach window as the miles swept by. Joshua Merryweather had fallen into slumber half an hour previously, Mary and Edith talking of inconsequential things.

As Nathaniel began to doze himself, a sudden commotion and raised voices commenced outside the coach. With a violent jerk the coachman halted the horses, a masked figure appearing at the window.

"My friends if you will kindly alight your carriage," demanded the man, grasping and turning the handle, tearing the door open.

Departing the vehicle, Nathaniel counted four men on horses, masked and brandishing pistols.

"This is an outrage," expostulated the MP for Portsmouth, "you'll hang for this."

One of the riders descended from his animal and approached Merryweather, his mouth set in a grimace, "And you, my friend, will die on the spot if you do not keep your mouth shut." Merryweather bristled, he was not used to be spoken to in such fashion.

"You don't frighten me, you thug, I will see you swing and that's a fact."

The highwayman smashed the butt of his pistol into the MP's temple with a sickening crack and he crumpled to the ground, bleeding copiously from a four inch gash. Edith Merryweather screamed and fell to her knees next to her husband's inert body.

" You cruel ruffian," she yelled.

"And don't think I'm squeamish about beating a woman either," the robber stated.

"Oh yes, a real man, aren't you?" cried Edith.

Lifting his weapon high, he was about to bring it crashing down on the woman's head, Nathaniel catching the arm as it swung in its arc towards Edith. Standing stock still he looked directly into the bandit's eyes, his own steely and steady as a rock.

"I don't think there is need of more violence, do you?" he said menacingly.

The robber was disconcerted, Nathaniel was showing no fear, indeed a slight smile adorned his face.

"Just keep her quiet," the thug ordered. His colleagues dismounted and joined their leader, who addressed the travellers, "Your money and valuables on the ground in front of me now, if you please."

In his riding position high on the vehicle, the escort reached surreptitiously behind his back for an ancient blunderbuss, Nathaniel catching a glimpse from the corner of his eye.

"No," he yelled.

It was too late. Two of the thieves fired, the man falling to the ground dead. One of the shots piercing his heart, he passed away instantly.

Removing the baggage from its fixings at the rear of the coach, two of the men rifled through it, tossing the contents of no interest over the earth. The travellers removed money from their pocket books, piling it in front of the gang's leader.

Spotting Mary the leader moved across to her, clutching her chin between thumb and forefinger.

"And here's a pretty prize," he laughed to his men. "Maybe I'll have some fun with this one."

"You have your booty so why not just go?" advised Nathaniel.

Walking up to him the bandit raised his pistol to the man's throat, "I'll tell you what, why don't I just cut you down right now and have done with it?" he threatened, forcing the barrel against the victim's flesh.

Remounting their steeds, one of them looked back, "He's right, Charlie, let's get out of here, we've got what we came for."

Shrugging his shoulders, the leader walked up to his horse and once in the saddle he addressed Nathaniel, "A piece of advice, when people like us attack you, it's best to show humility, my friend." With that he spurred on his horse, beating a path away from the scene, his associates following close behind. Joshua was coming round, face ashen and skin clammy to Mary's touch but he was recovering. Nathaniel's wife had found some strips of discarded clothing from the trunks and was binding his wound. The gash, open and weeping blood, looked severe but the flow was slowing mercifully.

Nathaniel bent to the man, whose head was resting in Edith's lap, "Joshua, can you hear me?" he pleaded.

The man's eyes opened fully, "Yes," he croaked, "there's no need to shout."

It broke the seriousness of the moment, carers laughing heartily, Edith's blended with tears of relief.

Merryweather was a dead weight as Nathaniel and the other male passengers lifted him gingerly, placing him in a recumbent position on the interior seat of the carriage, he lapsed back into unconsciousness and Nathaniel considered it a blessing.

It took the passengers some minutes to locate their strewn possessions, packing them back into the opened trunks and re-harnessing the baggage to the rear of the vehicle.

When the travellers were seated once more, the coachman whipped the horses into action and the journey continued. They had left the body of the escort in some undergrowth, intending to inform the first authority they could find, to have the cadaver recovered.

Nathaniel had lost some money in the incident though not a great deal. Mary and the baby were safe, that was what mattered to him. He had always retained money in England, a small but significant amount, enough to last them a few weeks until his South African moneys were transferred to his bank in Britain.

Merryweather moaned periodically, recovering his senses for a few minutes at a time, eventually waking permanently. Edith whispered things in his ears as if talking in normal tones might hinder his recovery.

"I understand from Edith that you stopped that cut-throat from attacking her, Nathaniel," his voice was reedy but understandable. "Thank you, my friend, you put yourself in great danger and I am forever in your debt."

"Nonsense," cried Nathaniel, who considered Joshua a bit melodramatic but the expression on the man's pale visage showed it was heartfelt. "It was my pleasure Joshua, believe me."

Beckoning him closer with a crooked finger, Joshua continued, "I promise this to you, Nathaniel, I will make representations on your father's case at the highest level of government."

CHAPTER 24

When their journey ended at the capital, Nathaniel was relieved the tedium of it was over. They had left the Merryweathers at a coaching inn along the way, where a doctor was called to treat Joshua.

The old man was despondent when the medical practitioner insisted he spend a few days recovering before continuing with his travel plans.

London's teeming populace scurried around the drab streets, going about their business resolutely. As Nathaniel and his family passed through the outskirts, street urchins loped alongside the vehicle begging for money, their tattered rags and blue feet from the cold tugging at Mary's heartstrings. She clutched the baby to her even more tightly, grateful that Toby would never grow up like the forlorn creatures outside the coach who had little hope of betterment in life.

In the seedier areas they passed through, the gutters flowed with human effluent, the smell overpowering. Nathaniel knew there was great wealth in England's first city but now he was seeing abject poverty on a scale he'd never before encountered.

A lurid sign greeted their eyes as the coach clattered into the yard of the Noose and Gallows coaching inn, its sign a dangling corpse watched by a crowd was hardly a welcoming sight for the visitor, but the premises looked salubrious enough and the cheerful owner, who had actually been an executioner until recent times, greeted them warmly and arranged a room for Nathaniel and his family expediently.

Two hours later, Nathaniel was standing outside the premises of Mathews and Wanley house agents, located on the bank of the Thames. Their offices, plush although a little dark inside, were hushed and studious as he walked in, heading for a lectern desk where a clerk sat scribbling furiously. Looking up the man laid his quill down slowly.

"May I help you, sir?"

"I understand you are acting for the sale of an estate in Northumberland named Thistlebrough," the visitor said.

Climbing down from his lofty position, the employee stood facing Nathaniel, stature small, head large and out of proportion to his frame.

"Indeed we do, are you interested in the estate?"

"It's possible," Nathaniel advised him.

"And your name, sir?" asked the clerk.

"Davidson," he replied, seating himself in one of the many chairs placed for visitors.

Scuttling away the clerk called back that he would fetch Mr Wanley directly, leaving his charge to scrutinise some inexpensive but competently painted landscapes adorning the panelled walls.

The managing partner of the firm had a shock of jet black hair and bushy eyebrows, which seemed to be moving across his face out of control. They almost met in the middle, Nathaniel finding them a distraction. More hair sprouted from the lobes of the ears in plant like splendour. He was around fifty without a hint of grey.

"Mr Davidson, would you step this way please," the partner instructed.

Sitting down in the chair proffered, Nathaniel gazed around the man's office. Magnificent bookcases encircled the room, containing an immeasurable amount of volumes with coloured spines, regimented in size and hue.

"I understand you are interested in the estate of Thistlebrough in Northumberland?" Wanley began. "I should inform you that the property was sold only yesterday, Mr Davidson."

The disappointment overcame Nathaniel like a freak wave engulfing a ship.

"Who bought it?" he demanded.

Wanley poured himself a glass of sherry from a decanter on his untidy desk.

175

"Mr Ezekiel Wilson, an American businessman who requires a home here in England."

"If it was only yesterday, then he hasn't taken possession of the estate yet, would he consider selling it again if I were to offer him a handsome profit?" suggested Davidson.

"The man is a multi-millionaire, Mr Davidson. He owns the largest tobacco plantations in Virginia," explained the house agent. "He's fallen in love with the estate so I doubt if he will be in disposition to sell it so soon."

Nathaniel rose, looking down at the man whose attitude was annoying in the extreme.

"Mr Wanley, where is this man staying in London?" he demanded, his voice almost shouting.

Wanley bridled but said, "He is patronising the Green Park Hotel in Half Moon Street, although he is intending to leave directly for Northumberland."

Without saying another word, the visitor was dashing from the man's office and the building, hailing a cab in the street outside, calling the destination to the driver as he climbed in.

The driver set off at sedate pace, until Nathaniel told the cabbie he would double the fare for a quicker trip. The man lashed the animals unmercifully, urging them to greater effort. Pedestrians on the capital's thoroughfares concerned at the speed as the vehicle tore by them. Men called to the driver to slow down as their ladies cowered away.

On the corner of Piccadilly, Green Park Hotel was a favourite haunt of literary figures and foreign royalty. The cab came to a halt, Nathaniel paying his fare and rushing into the ornate reception area of the edifice. People were milling around, he excused himself as he pressed between them to reach the main desk.

A man with the sharp features of an eagle was dealing with a balding gentleman. For a moment Nathaniel waited patiently for them to finish but when it became evident it would take some time he interrupted, "Can you tell me the room number of Mr Ezekiel Wilson?" he asked.

The hotel clerk blinked at him through small eyes, aghast at his impudence, looking down his hooked proboscis.

"Would you have the grace to wait sir," he demanded, "I am attending to this gentleman?"

"I apologise, sir," Nathaniel offered the customer, "but I am in a dreadful hurry."

With a smile, the gentleman turned to the clerk, "I think you had better look after this gentleman first."

"I am much obliged, sir," offered Nathaniel as the reception clerk directed him to room 212. He ran for the stairs, much to the disgust of the hotel employee. Nathaniel searched for the chamber on the second floor, discovering that it was located to the right of the stairs he had climbed. Reaching the door, he stopped to catch his breath, before tapping lightly on the wood. He stepped back, waiting for a reaction from within.

The portal opened, a scene of great luxury greeting him. This was no ordinary room but a suite, containing antique furniture the size truly staggering. With its beautifully ornamented ceiling, twenty feet above his head and elaborate wall coverings, this chamber would not have disgraced a royal personage.

"Can I help you, sir?" asked the liveried manservant, who had opened the door. Gazing up at him, Nathaniel was truly astounded by the man's height, he stood six feet six inches tall, a giant of a human being with a broadness to match his loftiness, and yet his voice had a distinct effeminacy about it.

"I would like to speak to Mr Ezekiel Wilson," exclaimed Nathaniel.

"And your name, sir?" continued the servant.

"Davidson."

Turning away the man regarded him cynically as he looked back.

"Very well sir, if you will please take a seat, I will ask Mr Wilson if he will see you."

He was left in the sumptuous apartment as the attendant disappeared through some high double doors.

Seconds later they reopened and a diminutive gentleman appeared, dressed in smoking jacket, his waxed moustache the prominent feature of the man.

A deep southern American accent, thick and musical, escaped thin lips, "May I help you, sir?" the man sat on a chaise longue in the centre of the room. "Please sit down."

Dropping into the closest chair, Nathaniel leaned forward, clasping his hands in front of him prayer like and began, "I know you have purchased an estate in the north of England called Thistlebrough" he advised the American. "I'll come straight to the point, I want you to sell the property to me today."

Ezekiel Wilson laughed out loud, "My friend, I only bought the property yesterday, why on earth would I sell it one day later?"

"Because," the visitor paused, "I will give you double what you paid for it, a one hundred per cent profit over one day is good business by anyone's standards, Mr Wilson."

Ezekiel Wilson was intrigued by the offer.

"Mr Davidson, money is not the issue here, my wife has fallen in love with the area and that particular piece of real estate," he smiled. "Now one of the things my old granpappy told me was never disappoint a woman, they have a way of making a man's life a joy or a burden and I have no intention of suffering the latter, besides I don't need the money."

Rising, Nathaniel sought to think of the best way to appeal to Wilson.

"There is more to this than just money for me too, Mr Wilson, please give me a few minutes to tell you and I hope you will listen to what I have to say." The young man's earnestness fascinated the tobacco plantation king, he retook his seat.

"Thistlebrough was my childhood home. My father, Sir Toby Davidson, owned the property by right from his father and it would have become mine in the fullness of time. My father went through problems, as a result of which we lost the hall but it remains the single thing in my life I wish to possess. My mother is buried in the vault there," his face demonstrated amply the pain of his mother's memory.

"The fact is Thistlebrough is in my blood, Mr Wilson, it has memories for me which have shaped my life and I really would like to own the estate."

Ezekiel Wilson's face frowned in sympathy, "And I commiserate with you, Mr Davidson, but my wife is adamant she wants the hall and its lands, so there is no chance of me selling it to you at any price, I'm sorry," he rose, a sign the meeting was over. "Now if you don't mind, I leave for Thistlebrough within the hour."

On the pavement outside the hotel, Nathaniel stood, dazed and disappointed by his failure to convince the man to sell. How could he tell Mary, he thought, but he had offered the man an unquestionably good deal, done everything he could and it had all been in vain?

A light rain began to fall. Turning up his collar, he flagged down a hackney carriage, spending the journey back to the coaching inn dejectedly, watching the glistening roadway sweep by.

Mary was occupied, sewing in their room. She was repairing some of his hose; as he entered she laid the material down, seeing the disenchantment on his face.

"He wouldn't sell, would he, Nathaniel?" challenged his wife.

"I'm afraid not sweetheart, and I tried, I really tried to get him to reconsider."

She engulfed him in her arms, sensing his despondency.

"Then we shall just have to make the best of it and find our own little hideaway and whatever that is, we will make it a happy home," she maintained.

CHAPTER 25

Two days later, Joshua Merryweather and his wife met the Davidsons in their Kensington apartments. The man had made enquiries through the coaching company as to the carriage's final destination, gladdened to discover the Davidsons were staying in London. His valet had been despatched to invite them to the Merryweather's home.

Joshua's head was heavily bandaged. Dismissing the doctor's advice, within a day he was heading for his London domicile.

"My friends," he gushed as they entered the sitting room. "We are overjoyed to see you once more, ah and the little chap," he said, pointing a bony finger at Toby in his mother's embrace.

Refreshments were brought, Edith pouring the tea personally, dismissing the maid.

Evening twilight spread through the room, drapes shut and lamps lit giving the chamber a distinctly cosy atmosphere. The adults played cards around a small green baize table. Speculation was everyone's preferred choice, the game continuing for an hour, only the ticking of the clock disrupting the silence.

"Whisky, Nathaniel?" prompted Joshua, rising from his seat at the end of a hand.

"That would be most acceptable," replied the visitor. Merryweather returned with two crystal tumblers, filled with amber liquid.

As the game progressed, conversation began to infiltrate the quiet. Nathaniel confided in Joshua about his failed attempt to secure Thistlebrough.

"I really wanted the old family residence, Joshua," he said.

"Sometimes we just have to accept disappointments, my friend," replied the MP. "You will have to move on and find an alternative I fear."

The baby began sobbing softly on a nearby sofa where previously he had been sound asleep. Mary excused herself, knowing the child needed feeding. Edith led them from the room so that she could feed Toby in privacy, the men clearing the card table and sitting in leather chairs on either side of the impressive fireplace.

"I take it you want to live in your native north-east?" Nathaniel's friend asked, staring into the flames.

"Indeed I do, Joshua and even though Thistlebrough is no longer for sale, we will travel to Northumberland and seek out alternative properties but I have not given up owning the hall at some point."

Merryweather leaned forward grasping the poker, "And when will you leave?" he inquired, raking the dying coals into flame.

"Tomorrow is as good a day as any," ventured Nathaniel, "we may as well set off immediately and sort out our life."

Returning, Edith and Mary found their husbands on their second drink, Joshua beginning to doze in the heat from the fire.

"My boy," said Joshua as they waited for the Davidsons coach to be brought to the front door. "Here is my card," a buff coloured rectangle was passed between them. "You rendered me great assistance on the road, if you need a friend in government, do not hesitate to call on me, my friend."

They grasped each other's hands, Nathaniel climbing into the carriage, where Mary and their son were already seated.

That night, Nathaniel sat in the lounge of the coaching inn, hands wrapped around a pewter tankard, peering into the ale, mood sombre from the day's events. It wasn't over he told himself, he would regain Thistlebrough one day. Whatever it took, however long it took, he was determined to acquire his childhood home.

Beginning the journey to Northumberland the following day, Mary was not looking forward to the gruelling trip. In the early light of a scarlet sky, they sought out a coaching company who plied their trade between London and Newcastle. Nathaniel paid over the requisite fare and they boarded the coach at 9.00am, along with a number of other passengers.

As the heat of the day rose, the smell of body odour increased in the coach. The sickly sweet aroma of sweat merging with countryside scents as they sped away from the capital.

Ten days later, they reached Tyneside, staying in questionable inns at the staging points, where horses and the drivers were changed.

Newcastle appeared in the distance at midday on the tenth day. Entering its quayside, coal barges were drawn up, awaiting loading of the black gold, which dominated the north-east economy.

A Sunday market was in full swing near the riverside. Familiar smells of newly landed fish, fruit and cooking food drifted tantalisingly on the breeze, noise of the crowd deafening as the sellers yelled their wares and prices at the tops of their voices.

Nathaniel realised how much he had missed the area, watching the bustling scene, the rich guttural accent of the populace added to his pleasure at returning and he walked Mary and Toby along the quayside, drinking in the spirit of the city. Wandering aimlessly for a while, they climbed the steep streets towards the centre. Passing St Nicholas' Cathedral, he drew Mary into the quiet grandeur of the edifice. Sitting in the sparsely attended religious house, he prayed for his wife and son and especially for his father.

In the Groat Market, seconds from the Cathedral, Nathaniel registered them into a small hotel, the Castle Buttress. It was comfortable but not opulent.

"Are you pleased to be back, my darling?" asked Mary.

"I am, sweetheart," admitted her husband. "I know we can't have Thistlebrough but Northumberland is rich with good property, we will find something that suits us."

Mary encouraged him to begin the search for a home immediately they were settled in their accommodation. They sought out the local property representatives. The hotelier pointed them in the direction of Hardwick's, some few streets away and Nathaniel led his family to the company.

One of Newcastle's greatest assets was its architecture, phenomenal building design everywhere. Hardwick's was an excellent example of the cosmopolitan architect utilising a number of designs.

Passing into the firm's interior, a man with bushy grey hair and wide staring eyes approached them.

"May I help you sir?" the accent was upper class with a hint of the local dialect.

"May we speak to someone about purchasing property?" inquired Nathaniel.

Davidson was taken aback at the man's reply.

"I am William Hardwick, owner of the company, perhaps I could help." Astonished, Nathaniel had thought the man a lowly clerk by his dress, he sensed Mary smiling at his discomfiture, amused by his mistake.

"Yes Mr Hardwick, you can," went on Nathaniel quickly. "My wife and I are looking for a substantial property in north Northumberland, do you deal in such estates?"

The company owner blinked at him with an expression of boredom, as though Nathaniel should know the stature of the company he was dealing with.

"Indeed we do, Mr…?"

"Davidson, Nathaniel Davidson," he appraised the house agent.

"Well, Mr Davidson, what kind of property did you have in mind?" probed Hardwick. Nathaniel and Mary took seats opposite the man's elaborate desk of massive proportion.

"My family were previous owners of Thistlebrough Hall," Nathaniel informed the agent. "Ideally that would have been the property I would like to purchase but it has recently been sold, so I am seeking an alternative." Hardwick's bushy eyebrows raised imperceptibly at the news.

"So your father was Sir Toby Davidson?"

"That is correct."

"Well I am afraid there are no properties of Thistlebrough's eminence for sale at present but we do have a number of lesser properties on the market," he offered.

For half an hour the men discussed the merits of various available options at the end of which there only seemed to be one he and Mary both liked the sound of.

Located just north of the market town Morpeth, Longland Manor seemed to offer the right size premises with a good amount of land attached.

"How long before this property will be available to move into, assuming we find it acceptable?" asked Nathaniel. Hardwick consulted documents.

"The property is already vacant, the previous owner has emigrated to Italy, so it can be taken possession of immediately."

"May we have a few minutes to discuss our thoughts, Mr Hardwick?"

The house agent rose, "Of course, when you are ready to talk further, please call me," advised Hardwick, leaving the room.

When they were alone, Nathaniel asked Mary her opinion.

"It certainly sounds like what we may be looking for, and it will do no harm to visit the area, my love, why don't you arrange for a viewing with Mr Hardwick?" she opined.

The agent arranged for a carriage to take them immediately to the property, joining them for the viewing.

Longland Manor lay among barren countryside, unseen by the visitors until they were almost upon it. Evergreen forests encircled the property, tall firs dominating the landscape, like huge sentries on guard. A track wound its way through the wooded area until it came to a clearing right in the centre.

The manor was magnificent at first sight, natural grey stone shining in the sunlight, which also glinted blindingly off the massive windows.

Entering the edifice, Mary's eyes widened. The panelling was majestic, biblical characters etched into the highly polished, dark oak wood. Sunbeams danced before their eyes, floating randomly as light streamed into the hallway.

Hardwick led them to a sitting room where the floorboards were bare, the clacking of their shoes on the treated wood, echoing loudly in the empty room.

When they completed touring the house, Mary was convinced it was the place they could be happy and whispered to her husband the fact as they surveyed the manor.

The agent invited them out of the house once more, asking them to observe the countryside in all directions.

"Everything you see, for as far as you see goes with Longland," he informed his clients.

Nathaniel asked Mary to leave the agent and himself to thrash out a mutually acceptable price for the property. She watched intently as they haggled animatedly some way from the bench on which she sat in front of the house. Toby slept in her arms, totally oblivious to his father's financial dealings with the agent.

Ten minutes later, the men shook hands and smiled, it was clear a deal had been struck.

Approaching her, Mary could see from his smile, he was happy with the outcome, his arm strayed solicitously around her shoulders, as he looked out on the loveliness of the district.

"Mary, we are home I think."

"Yes, my darling, I believe so," she replied.

CHAPTER 26

Seven days later, Nathaniel and Mary moved into the house, a whirlwind time of purchasing furniture and tying up the legalities of the purchase.

Two servants were hired from a company in Newcastle, specialising in the provision of domestic staff. Elizabeth Radford was one of four suitable candidates for the post of maid. Her cheerful manner securing the position, the others were too dour, thought Mary. This girl seemed to have the type of personality which Nathaniel and she could warm to. She was twenty-two years old and possessed a maturity far beyond her years. Her complexion was one any woman would kill for. The smooth alabaster skin and exceptionally blue eyes, the finest part of the girl's beauty.

Lionel Barron couldn't be considered handsome but seemed a stalwart, self-assured individual. At thirty he had gained experience from his former employer over a seven year period, in the role of valet, and Nathaniel decided on him immediately, without interviewing others.

An overweight individual, Barron had decided to reduce his bulk from its present nineteen stone to a more comfortable fifteen, Nathaniel detecting from his unwavering determination that he would achieve his goal.

For several days after the purchase of the manor, the owners and servants worked tirelessly to turn the shell into a home. The modern furniture suited the manor well. Mary had exceptionally good taste. Small repairs were carried out by local craftsmen on the minor structural problems they discovered.

Mary dragged her husband outside when the work was completed.

"Are you happy with it?" her husband asked.

She gazed at her new home, "Yes, darling, very happy," she smiled, kissing him full on the lips. "Thank you."

"My pleasure, my darling," returned her husband, grasping her tightly to his side.

It was a sunny day, warm with a gentle breeze, faintly motioning the trees. Nathaniel suggested a walk through some of the surrounding countryside and they set off hand in hand.

Walking through the nearby wood, the odour of fresh pine was overpowering, noise of animals scurrying in the undergrowth, faintly audible.

A stillness in the centre of the forest came about, the ramblers sitting, relaxing in the atmosphere. They rested in silence as the elegant form of a red deer moved into view. A magnificent creature, it grazed oblivious to the humans in its vicinity, remaining alert, constantly looking nervously about. Nathaniel knew if they were quiet, remaining still, the creature would happily carry on chomping on the undergrowth before them.

A choking cry rent the air that startled the creature, which bounded off, each loping stride straining the thin legs.

"My God, Nathaniel, what was that?" Mary said gazing in the direction of the scream.

It sounded again, a terrible shout of fear propelling Nathaniel into action. He ran in the general direction of the yelping. It was human, no doubt about that, the man thought. Mary tore after him, struggling to keep up with her husband's pace.

Bursting from the tree line, Nathaniel came upon a chasm. At the bottom a massive pool was being fed from a powerful waterfall, the water boiling over the edge to crash into the mere below.

Clinging to a rock, a figure flailed one arm, the other clutching the protuberance, the passage of water attempting to drag him over the edge, its power increasing.

"Mary, get back to the house and bring Barron with a rope," he yelled. Instantly she was gone, her husband searching for a way down to the site of the drama. He couldn't locate a natural pathway down to the pool, so eased himself over the edge, climbing gingerly down the sheer face.

Several times his feet slipped on moss covered rock, sending small boulders crashing into the greenish water. Dropping towards the bottom, his hands became bloodied from contact with the jagged rocks.

Reaching the edge of the pool, he could see across to the weakening figure. It was a boy about fourteen years old with blonde hair.

"Hang on," Nathaniel shouted, "I'm coming."

Panic etched the young man's face, he was trying desperately to get a purchase with his flailing limb, the strong current preventing it from happening.

Grasping overhead branches to steady himself, his potential saviour picked his way along the treacherous rim of the pool. Many of the rocks were covered with damp lichen, Nathaniel concentrating his effort on avoiding falling.

"Help me," screamed the victim in terror as Nathaniel closed on a position above him.

There was no way he could wait for Mary to return with the valet and the rope, the boy simply couldn't hold on much longer, the cold was bringing on weakness by the second.

Desperately, Nathaniel scanned the area for something that might help but nothing presented itself. The end of a rope snaked down to his side. He looked up to see Barron, peering over the precipitous edge above him.

"Grab that, sir," the valet called. As Nathaniel grasped the rope, Barron tossed the residue of it down to his master.

A gnarled tree trunk stood close to Nathaniel, he tied the cord around its girth, the free end around his waist. With a heave he jumped from the position above the boy, landing in the water awkwardly, swimming for all he was worth to the panicking child.

As he reached him, the boy's hand slipped from around the rock and his head disappeared below the surface. Nathaniel fished down, dragging the boy's face above the water, he was coughing and spluttering but he was alive. With monumental effort, Nathaniel swam away from the boiling edge of the falls.

In calmer water, Nathaniel looked up to see Barron standing near his anchor tree. The valet had brought a second rope and tethered it above, climbing down rapidly to assist his master. Now, he grasped the rope attached to Nathaniel and began to heave. The combined weights of the two bodies, coupled with the resistance of the water made the job excruciatingly difficult, Barron sweating profusely, veins throbbing at his temples.

Lapsing into unconsciousness, the boy's dead weight made it doubly difficult for Nathaniel to hold onto him but he reached the edge of the pool struggling to get the limp body over his shoulder.

He began to climb the sheer face, leaning out against the tautness of the rope and splaying his legs, ascending at an angle to the earth. After great effort on his and the valet's part, he scrambled untidily onto the ledge where Barron stood.

"Take him," Nathaniel instructed.

The big man laid the body down and bent his ear close to the bluish lips.

"He isn't breathing," he announced, setting to work to rectify the situation.

Nathaniel crouched, hands on knees, gulping great breaths. The effort had been immense and he felt giddy. He looked down on the boy, praying silently for his recovery.

With a gagging hack, a mass of river water, mixed with vomit, cascaded from the rescued boy's throat and he gulped air greedily.

"How did you get here so quickly, Barron?" his master queried.

"Your horse, sir, I found the pool yesterday when I took a constitutional late in the day," the servant informed him.

"Well thank God and amen to that," Nathaniel gasped. The youth's face displayed a greyish tinge which concerned his rescuer. "How are we going to get him up there Barron?" he indicated with a finger.

"I'll climb up first, sir," advised the valet, "you tie the rope around him and I will pull him up, it's the only way."

Nathaniel bent to the boy, who was conscious and shivering, "Are you alright?" he asked.

The youngster nodded and it seemed to Nathaniel that shock had overcome him.

Barron climbed with surprising agility to the upper level, despite his size, waving to his employer as he reached the safety of the flat ground.

Nathaniel tied the rope around the boy, waving back to the servant. The youth began to ascend slowly as Barron hauled him up. It took nearly ten minutes for him to reach the servant's position.

The rope was tossed down again and Nathaniel followed the rescued boy. Mary reaching the scene as he scrabbled onto safe ground, wrapping the boy in a blanket brought from the house and he seemed happier to see a solicitous female.

Sitting him astride the horse, Barron led it back towards the manor. Mary and Nathaniel walked on each side of the animal, in case the boy should slip off or pass out once more.

Elizabeth waited anxiously at the door, Barron carrying the boy to a room she had prepared. Ushering the Davidsons out, the maid took over the care of the young man.

Nathaniel and Mary went to their room where she removed his soaking wet clothes. As night fell, Nathaniel and Mary visited the boy, who had slept constantly since being put to bed by Elizabeth. Now he was awake, the Davidsons needing to question him, Mary cautioning her husband to be tactful.

Approaching the bed where the youth sat, propped up on feather pillows, his complexion had improved greatly, the ashen look gone, replaced by a healthy hue as the blood returned to the skin.

"I am Nathaniel Davidson," his rescuer said, "what's your name?" Nathaniel gently probed.

"Thomas Rutherford," replied the boy.

"And where do you live, Thomas?" Mary took over the interrogation, concerned her husband's tone might be wrong. The boy warmed to her, "Two miles away on a farm," he said.

Nathaniel looked toward the doorway where the valet and Elizabeth stood observing the scene.

"Have you discovered any farms around here yet, Barron?"

"There is only one that I know of, sir, just north of here."

Mary tucked the boy in, looking at her husband. "We need to let his parents know the situation as soon as possible, Nathaniel. His mother will be frantic with worry," she said.

Nathaniel and the valet saddled horses, setting off in the darkness to find the boy's home. A light rain was falling despite the closeness of the evening.

"You did exceptionally well today, Barron," Nathaniel informed the other rider. "What you did was much appreciated."

The valet dismissed the praise, "It's just good that the boy is safe, sir. Your effort was the one that saved him and his parents owe you a great debt."

Although their eyes had gotten used to the dark, the journey was difficult, horses stumbling on unfamiliar ground. The rain increasing in intensity, soaked the men through, Nathaniel was glad to see the milky yellow light of lamps through windows as the farm came into view. Awash with mud, the farmyard was a chaos of equipment. A plough seemed to crouch in the corner next to a wall, a kind of eeriness about it in the dark as if it were about to come alive and begin its work of its own accord.

Dismounting, the men tethered their animals to a fence stretching around two sides of the property. Nathaniel knocked loudly, hearing a chair being scraped over a stone floor as someone rose inside.

Creaking open, the door's hinges seemed reluctant to release the wooden slab from its closed position. An awesomely powerful man stood in the doorway. Nathaniel had never seen such a fit bulk in his life. Huge arms with upper muscles of phenomenal size, strained the shirt sleeves. It was a gruff voice that uttered, "Yes?"

"Is this the home of Thomas Rutherford?" inquired Nathaniel.

"It is," the giant's face softened. "Do you have news of his whereabouts?" the man begged.

191

A woman appeared behind him, small in stature with an agonised look on her face. At the sound of her son's name, Mrs Rutherford came forward.

"Yes," Nathaniel enlightened the man, "he is safe at my home," Nathaniel strove to allay their fears immediately, smiling in the woman's direction.

Mrs Rutherford broke down, "Oh thank God," she cried, crumpling into a chair next to the simple wooden kitchen table. She buried her head on her arms, resting on its surface, weeping unashamedly.

"Please sir, sit down, would you like something to drink?" Thomas' father kept his composure, though little signs were evident that his tough exterior had been breached, relieved at the news.

Nathaniel and his valet accepted the seats offered, declining refreshment,

"Your boy had a lucky escape today, he almost drowned, but he is well now," the owner of Longland Manor informed them.

"Was he at that damned pool again?" thundered Rutherford. "I've warned him time and again to stay away from there but he's headstrong and insists on going there."

"Yes I think the pool you refer to is where we found him today," advised Davidson.

The woman had recovered her poise and began to thank Nathaniel profusely, the man rejecting her gratitude.

"If you are happy for Thomas to spend the night at my home, Longland Manor, he is most welcome. You can pick him up tomorrow, my wife feels that he would benefit from not being moved at this time to give him time to recover."

Rutherford turned to his wife, who nodded her head imperceptibly. "Thank you, Mr Davidson, for your hospitality where Thomas is concerned, we appreciate it greatly."

"Not at all, Mr Rutherford. I'm only glad that we could be of assistance and your son is safe," he rose, Barron following him to his feet. "We will leave you now but please call for Thomas at anytime after breakfast."

Preceding them, the farmer drew open the door.

"Goodnight, Mr Davidson, and you too, Mr Barron." He bade them farewell and closed the door.

CHAPTER 27

Thankfully, the rain had ceased. Clouds dissipating to be replaced by a totally clear night sky. Glistening stars twinkled down in their millions, full moon shining intently on the travellers as they trotted through the countryside.

The journey back to the manor was much more comfortable for the men, taking little time to complete.

They halted in front of the moonlight drenched house, climbing from their mounts, Barron leading the creatures to the small stable behind the manor to dry and groom them. It would be an hour before he could seek his bed.

Mary was still awake, thrusting a glass of whisky into her husband's hand as he stepped into the sitting room. The liquid bit into his throat, pursuing its relentless path to the pit of his stomach.

"How did his parents take the news?" she inquired.

Nathaniel was exhausted from the day's endeavours. "Worried, of course," he yawned, "but happy when they discovered he was safe."

"Come with me, sweetheart, you need to sleep now." She dragged him from the chair, escorting him upstairs to their room.

The moment Nathaniel's head connected with the pillow he fell into an intense slumber, snoring loudly in the darkened room. As she looked down on his sleeping frame she thanked God for the day they had met. It seemed in the dim distant past now and she realised how contented she was with her husband and child.

Just after eight the next morning, Mr and Mrs Rutherford arrived at the manor. Nathaniel was showing Thomas the horses in the stable but as soon as the boy heard his parent's voices, he bolted from the block, rushing into his mother's arms.

Hugging him to her, she wept uncontrollably, Mary directing them to the house. Her husband had joined the boy's father in front of the manor and Rutherford spoke earnestly to him.

"The thanks we can offer seems scant reward for all you have done for our boy," explained the man. "He's our only child, Mr Davidson, the only one we have been blessed with and he means more to us than we can say."

"He's a fine boy," returned Nathaniel. "Have you breakfasted?" he asked the farmer.

"We came here straight away this morning. Ruth needed to be with Thomas as soon as possible."

Longland's owner led the man to the house, finding Mrs Rutherford and her son seated in the dining room, conversing with Mary as they ate the morning meal. Ruth was partaking of a slice of toast while the boy tucked enthusiastically into a full English breakfast, the day before seemed as though it had never happened as Nathaniel gazed on the munching figure.

The men gathered their food, joining the ladies and the boy.

"How long have you farmed here, Mr Rutherford?" asked Mary.

Between mouthfuls, Thomas' father stopped. "Going on ten years now," he informed her, "but we won't be here much longer."

"And why would that be?" said Nathaniel, taking over the conversation from his wife.

"I have been employed as estate manager to a property in north Northumberland, I take up my post in two weeks."

Nathaniel glanced at Mary. "And which estate might that be, Mr Rutherford?" he questioned.

"It's called Thistlebrough, would you happen to know it?" enquired the farmer.

"Indeed I do, my father used to own the estate and I was going to purchase it myself recently," notified the manor owner. "It occupies a great place in my heart."

Rutherford finished his meal, clinking the knife and fork down on the plate. "The American gentleman who owns it has made me an offer I can't ignore so we leave as soon as we can."

After breakfast, Thomas and his parents left for home, the adults making the decision to stay in touch with each other. Nathaniel liked the man very much, he was gruff, down to earth and as good as the day was long. Mary found Ruth a charming, intelligent woman who cared for her son above everything.

"Thomas," yelled Nathaniel as the horses trotted away, "you will stay away from that pool, won't you?" With a huge grin, the boy said nothing but waved cheerfully in the Davidsons direction.

CHAPTER 28

After the excitement of the past twenty-four hours, the house seemed strangely quiet, Toby had slept through most of the commotion and Mary disappeared to give him his morning feed.

Nathaniel dozed in his favourite chair, the previous day had taken more out of him than he expected. He was intensely weary.

Weeks passed, the work at the manor finally completed, he grew increasingly bored. Longland had reached the standard that Mary wanted, she was happy with the decoration of the house and had started to improve the garden outside. Nathaniel helped her for some days but he was itching to do some real work again.

By all accounts the businesses in South Africa continued to prosper, their financial standing growing constantly. The Davidsons were now very rich indeed but he needed the cut and thrust of actually running a company, day to day in some form. He broached it to Mary one evening as they sat reading.

"Sweetheart, I think I need to get myself into the swing of business again," he stated.

She looked up from the volume on her lap, "I wondered when you would feel that. What is it you want to do?"

"I'm not altogether sure, I just know that I need to occupy myself and working is the best way to do that."

She sympathised with him, "It's obvious you have a flair for managing companies, Nathaniel, why don't you establish one here?"

The thought had occupied his mind for weeks with an idea for a venture which he began to explain. "The horse farm in Africa is doing well, outstripping all our expectations, so I thought I may set up a stud farm to produce thoroughbred animals here," he advised her.

She rose and crossed to him, kissing him lightly on the mouth. "That's a wonderful idea darling, I want you to be happy and if that will make you content, then I'm glad, besides it's a trade you are very knowledgeable with now."

The work at the manor had exhausted them both. It had been a week since they last made love. Now he wanted her very badly, the passion rising in his frame.

"Let's go to bed," he breathed huskily, "I need you, my angel."

Mary pulled him upright from his chair and led him to the staircase, his arm tight around her waist, they were kissing hungrily.

Falling into each other's arms in bed, they drank heavily from the pool of passion, which hadn't diminished one iota in all the time they had been married. It was only exhaustion which dampened their ardour.

Awakening next morning, he found his wife no longer next to him. Reluctantly he rose, washed and shaved himself, then descended to the dining room.

Mary was glowing, a look of rapture and contentment covered her face and he bent to kiss her while she ate breakfast.

"You realise how much you mean to me?" he started. "You and Toby are my life."

"Of course I know, Nathaniel," Mary replied as she gathered some food for him from the silver trays on the sideboard. "Today is the start of your new business undertaking, you start immediately."

The first task would be to expand the stable block and create a good size paddock. He rode to Morpeth after breakfast to seek out a builder who could construct the right size of facility to house up to twenty horses initially.

A small but stunning clock tower dominated the town as Nathaniel rode into Morpeth. The town was exquisitely set in a depression amid spectacular countryside, one of the most beautiful scenes he had ever experienced.

Even at this early time of the day, the town was alive with people making their way to work. A man stood, cap on ground, playing Northumberland pipes, the haunting sound drifting evocatively over the teeming display.

He continued on through the town, gazing with admiration at the architecture of the buildings, before coming upon the 17th century bridge spanning the river which flowed through Morpeth. The water bristled with screeching ducks, males bickering over females in season.

Bennett's builders was set back off the road, hidden by trees, only identified by a peeling board, erected outside rickety wooden double gates.

Entering the yard, he dropped from his horse. Several labourers congregated around a low slung building, piling materials onto carts, ready for the labours of the day.

"I'd like to speak to the owner if I may?" called Nathaniel to the men. From the building a man of about fifty exited. He was sun tanned, the deep nut brown of his skin prominent against the white hair and magnificent sun bleached whiskers adorning his face.

"I'm Bennett," he said, "how can I be of assistance?"

"My name is Davidson, I'm the owner of Longland Manor. I require some building work carried out, Mr Bennett, I hoped you might be able to assist me," Nathaniel stated, noticing the labourers had disappeared to their work.

At the sound of Longland Manor, Bennett's ears pricked up, realising it could be a lucrative commission. "Perhaps we should step into the office and discuss it further," the builder declared, leading his visitor inside the building.

It was dark inside, the windows encrusted with brick dust and general filth. The atmosphere choked the visitor. Residual particles from sacks recently humped from the confines of the building, floated around in massive clouds, making Nathaniel sneeze, powder invading his nostrils.

"Please sit down Mr Davidson, may I offer you some wine?" proffered the builder. Nathaniel declined with a wave of the hand, both men taking seats in the small chamber which acted as the company office.

"What kind of work did you have in mind, sir?" asked Bennett obsequiously.

Over the next five minutes Nathaniel outlined his plans for extending the stable block, the builder made brief notes as he talked.

"In order to give you a price for the work, I will have to visit the site and see what is involved for myself, Mr Davidson," advised the builder.

"When can you call to make the estimate?" he inquired.

"As it happens I can do it later today if that is acceptable," smiled Bennett.

It was past four when Bennett rode into the site of Longland Manor, he regarded the building with a craftsman's eye, impressed by the grandeur of the house. Elizabeth answered the door, guiding him to the sitting room where Mary sat.

"Mr Bennett, ma'am," the maid stated.

"Do sit down, Mr Bennett, my husband will be here directly, he's dealing with a small domestic problem at the moment," explained Mary.

After a few minutes small talk between the builder and Mary, Nathaniel swept into the room,

"Ah Mr Bennett, so good to see you once again, let me show you what I need," saying that he exited the room.

Bennett trailed him, turning to Mary as he left, "It was a pleasure to meet you, Mrs Davidson," announced the man.

Now that the builder could see first hand his client's requirements, he could make a quick estimate for the work, Nathaniel happy with the figure quoted.

"When could you begin the work, Mr Bennett?" he asked.

"Shall we say three days from today, I will need three men working full-time to complete it in the time frame you want?" It suited Nathaniel, in the meantime he could fence off the paddock with Barron's help.

He escorted Bennett to his horse, "I'll look forward to your men arriving on Thursday, Mr Bennett," he called as the man trotted away from the manor.

"Rest assured, they will be there, Mr Davidson," he returned. Mary joined her husband at the front of the manor, the grey tinted sky showing twilight inexorably approached. Slipping his arm around her shoulder, the pair looked out over the breathtaking countryside.

"So your project is underway, my sweet," she enthused.

"It is, I only hope it's successful," answered her husband.

CHAPTER 29

At nine o'clock on the prescribed day the work began, the builders arriving led by Bennett himself, who had decided to oversee the build personally.

They began by knocking down a side wall of the block in order to construct lengthwise, great chunks of masonry were pounded out of the wall relentlessly, the men's features were grotesquely changed by a white mask of powder covering face and hair, giving them the appearance of wraiths.

The men toiled ceaselessly, despite the searing heat of the day. At lunchtime, Mary instructed Elizabeth to prepare a meal for the workforce.

A table was set up for them at the rear of the manor, where they tucked gratefully into pork pie and pickles. Mary provided enough ale to quench their thirst, the gesture much appreciated by the workforce, who guzzled the beer greedily.

Nathaniel chatted with the men over lunch, finding them delightfully amusing, their broad Northumbrian accents thick and difficult to decipher.

By evening, he was impressed by the amount of work they had gotten through, a gaping hole created had been cleared of all debris and the brickwork of the surround was ready to build on to.

They left in the same cheery fashion with which they had conducted the day's toil.

It took two weeks to complete the work, in the meantime Nathaniel scoured the north-east of England for suitable animals. Only eight could be found of the right quality to start the lineage, two stallions and six mares but they were exceptional creatures, sturdy and sleek to the eye. His acquisitions had been expensive but worthy animals.

At the completion of the work on the stable block, Nathaniel toured the interior with Bennett. It was a magnificent job, now it had been furnished with the requisite tools and ancillary paraphernalia. Nathaniel installed the horses, which had been held in temporary quarters in an outhouse.

"Are you happy with the result, Nathaniel?" asked the builder, now on first name terms with his client.

"Very content, Abraham," replied Longland's owner. "We would like to reward your men for their efforts over the last two weeks, I have set up a meal and some refreshment for them if you don't mind."

"Not at all, my friend, I'm sure they will be very grateful," the builder advised him, leaving the block to inform his men of the good news.

Nathaniel heard the small cheer as he stood admiring his extended accommodation for the horses. The animals seemed happy in the stalls provided. Soon the mares would be let out into the paddock for the stallions to do their duty, even though it was the most natural procedure in nature, there was still some delicate rules to follow to achieve the best results.

Bennett and his cohorts were already drinking ale at the table, Nathaniel impressed by the amount of ale being quaffed. These were hard physical men who partook of alcohol in the same tough fashion as they performed their work.

They toasted Nathaniel and his wife, they toasted Toby, they toasted the erection of the block and in truth some of the other toasts were even more tenuous in there subject matter. Like the toast to the wart on Billy Short's nose, he sat smiling drunkenly at the attention and for the first time in his life he wasn't conscious but proud of the protuberance.

The party well under way, Nathaniel was feeling quite merry himself when he turned round, receiving an enormous shock. Ebenezer Smith leant against the side of the house, smiling broadly at the sight of his tipsy friend.

Nathaniel bounded to him, grasping him in a bear hug which the visitor returned. Male banter sounded behind him as the men cast doubt on his sexuality with the display. It was all good natured fun and Nathaniel was pleased that Mary was not in earshot.

"My God, Ebenezer, it's good to see you," the manor owner stated. "How in the world are you here?"

"I do read my correspondence, Nathaniel. Mary wrote to us to tell us of your purchase of the manor. I'm so sorry you couldn't acquire Thistlebrough; who knows maybe it will come on the market again soon."

Joining the men at the table, Nathaniel poured them both a tankard of ale. Ebenezer told his friend about the transportation of his horses from the farm in Africa.

Several drinks later, they were very much the worse for wear, joining in the loud singing of the labourers.

The celebration broke up and the builders set off for the last time, Nathaniel leading his friend to the house. Mary sat with Sally, who was bouncing young Toby on her knee. At the sight of the men she rose, greeting Nathaniel with a light kiss on the cheek, "Lovely to see you again," she purred.

"Tell me about your acquisition of the manor, old friend?" asked the Captain, flopping into a comfy chair.

The four talked for an hour, Nathaniel delighted to discover they had accepted an invitation from Mary to stay at the Manor rather than find a room somewhere in Morpeth.

Dinner was a relaxed affair, Elizabeth and Barron handling the first such party with aplomb. Mary felt pride in their performance. Like most women, the management of her household was extremely important to her, she preened herself at the success of the meal.

The ladies rose and retired, leaving the men to their port. Pouring himself one of the ruby liquids, Nathaniel passed the decanter to Smith.

"If your venture here is as successful as the ones you have overseas my friend, you will be a rich man indeed," advised Ebenezer.

"How are you and Sally, Ebenezer?" Nathaniel asked, pouring another port for himself and the Captain.

"She's everything I could have hoped for in my life," he said, "beautiful, lively, witty, charming and loving, what more could I possibly want?" He sipped the fortified wine, the clock sounded relentlessly in the room, its ticking rhythmic and loudly ominous.

They sat in silence a few minutes, Ebenezer eventually breaking the silence.

"Is there any news of your father, old friend?"

"My new found acquaintance, the MP for Portsmouth wrote to me recently, telling me he'd made representation to the Prime Minister for a pardon," Nathaniel informed him.

Ebenezer leaned forward, "Is there a chance that it will be granted?"

"It cannot do any harm to have a government back bencher making petition on his behalf, but he has given me no indication if it might be successful."

Smith regarded him with enthusiastic eyes, "Then there is a chance for him. However, small that chance may be, you must hold onto it positively."

Nathaniel rose and poked thoughtfully at the fire, it had become chilly as the night progressed. Manipulation of the coals prompted the flames to burst into life, throwing unearthly shadows around the room.

"I take one day at a time, my friend, if he is released then no one will be happier than I, but I must look on the situation at its bleakest, then I cannot be disappointed if the outcome is not how I want it to be," announced Nathaniel.

The women returned after a discreet time to say they were retiring; after they had left, the friends sat for half an hour reminiscing about Africa before ascending to their beds.

A miserable day greeted them the following morning, ominous dark clouds hung threatening and stationery in the sky, incessant rain beating down remorselessly on the landscape, misting the hills with a foggy curtain in the distance.

The atmosphere of the morning seemed to permeate the characters at breakfast. Nathaniel and Ebenezer were suffering from the alcoholic involvement of the previous day, both faces pale and their appetite nonexistent, although Ebenezer ate a piece of toast, Nathaniel could face nothing but tea.

Gazing out of the windows it seemed as though the precipitation would never cease. A shepherd in the distance tended his flock, Nathaniel marvelling at the man's determination in the teeth of such conditions.

It remained a quiet morning, little conversation was attempted by anyone with the men particularly reticent in view of their hangovers. The ladies sat reading; about 10am Elizabeth entered the sitting room.

"A gentleman to see you, Mr Davidson," she announced.

"Who is it?" the man enquired.

"A Mr Rutherford, sir."

Nathaniel's demeanour improved markedly, "Please show him in."

The man almost vaulted into the chamber. "Nathaniel, I have urgent and wonderful news for you," he bellowed.

"How is Thomas?" interrupted the owner of the manor.

"He is well, my friend, very well, but you must hear what I have to say," enthused Rutherford.

"Alright, Jonas," it was the first time Nathaniel had used the man's Christian name. "Sit down and tell me."

The estate manager eased his bulky frame into a chair. He seemed as excited as a schoolboy at the end of term.

"Ezekiel Wilson is leaving England for good, he's looking to sell Thistlebrough," he was so aroused his voice stammered the words.

Nathaniel couldn't take in the information. "But he has only just acquired the estate." Now it was his words that were faltering with emotion. "Why is he leaving?"

Jonas Rutherford perched on the edge of the seat like a bird spying prey from a branch.

"It seems that he had been travelling extensively throughout Europe for some time and had left his plantations in the charge of a manager," he paused to draw breath. "Apparently the crop became blighted and the manager kept silent about the extent of the problem and it got much worse, now Ezekiel Wilson is facing bankruptcy."

"My God, Nathaniel, I know I said yesterday that the estate may come on the market again but even I could never have foreseen this, it's everything you could have hoped for," laughed Ebenezer, who had listened to the news avidly.

The owner of Longland's mind was in turmoil, he couldn't grasp the enormity of the news. It was something he had set his heart on but he had just bought the manor and Mary seemed deliriously happy. How could he uproot her now he thought?

"Sweetheart," his wife began, "I have an idea what you are thinking about and I want you to know that I am fully behind you if this is what you want."

It was the endorsement he was hoping for. He gathered her up in his arms, kissing her fiercely and then laughing uncontrollably.

He and Ebenezer saddled horses and joined Jonas Rutherford, galloping away from Longland as the rain pelted down without let up. Smith suggested Nathaniel approach the American with all haste.

"My friend," he started, as they journeyed to Thistlebrough. "Don't get your hopes up too high until you speak to this man, he may be unwilling to sell to you or inflate the price if he has other interested parties."

"I will have it this time, Ebenezer, whatever it costs or whatever I have to do, the estate will be mine," the Captain's friend replied.

Smith looked sideways at his colleague as they rode along, concern etched on his face. He was so adamant about the ownership of the estate that the Captain felt disquiet, wondering how his friend might take it if he lost out on the purchase a second time.

Out of the misty atmosphere, Thistlebrough appeared. As soon as Nathaniel looked on its imposing frontage, he knew why his heart was so set on its procurement. It had not changed in any respect since the last time he had seen its grandeur, the impressive nobility of the house dominated the landscape. Joshua disappeared before the estate hove into view. It was best they all thought, if Wilson didn't know his Estate Manager had approached Nathaniel.

The two men allowed him a discreet length of time to return to the house, waiting in a nearby copse, rainwater cascading down from the trees above in a depressingly rhythmic fashion.

"It's a magnificent structure," murmured Smith, gazing with rapture on the scene before him, "no wonder you want it so badly."

Looking down on the house which had served as his childhood home, Nathaniel stirred nervously in the saddle.

"There are many reasons why I want Thistlebrough, my friend, the architecture is only one of those motives but in truth, I want my father to end his days in the place he loved so much," he stared unblinkingly straight ahead. "I know the chances of that happening are slim at best, but I hold out the hope he will receive a pardon."

An hour later they judged Rutherford would be safe from criticism, the two men approaching the hall. The rain had lightened but fell persistently, its coolness chilling them to the bone.

A liveried footman appeared at the huge double doors, looking disdainfully on the dishevelled and dirty visitors.

"May I help you?" the voice was nasal and betrayed his sneering demeanour vocally. Irked by the man's attitude, Nathaniel's own voice returned the compliment.

"We wish to talk to Mr Ezekiel Wilson; my name is Davidson and this is Captain Smith."

"Perhaps you would step this way," he ushered the men inside, embarrassed to have anyone see them calling at the main entrance to such a magnificent building. "Please sit and I will announce your arrival," he sniffed, pointing at some chairs.

"A particularly likeable individual," Ebenezer commented sarcastically.

The church like quiet of the massive entrance hall was something Nathaniel had forgotten.

A sight of extraordinary elegance glided into the hallway, perfectly coiffured hair and well cut clothing accentuating the form perfectly.

"Gentlemen, I am Mrs Wilson, how may I help you?" the accent was English upper class.

"My name is Nathaniel Davidson and this is Ebenezer Smith, I would like to speak with your husband on a matter of great urgency, if I may?"

"I'm afraid my husband left for Newcastle a few hours ago, perhaps I could help you, Mr Davidson."

"I attempted to purchase Thistlebrough from your husband recently and I understand that he is returning to the United States and wants to sell the hall," stated Nathaniel. "I am hoping to persuade him to sell the estate to me on this occasion."

They had risen from their seats on the appearance of the lady, who selected a chair for herself and sat, Nathaniel and Ebenezer re-seated themselves.

"Ezekiel has gone to the city to negotiate the transaction of Thistlebrough with the Duke of Northumberland, who wishes the hall for one of his family," Mrs Wilson informed him.

Nathaniel became agitated, "Do you know where they propose to meet, Mrs Wilson, I must speak with your husband as soon as possible?"

"They are meeting with our solicitor in the morning," she rose once more. "Lambert and Hodgson situated on Grey Street."

The news was important to Nathaniel, he wanted to seek out Wilson before his meeting.

"And tonight, where is he lodging this evening?"

She thought hard, "A tavern; the Coach and Horses I believe, it's somewhere near the river."

"I am much obliged to you, Mrs Wilson," the visitor asserted. "Thank you for your help."

The men remounted their steeds, Smith looking at his friend, "Where now?" he asked, "back to Longland."

"No," Nathaniel called galloping away, "Newcastle and the Coach and Horses."

CHAPTER 30

Whipping their horses to the gallop, Smith struggled to remain in contact with Nathaniel, whose horse was the fastest of the pair. The miles diminished inexorably, darkness falling as they reached the outskirts of the city.

A man was walking a mangy dog along the road, his coat buttoned to combat the biting wind. Ebenezer challenged him for directions to the inn. The individual informed them that the Coach and Horses stood alongside the river, at the lower end of the city.

It was a welcoming atmosphere inside the inn, warm and well decorated. After enquiries they discovered that Ezekiel Wilson was indeed residing there but had gone out to dinner, no one knew of his expected time of return.

Nathaniel was frustrated in the extreme. It seemed as though the fates were conspiring against him, and he voiced his concern to Smith.

"Be patient, my friend, we'll wait for him until his return and you can tackle him then, in the meantime perhaps we should dine."

Smith attempted conversation, small talk throughout the meal but Nathaniel's mind was elsewhere. It was after 11pm when the object of their wait arrived. Wilson, accompanied by two men, entered the inn as his escorts said their goodbyes.

He headed for the stairs to his room, Nathaniel waylaying him, "Mr. Wilson, I wonder if I may have a word with you?"

Ezekiel Wilson's eyes narrowed, searching the confines of his mind for the man's name and with sudden recognition he began, "Mr Davidson, it's a great pleasure to see you again, but what are you doing here?"

"I own Longland Manor in Northumberland now, I purchased it following our last conversation," he indicated a chair at his table. "Would you care to join myself and my companion for a nightcap?"

He introduced Ebenezer to the American, who warmed to the Captain immediately and they discussed various ports in the United States which Smith had visited in the course of his voyages.

"This isn't a coincidental meeting, is it Mr Davidson?" hinted Wilson after a time.

"No it isn't, and I hope you will call me Nathaniel."

Ezekiel ordered whisky and soda, the others joining him in his choice, "Then enlighten me as to the reason for this meeting, Nathaniel," persisted the gentleman from the United States, "although I think I can guess its nature."

Davidson felt uncomfortable as he began speaking, "I can't tell you how I have heard this news but I believe it is the case you are returning to your country and want to sell Thistlebrough, correct?"

A fleeting look of annoyance swept over Wilson's face but it passed quickly.

"Yes it is true, Nathaniel, I daresay you want to purchase the estate again, am I right?"

"You know my feelings regarding the hall Ezekiel, it means a great deal to me," pleaded Nathaniel. "Surely you will give me the opportunity to buy it on this occasion."

Wilson tossed the amber fluid into his mouth, the biting warmness enfolded his throat as he swallowed, "I am here to negotiate the sale of the property to the Duke of Northumberland," he commented, "we meet in the morning with my solicitor to finalise details."

Leaning forward, Nathaniel beseeched the American, "Then the deal is not yet done, my money is as good as anyone's isn't it?"

Wilson eyed him curiously, "Indeed it is, Nathaniel, but with my business interests in the United States, the Duke offers his name as a director of my company. Having a member of the British peerage appear on my list of directors provides me with great prestige," he paused. "And that type of endorsement is better than money in the bank to me." The argument was compelling, Davidson feeling deflated. It looked as though he would lose the opportunity of buying his dream a second time.

As he looked at Smith, Nathaniel could see defeat written in the seafarer's eyes.

"I will double whatever the Duke is offering," blurted Nathaniel.

"You aren't listening. It's the endorsement which is important to me and gives the Duke the edge," instructed Ezekiel. "He will pay a fair price for the property and I will make much more from his name."

The crestfallen expression on the man's face touched the American.

"I'm Sorry, Nathaniel, but this has to be a commercial decision, now if you don't mind, gentlemen, I must retire."

It was too late to return to Longland and Nathaniel still had the desire to fight for the ownership of the estate. They booked rooms in the inn, knowing their wives would understand this was a real possibility and wouldn't worry unduly if they did not return.

After a comfortable night, they descended to the dining room, where Ezekiel Wilson was already partaking of breakfast, nodding in their direction as the men took seats at a nearby table, he carried on eating.

Twenty minutes later, Wilson rose to leave, Nathaniel deciding to tackle him once more to try and change his mind a last time.

"Mr Wilson, I implore you to reconsider your position; if I can persuade the Duke to endorse your company despite losing out on the hall, will you consider my offer to buy Thistlebrough?"

"And how do you intend to perform that feat, Nathaniel?" asked the American.

Davidson smiled. "In truth, I have no idea, but I'm willing to try," he said. Wilson smiled back, he could see some of his younger self in the man.

"Alright, if you can accomplish that feat, I will think about selling the estate to you."

The first thing was to locate the member of the aristocracy.

"Where are you meeting with the Duke, Ezekiel?"

Reseating himself, the American advised, "At the County Hotel where he is staying," he consulted his watch. "At ten o'clock which gives you little over an hour to achieve your goal."

Nathaniel and his companion rushed from the inn and ran towards the centre of the city, location of the establishment.

Elaborate floor tiles with rich floral designs welcomed the men as they dashed into the hotel foyer. Elegant wall coverings and drapes of deep red hue, decorated the structure inside, an imposing oak reception desk stood in the centre of the floor, occupied by a young but imposing man.

"May I speak with the Duke of Northumberland?" inquired Nathaniel, "I believe he is staying in the hotel."

"I'm afraid I have strict instructions not to admit anyone to the Duke's presence without an appointment," advised the employee. "Do you have an appointment?"

Nathaniel's frustration boiled within him, "No I don't, but this is a matter of urgency," he yelled.

"Yes sir, I'm sure it is," sneered the receptionist with an air of superciliousness.

A man crossed the floor, having descended the stairs, "May I help you sir, I am the Duke?"

"Your Grace, I apologise for the intrusion, but I am in the process of having these men removed," the receptionist fawned.

The Duke raised his hand to halt the man's chatter, "It's quite alright, I will talk to these gentlemen, although I have to advise you that I have a meeting in less than an hour," he advised Nathaniel and Ebenezer.

"May we sit, Your Grace," pleaded Nathaniel.

They selected seats in the foyer, "And how can I help you?" queried the member of the peerage.

"Your Grace, I know you are meeting Mr Ezekiel Wilson very soon to discuss the purchase of Thistlebrough estate," he continued speedily. "My father used to own the estate, perhaps you know of him, Sir Toby Davidson," said Nathaniel.

"Indeed yes," replied the Duke, "how is he?"

"I'm afraid my father was transported on a charge of murder Your Grace."

"Good God," exclaimed the Duke, "was he guilty?"

"He was protecting me, Your Grace, but could we talk about that another time, I need to talk to you about Thistlebrough."

"Carry on Mr Davidson, how can I be of assistance?"

Nathaniel gathered himself. The next few minutes would determine if he could purchase the estate, he chose his words carefully.

"Ezekiel Wilson is anxious to be rid of Thistlebrough as he has to return to America, he has tentatively arranged to sell the property to you in return for your endorsement of his tobacco company," Nathaniel examined the man's eyes for any indication of mood, seeing a blank expression. "I am desperate to buy the estate and he will not sell it to me because he feels that you will reject the opportunity to give your seal of approval to his concern."

"And he is right, Mr Davidson," the member of the peerage replied. "As you probably know, I am purchasing this for a member of my family. I will get it at a favourable price because of the man's need to sell quickly and my name on his company rolls."

Nathaniel thought hard. "Your Grace, you have many properties here in the county and one of those would suit the needs of your relation well I'm sure and it would be in your interest if you appended your name to his company regardless of any purchase of Thistlebrough. Everyone knows that tobacco is one of the growing and most successful of businesses in the future."

Suddenly, Ebenezer Smith interjected, "My apologies, Your Grace but I wonder if I might have a word with my friend in private, it might be of mutual benefit."

"By all means," the Duke retorted.

Smith led Nathaniel away from the man whispering, "My friend, you really want this more than anything, don't you?"

"You know I do, Ebenezer."

"So offer him a directorship in your businesses in South Africa on a non executive basis and pay him a bonus once a year, for say ten years," Smith continued. "That should sway him, with the undoubted contributions he will be receiving from Wilson, he should be more than satisfied."

Nathaniel grasped him by the shoulders, thanking him profusely, returning to his seat near the Duke. "Your Grace would you consider a business proposal from myself that might compensate you for your loss of Thistlebrough?"

"I am always open to any offer which might improve my wealth and standing," smiled the Duke.

"I am a very wealthy man in my own right, I have successful businesses in South Africa dealing in thoroughbred horses and quality wine which are exported around the world." He considered how to make the approach. "I will make you a director of those businesses in a non executive capacity and pay you a bonus of five per cent of the profit over the next decade for your withdrawal on the sale of Thistlebrough. That with your endorsement of Ezekiel Wilson's company should compensate handsomely for pulling out of the purchase."

With surprising alacrity the Duke nodded, "Yes, Mr Davidson, if your businesses prove as successful as you seem to think they are, then you have a deal, I will need my solicitor to investigate your claims very thoroughly." He held out his hand and Nathaniel grasped it, knowing that the gesture was sufficient endorsement of his word. "We have one problem, however, and that is the speed with which Mr Wilson needs to sell, I suggest we meet him now and you conduct business to buy the hall; we will have a contract written to the effect that, if your businesses do not prove to be as beneficial to me as you say, you will sell the hall to me at the price you pay for it."

"With pleasure, Your Grace," Nathaniel couldn't believe he had managed the feat, all due to Smith's suggestion.

Ezekiel Wilson was satisfied with the arrangement. The men's legal representatives met in Newcastle in the afternoon to finalise details of the proposals.

Nathaniel's solicitor was the last to arrive, he had been conducting business in the morning and with his arrival the sale of Thistlebrough could be completed.

Wilson shook hands with Nathaniel at the conclusion of the transaction.

"It seems appropriate that you have finally gained tenure of Thistlebrough, my boy, you've fought so hard to get it," the American declared.

"It's the realisation of everything I've ever wanted," he explained, "and you have the endorsement you want, which makes us all winners."

"Gentlemen, perhaps we should conclude business with dinner," declared the Duke, "I would be honoured if you would join me as my guests, shall we say 7.30 at the Northumberland Hotel?"

The men agreed, going their separate ways until the evening. Nathaniel and Ebenezer were without the appropriate attire, seeking out a company specialising in hire.

Grant's Gentlemen's Outfitters was situated on Northumberland Street, the city's main thoroughfare; it had an air of bleakness, dingy and dusty within but had an enviable reputation for the provision of evening attire.

Nathaniel had rarely seen clothes of such an expert cut and the fitting was superb. Their garments could have been made to measure, such was the closeness of the measurements.

At the appointed hour, Nathaniel and Ebenezer walked into the lavish Northumberland Hotel, met in the dining room by the Duke and Wilson. It was a sumptuous chamber, gleaming silver cutlery set in military precision on crisp, pure white table linen. Daubs of shimmering light covered the walls where the reflection of the lamps in the silver fell.

They began with smoked salmon, the texture of which was of just the right consistency and taste. Delectable roast beef formed the main course and to finish they partook of fresh strawberries and cream.

All Nathaniel could think of, as the meal progressed, was of returning to Longland and telling Mary the good news but niceties had to be observed.

"Now that you have attained Thistlebrough, what are your plans, Nathaniel?" enquired the Duke.

"That is easy, Your Grace," retorted Davidson, "my next goal must be to have my father pardoned, his conviction was a travesty of justice."

"How will you manage to achieve that, my friend?" Ebenezer asked him, sipping at a fine Madeira.

"That will be my most difficult task to date, but I do have Joshua Merryweather, the MP for Portsmouth, making representation to the Prime Minister on my father's behalf, I hope that may help," advised Nathaniel.

"Perhaps if you explained the situation to me, I might be able to attack the establishment from a different direction," offered the Duke.

Total silence fell as Nathaniel recounted the episode to the men, it took fifteen minutes to describe the night in question and the circumstances which led to Philip Brent's death.

At the end of the account, the Duke leaned towards the new owner of Thistlebrough.

"I shall be glad to take up your case in the Lords, my boy," he advised. "I will speak to my fellow peers; I am confident they will support me in my efforts."

Tears pricked the eyes of Nathaniel, the backing of the Duke was more than he could have hoped for.

CHAPTER 31

In the orange glow of dawn, Nathaniel and his companion set out for Longland. Although he was anxious to give Mary the news, they did not rush back.

As if to reflect Nathaniel's excellent news, the sun shone brightly down on the men all the way back to Longland.

It was mid afternoon by the time they rode into the grounds of the manor, the day calm, droning bees buzzed haphazardly around the flowers in his wife's garden. Nathaniel entered the house to find it deserted.

Two hours later, the household returned from a picnic in nearby fields, Mary had taken advantage of the good weather to have the outing.

His wife entered, Nathaniel leaping to his feet. "Mary, I have it," he cried, laughing. "Thistlebrough is finally mine."

His wife smiled broadly, she had desperately hoped for the result, but in truth did not really believe it could be achieved.

"That's wonderful news my angel, I'm so pleased for you."

"We can take possession of the property in two weeks," continued her husband. "Ezekiel Wilson will be leaving for the United States then."

Sally crossed to him, grasping his hands. "The news is truly marvellous, Nathaniel, I'm sure you will both be very happy there," her knowing smile demonstrated true delight at the information. The memory of their brief liaison flitted briefly through her mind, he had changed so much in so few years, she thought.

Toby began to cry softly in the arms of his mother, Nathaniel lifting him gently from her grasp.

As invariably happened on these occasions, Toby ended his sobbing the moment his father looked down and smiled at him.

Life over the next two weeks proved hectic, so much organisation was necessary that time seemed to fly by.

On the day of their relocation, Nathaniel woke before 5am. He had slept little, fitful episodes lasting no more than half an hour at a time.

The kitchen of Longland was still at the ungodly hour and Nathaniel brewed tea, sitting sipping the strong liquid, lost in thought.

Elizabeth and Barron walked into the room an hour later, in preparation for the move, surprised by the seated form of their master.

The valet addressed Davidson, "Today is your day sir, I'm sure you must feel very proud to take back your family's estate."

Nathaniel felt a warm glow. "Yes, Barron, it is a great day for myself and for my family but I know when you see it you will fall in love with Thistlebrough too."

In his mind there was a little sadness at leaving Longland. It had been a beautiful place in which to live, despite the shortness of their tenure. He walked outside, drinking in the atmosphere of the manor grounds and gazed over Mary's patch of flowers, which she'd spent so much time nurturing.

The extended stable block and newly fenced paddock were testament to his vision, he knew the business would be well run by the new inhabitants of the manor. Jonas Rutherford had been instrumental in the acquisition of Thistlebrough, Nathaniel rewarding him by giving him Longland for his home while he looked after Nathaniel's business interests.

Nathaniel and Mary left with the servants after breakfast, Ebenezer and Sally joining them on the journey to their new home. Rutherford and his family had arrived at Longland before eight, eager to move into the plush edifice, which was to be their home from that day forward.

Their son was like any normal boy, the experience at the waterfall no longer a thought in his head.

"Thomas," shouted Nathaniel, the boy trotting over to him. "How are you, my boy?" asked his saviour.

"Very well, Mr Davidson, I never really thanked you for that day when you saved my life but I thank you with my whole heart now," his face belied genuineness and the statement brought a tear to Nathaniel's eye.

"Think nothing of it," stammered Davidson, "just you justify my actions by looking after your mother and father, understand?"

"I will," yelled the boy, galloping away to explore the grounds of his new home.

Mary gazed back on Longland Manor as the carriage pulled out of the driveway, her mood sombre at the departure but she had married Nathaniel and determined to make him happy, wherever they resided.

She looked away from the manor house, glinting in the sunlight, fully recovering her composure and eagerly looking forward to her new life at Thistlebrough.

It was an uneventful journey, the day warm and full of sounds of the country. Sheep bleated their staccato cries throughout the trip and there was a rustling in the trees, where a stiff breeze sprang up, swaying the branches with metronomic rhythm. An hour later, the party halted, Elizabeth and the valet opening a picnic basket, handing out food and wine to the travellers. The wine was tepid and bitter to the taste, warmed by the heat of the day.

Nathaniel's impatience was getting the better of him as his wife ordered the stop.

"Is this strictly necessary, my dear?" he questioned her.

"Thistlebrough will still be there, Nathaniel, don't worry. It's stood for generations now, so I hardly think it will fall down before we get there," she smiled. "besides it's a beautiful day and I just thought we might take advantage of it."

"Yes, my dear," her husband allowed sheepishly, realising the pettiness of his actions and the smirk on Ebenezer's face.

"Mary is right, my friend," the Captain smoothed, "enjoy the day, we'll be there soon enough."

Twenty minutes later, the carriage moved off, Nathaniel feeling much happier. When the estate finally appeared, his heart almost leapt with joy. Even though it had not been too many years since residing there, the knowledge he was returning in ownership overwhelmed him.

There was one person left at the hall, she introduced herself as Mrs Trent. Nathaniel deciding he had never seen such a craggy face on a woman before; it was like a rock face. The Wilsons had left the day before, leaving instructions with the woman to remain until the new owners arrived.

Sensing he would like to enter Thistlebrough alone as the new owner, Mary, Ebenezer and Sally supervised the unloading of the cart, Barron and Elizabeth had travelled on, removing the Davidsons possessions.

Nathaniel looked up at the ornate designs on the roof of the cavernous hall, staring for some minutes at the benevolent scenes from the Bible on the ceiling. It was difficult to accept the sense of contentment he felt. He wandered the lowest storey of the house, familiarising himself with the hall's topography again.

There was one task he wanted to complete with all his being. Exiting the hall he walked to the mausoleum where his mother was entombed.

Falling to his knees in front of the structure, Nathaniel broke down, sobbing unrestrainedly. The first time he had the opportunity to be near his mother since her death was almost too much for him, his hands stroked the icy stone block, as though somehow the touch could be felt by her spirit.

Nathaniel lost himself in grief for an hour, talking to her, letting all his pent up emotion flow into his loving words.

The area around the crypt, overgrown and untended, needed much attention to return it to its former magnificence. That would be one of his first tasks. It would be returned to its original state he determined.

Sitting cross legged on the grass beside the monument, he spied Ebenezer coming towards him from the house, rising slowly, as the man neared.

"My friend," the Captain began, "Mary requires you back at the hall, some domestic matter I think," he laughed.

Showing his companion the place where his mother lay, the man's demeanour changed to one of respectful reverence.

"I'm sure she knows how you feel about her, my friend, but your place is with the living, you have a wife and child to care for and now you have the prize you always wanted." He placed his hand on Nathaniel's shoulder. "The best thing you can do for your mother now is occupy the hall and continue your family tradition."

They walked slowly back to the hall, Nathaniel lost in thought about his mother. Inside the house, Mary was occupied changing furniture around to suit her taste. Her husband had purchased the property complete with fixtures and fittings, he was delighted to note everything from his childhood remained. The Wilsons had purchased some items, but the majority were left from his mother's days. Despite his gladness to be back, there was sense of unfamiliarity in his soul, though he knew that would pass.

Mary found him in his childhood bedchamber, holding a lead soldier which he'd hidden many years before under a loose floorboard, a legacy of inclement days spent planning campaigns on his bedroom floor, at a time when his ambition was to be a General when he grew to manhood.

Paint was peeling off the Guardsman and diaphanous cobwebs shrouded what was left of the colouring but her husband held onto it tightly, like a precious jewel, a memory of his youth.

"Nathaniel, let's go for a walk," his wife suggested.

They walked around the paddock in which Nathaniel had broken the horse the fateful day he had left Thistlebrough.

"I have some news, my darling," said Mary breathlessly, "I'm pregnant again, my love." The day was proving to be one of the best in his entire life.

"That's wonderful," gushed Nathaniel, "God is certainly blessing me in many ways today."

Hugging his wife tightly to him, they kissed as the man took in the news of a second child.

"You are happy about this, aren't you, sweetheart?" Mary's face showed concern which baffled her husband.

"Of course I am, Mary, why wouldn't I be?" he replied.

"It's just that a lot of things have happened recently, I didn't think the timing was ideal," she advised him.

Nathaniel laughed heartily, "It's the best news I could have, our family means more to me than any property, my darling," the look on his face dispelled any reservations the woman had.

Ebenezer Smith and his wife climbed the gentle slope of the hill, the woman carrying Toby carefully in her arms, husband supporting her as they ascended. When they reached their friends, Mary lay the child on the earth sitting next to Sally on the grassy hilltop.

"My friends, I have some wonderful news, Mary is with child again," blurted Nathaniel.

The Smiths looked at each other and began to laugh.

"That's excellent news," Sally offered, "because Ebenezer and I have been blessed with the same news."

Nathaniel Davidson thought on his son by Sally. The boy had been left in the charge of the first officer of the Adventuress, he would be glad of a sibling, Nathaniel was sure.

He began to reminisce about his life and the twists and turns it had taken to this point. Christian Davenport was a big miss in his world, a true friend and confidant, the man would have been delighted with the progress his friend had made.

He thought of his liaison with Sally as a younger man, his first experience of a woman, and a warm glow came over him. It may have been the first inexperienced fumbling of youth, but it was an important aspect of his life. Nathaniel stole a glance at her. She meant much to him as a friend but any love for her was long since gone. She could never replace Mary and he was delighted she had found true happiness with the other loyal friend of his life.

Thoughts of the wonderful time he'd spent in Africa occupied his mind too, the sunrises and sunsets over Table Mountain, an enduring memory. He knew one day he would have to return to the wonderful land once more.

Toby gurgled in his mother's arms and he looked proudly on his son, knowing he would die for him if the necessity arose. The boy meant the world to him, as did his unborn child.

Nathaniel gazed around the estate from his vantage point on the hilltop, taking in his mother's resting place and the gnarled oak, around which he played as a child.

His old friend joined him, the men walking away from the ladies, who were deep in conversation about their yet to be born children, smiles broad as they talked of the future.

Out of earshot, Ebenezer turned to his friend. "Nathaniel, as you know I am not a man given to sentimentalism, but I want you to know that I greatly esteem your friendship, we have been through much together; I would not have missed it for the world."

"Nor I, my friend," reciprocated Davidson, "your companionship is a constant pleasure to me."

Nathaniel looked down on Thistlebrough as owner, its architecture still fascinated him after all the years he had experienced in the building's precincts, something he knew would never leave him.

"And who is this coming to call?" piped up Smith. Following his friend's gaze, Nathaniel noticed a small speck, which gradually emerged as a carriage, trundling toward the hall.

Sheep scattered off the muddy track as the vehicle approached, with their ungainly movement. The animals descended the slope on either side of the wagon, one of them stumbling and falling, lying on its back, its displaced stomach preventing it from rising again. Nathaniel knew someone would have to help the poor creature to its feet.

The carriage swung through the gateway, up to the hall where the driver reined in the horses.

Joshua Merryweather descended from the interior. It was clearly him from his gait and Nathaniel blinked in stunned surprise as a second figure climbed out. It was his father. Nathaniel's head bowed, tears flowing.

CHAPTER 32

There was an oppressiveness in the room which could only be associated with death. No chink of light escaped into the chamber through the heavy velvet curtains, closed and barring out life itself.

Ruffled bedclothes betrayed the previous thrashing of the man, nearing the end of his life, his breathing laboured, body emanating a pungent aroma as internal organs began to break down.

Bending once more to the patient, the doctor held his breath, keeping the rotting stench at bay. He clasped the wrist, feeling desperately for the pulse, when he found a murmur it was thin and intermittent. Looking at the people gathered around the bed, he silently shook his head, testament that the patient was fading fast.

The old man's eyes flickered open, his watery gaze settling on his son. Opening his mouth to speak, Nathaniel fell to his knees next to his father, placing his ear next to the flaky lips, straining to pick up the words.

When they came, it was as if from another man.

"My boy," the effort was almost too much, "I know we haven't always seen eye to eye, but tell me I have been a good father?" the grip placed around Nathaniel's arm was astonishing for a man so close to his demise.

"Of course you have, Father," he replied, "I only hope I have given you opportunity to have pride in me." No answer was necessary, the thin smile showed the son more than words ever could that it was the case.

"Nathaniel," croaked Sir Toby, "I need to see the sun once more, open the drapes."

Striding purposefully to the massive window, Toby's son threw back the curtains, light sweeping majestically into the room, flooding the chamber with an immediate warmness.

226

Nathaniel began a commentary on the grounds of Thistlebrough Hall below. His father would appreciate the gesture.

"I can see the horses in the paddock, Father, Blaze is nuzzling Beauty, she is responding; Evans, the gardener, is tending the vegetable patch…"

The doctor emitted a revealing cough behind him, the sort that speaks of bad news. As he turned to look at him, he knew the worst immediately.

"I'm afraid your father is gone, Nathaniel," the physician stated.

Sir Toby lay at peace, the agony of the previous twelve hours no longer evident on the face. Where previously wrinkles of pain had been evident, the skin was smooth, expression contented.

Nathaniel had seen death before of course, the same thought always invading his mind. A light in the person had been extinguished, leaving an alabaster shell behind, void of the spark of life.

Taking his father's hand, it was warm but he knew in a very short time the body would resemble an icy marble statue. Looking down at the cadaver his mind raced back over the years, remembering the good and bad times.

Venturing toward him, Mary slipped her arm around his waist. Twenty years of good living had expanded the girth but she liked the extra pounds he had acquired.

"I'm so sorry, sweetheart," she said, "but he is at peace now."

Clinging to her in return, trying to extract every ounce of compassion and comfort from her warm body, the tears began to flow, hot on his cheek, salty to the taste, as they splashed on his lips.

Suddenly, he wanted time to grieve alone with his father,

"Mary," he rasped, "please don't misunderstand me but I wonder if I might be alone with him for a few minutes."

"Of course, my dear." Motioning to the doctor and the servants in the room to vacate, she crossed to the door, standing for a moment to look with compassion on the sunken frame of her husband.

The room empty, silence boomed out. Nathaniel crossed to his father, looking down, reciting the Lord's prayer to himself over the inert form.

Mary escorted the physician to the library, ordering tea from the maid. They fell into conversation, although she occasionally glanced nervously at the ceiling, wondering how her husband was coping in the room above.

The doctor began in formal fashion, "Mrs. Davidson, there is nothing further I can do for your father-in-law; I am concerned about Nathaniel, however," he paused to sip the tea recently placed before them by the maid, the girl slipping out of the room like a thief in the night. "He is much troubled about his father's death and is a sensitive man, how do you think he will cope with the loss?"

"In truth I have no idea, Doctor. I know that my husband and Sir Toby had a difficult start in life, but in the last few years there has not been a more loving parent and child relationship." She searched for a decision which would placate the medical man. "Nathaniel has lost people close to him before." Finally she made up her mind. "The fact is I believe he will cope badly."

"Mmm," mused the doctor, "it's much as I feared, please keep a close watch on him and let me know if he has further problems coming to terms with his father's death." The man took out his watch. "And now I must go, there are other patients to see, my sincere condolences on your loss, Mrs Davidson," he gave a pain filled bow and left the room.

Mary occupied herself with sewing until at last the library door swung open, Nathaniel entering, looking haggard and thoroughly defeated.

Mary was unsure whether to speak, if he wanted to talk, he would begin the conversation so she bent to her embroidery once more.

"I don't know how to face this, Mary," he blurted. She looked at him as a mother looks at a child.

Early morning mist eddied around the base of the marble crypt, freshly opened to accommodate the body of Sir Toby. He would be reunited with Nathaniel's mother after so many years apart. As he stood looking on the scene clasping the waist of Mary, tears began to flow for the umpteenth time.

Reverend Bottomley conducted the service as briskly as was decent in the circumstances, aware of the chilling temperature and the man's feelings.

"We therefore commit his body to the earth, in the sure and certain knowledge of the resurrection of the spirit to God's holy grace," the churchman intoned. Nathaniel's son placed his hand on his father's shoulder in a gesture of compassion. Young Toby was coming up on his twentythird birthday, growing into an Adonis, much coveted by the young women of the district. Nathaniel's youngest son, Edward, looked on in silence.

The service ended with the internment and a period of uncertainty as to what to do ensued. Bottomley approached the Davidson family.

"He was a good man, Sir Nathaniel," he advised, melting into the background, leaving them to a few moments contemplation at the grave site.

Nathaniel realised that the hereditary peerage had passed to his shoulders, in that one sentence, it sounded incongruous to hear himself referred to in such fashion.

Nothing remained but to head back to the hall, the few mourners trooping away in the direction of tea and breakfast. Nathaniel regretted the fact so few people could attend by virtue of the burial's swiftness, he had hoped by its speed that the pain of his father's death might be assuaged.

Reaching the hall, he realised he could not mingle with the mourners, listening to platitudes and stories of his father's life, so Mary and their sons assumed the responsibility, while Sir Toby's offspring headed for his study.

Pouring himself an enormous whisky from the decanter on the bureau, he fell despondently into the seat behind his desk. The tranquillity of the room was a godsend, far enough away from the gathering to be silent.

As he sat, he reflected on his future. Three hours elapsed before Mary entered the room, looking exhausted from entertaining and the sombreness of the day's events. She had been his rock all these years, time doing nothing to diminish his feelings. Time and companionship, had perpetually strengthened the love between them.

She sat on his knee, something she hadn't done for years, placing her arms around his neck.

"I can't stay here, Mary," he cautioned her. "Thistlebrough will hold too many painful memories for me, at least for now."

The intuition of a wife prepared her for this eventuality, she had suspected it might be coming, knowing she would follow him anywhere he asked her to go.

"I know you are unhappy at the moment, sweetheart," she soothed, "but don't you feel that you should take a few days to allow your grief to diminish before you make such a major decision?"

Mary hoped with the passage of time Nathaniel might change his mind, but his resolve to leave hardened over the next few days.

They were sitting one evening, Mary sewing, her husband reading, when suddenly he raised his eyes from the page.

"Mary, I think we should return to Africa," he ventured. It was the logical choice but the decision was a blow to her. She enjoyed a comfortable and good life at Thistlebrough, and would loathe to give it up.

"Alright Nathaniel, if that is what you want, then we will do that," she replied magnanimously.

It was a sacrifice for his wife and it made him proud to know that she was prepared to give up her happiness for his welfare.

Two weeks later they were ready for the journey, Toby decided to join them, leaving his position as clerk in the solicitors for which he worked.

Climbing the gangplank to the ship's deck, Nathaniel's mind was transported to the day when he and Christian Davenport had begun a similar journey and their fortuitous meeting with Ebenezer Smith, his greatest remaining friend. Their son Edward stayed for the remainder of his boarding term at school.

The ship larger and the crew less friendly than the one on the Lady Bamburgh many years before, he stood at the rail with his wife and son, wondering what this new chapter in his life would bring.

CHAPTER 33

The ship ploughed toward the harbour, crewmembers reducing sail until only that necessary for the barest manoeuvring was left. Dropping speed rapidly, the vessel cruised to a suitable spot in the bay, the huge anchor slipping from its mooring, plunging into the tranquil water.

Cape Town had not changed much since the day Nathaniel left all those years ago. He gazed over the scene with regret, thinking of Christian's death and his father's incarceration and subsequent deportation to the penal colony of Australia.

"It looks no different," he muttered to Mary. "Still a jewel in Africa's crown."

Mary followed his stare, "Are you happy to be back, sweetheart?" she inquired.

"Very happy, and you?"

His wife had more than a few reservations about returning, she realised Nathaniel's contentment was paramount, almost believing herself when she uttered the word, "Yes."

Toby joined them at the rail, the first look at his new home filling him with excitement. What captured his imagination most, was the exoticness of the bustling city, it generated feelings of adventure in his soul. Life could be good here, the young man mused.

"Father, can we go ashore now?" His youthful zeal awakened the same feelings Nathaniel had experienced on his initial visit to the continent.

"Be patient, my boy," he laughed, "as soon as the Captain secures his ship, he will allow us to leave."

By the time the ship was closed down from sea duty, it was an hour later. Time enough for the Davidsons to gather their possessions and prepare for disembarkation. Toby was almost beside himself with desire to set foot on terra firma. When a member of the crew invited them to the boat station, he bounded up the companionway, into the glaring sunshine.

Half an hour later they were standing on land, Nathaniel immediately casting around for suitable transport for themselves and their effects; once loaded they set off for the vineyard.

Abundant fruit burdened the slopes as they approached; clearly this year's harvest would be a good one.

From the first glance at the exterior, the house remained the same, but the inside had been completely redecorated by the Estate Manager. It was unfamiliar to Nathaniel, who knew Mary would require a complete change when the employee had been rehoused. Jeremiah Brown had been manager over ten years and under his direction the business had expanded year on year, giving the Davidsons the lifestyle they had come to expect. Nathaniel provided Brown with the best remuneration any vineyard manager could expect. As a result, he was well off in his own right.

Brown by name and brown by sight, the stocky individual bounded into the house. Years of exposure to the burning sun contributed to a swarthy complexion.

"So good to see you again after all these years, Mr Davidson," the voice rich and booming. "And this must be Mrs Davidson and young Toby," he laughed, pumping hands all round.

As Mary and his son settled into their rooms, Nathaniel and Brown reclined with drinks.

"May I have a report on the activities of the business, Brown?" asked the owner.

"Well, sir," the manager began. "This year promises to be the best harvest yet, it seems the longer we grow in the soil here, the richer it gets," he sipped at the liquid. "The workers are longstanding and expert at their jobs."

"Then are we looking at expansion now, Jeremiah?"

"I think we are, sir, yes," replied the Manager. "There is no spare capacity on the estate as it stands, Mr Davidson, so if you wish to advance the business we will need more land and consequently more workers." Nathaniel liked the man's forthright manner, there was something in his character which showed him he could be a good friend and well trusted.

"How many workers do we have at present, Jeremiah?"

"A hundred and six, sir; seventy-two men and thirty-four women."

"I will settle in today, I know you will have duties to attend to, I will see you at dinner, Jeremiah, and we can continue our discussions then."

The man returned his whisky tumbler to the tray, moving to leave.

"It's good to see you here, sir; I'm sure the business will go from strength to strength now," he commented and was gone.

Mary returned to the room from her unpacking, looking hot and flustered, observing the drink in his hand,

"So that's the way of it is it," she smiled, "I work and you drink, what about one for me?"

"This was purely a business drink with my Manager," he grinned in return.

It took several days for Nathaniel and his family to establish a routine of living at their new home. Jeremiah had been found temporary accommodation on the estate, Nathaniel retaining a building company from Cape Town to construct a new home for his company supervisor.

The men sat astride horses on a ridge above the vineyard, discussing future plans in the warm, early morning sunlight.

"West would seem the best direction in which to expand the estate, don't you think, Brown?" The man gazed in the direction indicated.

"Yes, sir," he replied, "the slopes seem eminently suitable."

"Good, we will start at the beginning of the next growing season," Nathaniel decided.

For a large part of the day, he and Jeremiah toured the slopes, fully acquainting the owner of the state of his property. He noticed the vines thriving, producing at least fifty per cent more yield than when he had purchased the estate.

Pendulous grapes, bursting with juice, hung precariously from the vine in the bright sunshine, waiting to be plucked before the bounty began to turn and rot.

They neared the house at the end of an exhausting day, a state of agitation there evident as they approached. Servants were running back and forth, as if terrified by some unseen adversary.

Nathaniel and Jeremiah spurred their mounts into action, riding the last two hundred yards in seconds.

Mary burst from the house as the men dismounted, her expression bringing dread to her husband's heart.

"Oh my God, Nathaniel," she sobbed, "Toby has been taken."

At first he couldn't take in what he was hearing, couldn't understand what she meant, until she thrust a piece of paper into his palm. He read the words, heart sinking. The message brief and to the point, stated that, if he wished to see his son alive once more, he would need to pay £20,000 for the privilege. Whoever had sent the missive said they would contact him again but, if the authorities were informed, then Toby would die. He passed the note to Brown.

"God Almighty," expressed the man, "who would do such a thing?"

"You may well ask," retorted Davidson, "have you any ideas?"

"You've only been in the Cape a few days," Brown replied, scanning the note again as if he couldn't believe what he had read. "No I can't think of who this might be; a spate of kidnappings have occurred over the years."

Nathaniel held Mary to him, her sobbing rhythmic but a little quieter after the initial shock.

"One thing is abundantly clear, we can't inform anyone in authority about the situation."

"Are you sure that's wise, sir?" asked Brown. "Maybe they are bluffing."

"And maybe not," said Nathaniel vehemently. "No, I can't take that chance with my son's life at stake."

He led his wife into the house, pouring her a brandy to combat the shock but she continued to weep desperately, despite drinking down the liquid in one. It would be a long night, thought her husband.

At some point through the night, Nathaniel must have fallen asleep. He wouldn't have believed it possible he could, but the pull of Morpheus was overwhelming. The sun was rising over the vineyard, when his eyes flickered open and he lifted his head from the kitchen table, where it had rested all night. Mary had managed sleep upstairs in the comfort of their bed and she dozed on fitfully as night wore on into day.

Venturing to the door, opening it to the early morning sunshine, he immediately noticed the note pinned in a haphazard fashion to it, a dirty, off white sheet, the writing an almost illegible scrawl. Ripping it from its anchor, he scanned the words slowly, aware of Mary coming up behind him.

Nathaniel handed her the note without saying a word returning to the interior of the house, while his wife perused the communiqué. Mary's eyes clouded as she ploughed her way through it, "What do you intend to do, Nathaniel?"

"Just what it says, I will withdraw the amount of money they are demanding from the company accounts here and pay them," he said resignedly. "Anything for the return of Toby. You agree, don't you?"

Mary nodded, "Of course I agree, but the note says it is to be paid next Saturday, that is six days away," she looked panic stricken, "I will be a nervous wreck by then."

Her husband comforted her, "There is nothing we can do about it, Mary, they have the upper hand, whoever they are, but once we have our son back, I am going to hunt them down and make them pay for what they have done." Brown arrived a few minutes after seven, taking breakfast with his employers, they showed him the latest communication and explained that they were going to pay the figure asked.

"Perhaps we could find out on Saturday where they are holding your son," the Estate Manager suggested.

"Nothing must be done to endanger Toby," the boy's father cautioned.

"I realise that," the answer came back, "but I have a plan that might work without putting Toby in jeopardy." Mary looked uneasy but her husband was willing to hear the man out.

"Go on, Jeremiah," Nathaniel instructed.

"It says in the note that a man will be waiting to pick up the money outside the banking offices in the city, that he will make himself known to you on your exit," Brown continued on. "It's probable that whoever this is knows everyone on the estate here; it would be impossible to follow the man after he gathers the money, but I have a friend in the city who can be trusted to shadow the contact discreetly to find out where he goes."

"And if we try and recover my son, they will have a chance to kill him. No," Nathaniel decided. "We can't take that chance."

"Mr Davidson, we don't try and get Toby back then," explained the Estate Manager. "They say they will release him four hours after the money is transferred to their keeping, so we wait to see if they keep their word and once your son is safe, we alert the authorities to the location of their hideout," he paused. "We may even recover the money."

Nathaniel glanced at Mary. "We need to think carefully about this, Jeremiah, if we go along with it, the outcome could be disastrous," he explained.

Mary and her husband agonised over the plan for a day, their decisions fluctuating wildly. Sometimes Brown's plan seemed foolproof, at other times, doomed to failure. Eventually, after much soul searching, Nathaniel took the initiative.

"Sweetheart, we must make a decision," he implored her. "I say we go with Jeremiah's idea." His wife looked haggard. Loss of sleep and the tautness of her emotions had brought her to the point of collapse.

"Very well, Nathaniel, I leave it in your hands, you will have to decide for both of us."

237

He would have preferred a much more supportive role from his wife but was happy to have the matter resolved.

"I'll speak to Brown this morning and get him to contact his friend," he advised her.

Immediately after breakfast, he sought out the Vineyard Manager, bringing him to the house.

"We have decided to go with your plan, Jeremiah, can you have your friend come and speak with us?"

A look of satisfaction crossed the man's face, "May I make a suggestion?" he broached.

"Of course," replied the employer.

"We don't know who is involved in this," Brown said. "They could be workers here or people watching the vineyard constantly, can I suggest that we visit the city and my friend during the night."

Nathaniel was impressed with the logical manner of the man. "Of course you are quite right, Brown, set up the a meeting will you?" Nathaniel requested.

CHAPTER 34

The meeting was set for Thursday night prior to the proposed day of payment. In the dead of night, the men mounted horses, setting off for the rendezvous with Brown's colleague, carefully observing the route as they rode, to ensure no one was following.

It was a full moon with no cloud. After a few minutes in the darkness, their night vision improved, the silvery landscape becoming a better acquainted friend.

Entering the confines of the city, Nathaniel realised they were not heading for a fashionable area. Narrow, litter strewn streets characterised the district. Nearing the urban sprawl, the men had fallen silent, not drawing attention to themselves. After ten minutes negotiation of the run down streets, Brown reined in his horse outside a dirty, run down building, dismounting, indicating to Nathaniel he should do likewise.

A sickly yellow glow emanated from the window, scarcely throwing any illumination into the thoroughfare.

"Good God," whispered Nathaniel, "where are we?"

Brown tethered his horse to a nearby post. "I realise these are not the sort of neighbourhoods you would be used to, Mr Davidson, but the person we need is a fairly dark character and they tend not to reside in the more affluent areas. After all, his particular talents are normally employed in the criminal fraternity," instructed Jeremiah.

The owner of the vineyard was uneasy as Brown barely knocked on the sturdy door, his quick glances checking the back streets for signs of life. When the door cracked open, a pair of suspicious eyes bored into them.

"It's us, Pierre," Brown advised the shrew like individual, positioning himself into the scant effulgence for the man to fully recognise him.

A second later, the door swung wide, the men passing discreetly through. Inside the house was as dilapidated as the area it stood in, the clutter had to be seen to be believed.

Pierre himself was not much better. A great slob of a man, but the type Nathaniel knew would satisfy their requirements.

The men sat for some seconds in silence before Pierre spoke in a gruff tone, "So, Jeremiah, what is it you want me to do exactly?" he demanded.

The Estate Manager outlined the plan to Pierre, Nathaniel inputting occasional snippets of information to guarantee the man knew precisely what was required of him. Pierre smoked during the explanation and the room became heavy with acrid tobacco fumes.

"It seems an easy enough prospect," spouted the man, "but what is in it for me?" he demanded.

Nathaniel was sickened by the mercenary attitude. "You will be well rewarded," he spat, "of that you have no fear, I give you my word."

"Well in that case," Pierre grinned, "I will be outside the bank a full half hour before the transaction is to take place and I will not fail to locate the man's destination. After that it is in your hands."

At that point, Nathaniel gazed around the hovel and wondered whether he had chosen the correct course of action, but at this stage, the die was cast.

The journey home was completed in silence but as the two men trotted through the silvery brush, Jeremiah spoke up.

"You are not completely happy with this, are you, Mr Davidson?" he ventured.

"Not completely, no," retorted the Englishman, "so many things could go wrong; I don't want to lose my son."

The hours dragged by until the time of the handover. Nathaniel and Jeremiah riding into the city at the appointed time, the estate owner climbing the steps to his bank. It took a massive effort of will not to peer around the surrounding streets, trying to locate the possible contact who would relieve him of the money. Inside the cavernous foyer of the monetary institution, it was cool, marble pillars adorning the structure. Nathaniel headed for the teller who traditionally served him, greeting him with a forced cheery good morning.

"I would like to withdraw £20,000," Nathaniel casually demanded. The teller looked perplexed.

"That is a great deal of money, Mr Davidson, perhaps you would care to wait while I ask the Manager to deal with your request."

The clerk scuttled off, leaving Nathaniel to fume in frustration, nervousness at the delay evident. Presently the man returned with a tall, cadaverous looking individual, he knew to be John Gascoigne.

"Mr Davidson, how very pleasant to see you once again," the Manager gushed. "It's a very pleasant day."

"I am afraid I have no time for pleasantries today, Mr Gascoigne, I need to conclude my business rather rapidly."

"Ah yes, the small matter of a £20,000 withdrawal," the man self-consciously cleared his throat,

"While you are of course entitled to your money, it may take us a few minutes to gather it together, perhaps you would join me in a glass of sherry in my office while you wait?"

Nathaniel's patience was at breaking point. "No, I would not," he exclaimed curtly. The Manager was taken aback at the vehemence of the retort, but had the good sense to instruct his teller to collect the currency rapidly.

"I take it," he asked, as the man scurried off to his duty, "that you require it for a business venture?" he enquired of Nathaniel.

"It is of no consequence to you, what the money is for, Mr Gascoigne."

Gascoigne was looking uncomfortable with the atmosphere, he couldn't resist rebuking Nathaniel.

"Really, Mr Davidson, I am only making polite conversation here, I do feel that you might consider my position here in the bank."

Nathaniel's attitude softened, "I apologise, Mr Gascoigne, I have some personal family problems which need addressing and I am afraid I have let the frustrations of those cloud my manners."

The next few minutes were spent in frosty silence, the bank employee clearly refusing to accept Nathaniel's excuse until the teller appeared from the area of the vaults, clutching a small case. He placed it in front of the customer, inviting Nathaniel to count the money, which he declined to do. With a rapid farewell, he hurried from the bank and stood on the steps, wondering what would happen next.

Many people crossed his path, going about their business. A cough sounded behind him and the tramp Nathaniel had noticed lounging against the column of the bank frontage on his exit, now stood directly behind him.

"Mr Davidson," the voice was surprisingly clear and strong. "Place the bag on the floor and leave, don't look back if you wish your son to live. Now go."

From the corner of his eye, Nathaniel could see Pierre in conversation with a woman on the opposite side of the street. It seemed like an animated discussion between the pair, the man not looking directly at the bank or the transaction taking place. Nathaniel just hoped his mind was on the job.

Walking purposefully down the street and round the first corner, heading for the hotel where Brown waited patiently for him, and where Pierre would seek them out at the end of his task.

As the Estate Owner arrived, he observed Jeremiah sitting in the foyer of the hotel, drinking coffee. The man indicated to the staff he required another beverage, Nathaniel sitting opposite him.

"All we can do is wait," Davidson notified his estate manager.

"Pierre won't let us down Mr Davidson, you can be sure of that."

An hour passed, seeming to Nathaniel like a year. Although he was agitated, both he and his estate manager drank only one whisky each, waiting for the arrival of their agent.

As Nathaniel's reserve was weakening toward another drink, Pierre entered the hotel bar, sitting down at the table. Looking flushed from some exertion, he ordered a glass of water, gulping it down.

"He went to a house on the outskirts of the city," his breathing laboured. "It's in a middle class neighbourhood, but there was no sign of the boy."

"The question is what do we do next?" Jeremiah ventured.

"There is about another three hours until the time they said they would release Toby, but the question is do we wait and see if it happens or do we act now?" the boys father asked.

Jeremiah and Pierre agreed that the best course of action was to get the boy where they suspected him to be, they were reasonably sure he was still alive. Impressing their feelings on Nathaniel, they urged him to accept an immediate course of action, but Toby's father still prevaricated.

"Mr Davidson," began Pierre, "I live and work in the underworld of the city. If I had captured your son and been provided with the money, I would have no compunction killing the boy." He continued, "I urge you to consider my experience in these matters; rescue the boy now."

Jeremiah nodded in his employer's direction, "Take his advice, Nathaniel, don't wait and be faced with the death of your son, knowing that acting early enough may have saved him."

"Very well, we will inform the authorities of my son's whereabouts and leave them to their task." Pierre looked concerned at the course Nathaniel was proposing.

"With all due respect, Mr Davidson, I feel the authorities are not the best people to deal with a situation of this sort," Pierre pointed out, downing a whisky which had been ordered for him. "I think we could handle this undertaking in a much more covert manner, along with some people I know."

Nathaniel was troubled at Pierre's plan, "What people?" he queried.

"People who act in this environment all the time. People you would not normally associate with, but people whose talents exactly match the requirements we need, stealth and, let's be honest, violence." The man sat staring at Nathaniel, almost daring him to refuse his proposal. His reservations were well founded as Nathaniel did indeed reject his proposals.

There was no time left for contemplation and Nathaniel was acutely aware of it.

"No, Pierre," Nathaniel was adamant, "we will use the correct agencies and may God have given me the correct judgement in this."

Pierre dashed from the hotel, returning twenty minutes later with a number of soldiers from the nearby garrison, heavily armed and commanded by a Lieutenant Wright, a fresh faced young officer. There were eight in the party, looking capable of handling the situation.

Horses had been brought to the exterior of the hotel, where the men milled around. At the officer's command, they mounted their animals, Nathaniel, Jeremiah and the officer of the group in the lead.

Nathaniel's mount obeyed his gestures as though the creature had been his forever. The cobbled streets proved difficult to negotiate at the speeds they were achieving, and sparks flew haphazardly from the metal shoes in contact with the smooth stones.

Fifteen minutes later, the officer held up his hand to indicate a halt, dismounting and ordering his men to do likewise. His feet hit the floor.

"We are two streets away, Mr Davidson," he stated. "Close enough to formulate a plan and not be detected by whoever it is that has your son."

The soldiers ambled up after dismounting, gathering in a well-drilled half circle around the officer, Nathaniel, Jeremiah and Pierre easing their way to the front of the throng.

Nathaniel was prepared to let the Lieutenant instruct the others in the course of the plan, even though he desperately wanted to take charge of the situation.

"Men," Wright began. "This is a dangerous business, we have no idea how many people are in this house or their strength; I know we all appreciate the prospect of a good scrap; I am telling you now that we rescue this boy by any means, if that means killing his captors, then so be it." The next few minutes were spent making his dispositions, some to the rear of the building and some on a frontal assault including himself. "Mr Davidson, you, Jeremiah and Pierre come along with me," he instructed the vineyard owner and by implication his manager and the other man too.

From the professional way that the men set off to carry out their duties, it became obvious to Nathaniel they had undertaken similar operations before.

The finger of fear climbed inexorably up the vineyard owner's back as Nathaniel, his colleagues and the soldiers charged down the street towards the edifice. Cold sweat ran in rivulets which coursed down his spine as they neared their objective.

No ceremony was indulged in when they encountered the door. Pierre's well-placed boot crashed the wood from its hinges, shattering the lock from its mounting and slamming it to the wooden floor. Immediately the rear entrance suffered a comparable fortune.

The moment they entered the building, all hell broke loose. A man charged at them and was shot dead in his tracks, the bullet entering the head centrally on the forehead, pitching him backwards, pole axed like a fateful cow in an abattoir. Chaotic shouting accompanied the entry and more by luck than judgement, the invaders failed to injure each other. Wright continued to lead the frontal assault, Nathaniel and Jeremiah hot on his heels as he hurtled through the ground floor chambers.

Without warning, an individual appeared at the door of a side room just as the leader hurried past. He was clutching a rifle, aiming at Wright's back. Nathaniel thought nothing of his actions as he blasted the individual in the chest with the shotgun he carried.

Blood spattered from the enemy's back, spotting the door lintel, the body crumpling to the floor, dead before he became intimately familiar with the wood.

Gunshots echoed around the dwelling as Wright's colleagues rampaged their way throughout.

"We have him," came a shout from the upper floor, Nathaniel charging up the stairs, searching the rooms which were now secure. Wright's small army had performed commendably, the father entering the room where his son lay on a bed, hands tied to the wooden bedposts. Several men had fanned around the boy, protecting him from any possible counter attack.

Nathaniel released his son from the bonds, hugging him in sheer relief.

"Thank God you're alright, Toby, your mother has been beside herself with worry," he said.

Jeremiah entered the room, placing a bag on the bed next to the father and son. "We recovered the money too," he grinned, "every penny of it."

The vineyard proprietor thought over the carnage they had left in the house. No doubt others were killed which he knew nothing about at this stage. He worried over his, Jeremiah's and Pierre's involvement in the action.

Pierre entered with two of the soldiers, smiling broadly, clearly happy with his day's work.

"How many dead?" enquired Nathaniel.

"Eight and that is all of them," replied Pierre.

"No survivors at all?" he queried.

For the first time, Pierre looked a little uncomfortable. Nathaniel's pleading was not the reaction he'd expected, he went on the offensive.

"Mr Davidson, these are people having no compunction at kidnap and murder for money, are you sure in all conscience, you would have liked any of them to have escaped to wreak their deeds on someone else, which is precisely what they would have done?" his face challenged Toby's father to disagree.

"I suppose not," returned Nathaniel, "but I never expected summary killing on this scale."

Pierre moved closer to him threateningly. "Yes you did, it's only now that you have pontificated in this manner, when your son and your money is safe, beforehand you were happy to get Toby back under any circumstance, right?"

It made Nathaniel uncomfortable to say it but he had to assent, "Yes," he muttered, "I have to agree with you."

The man spun on his heel, stomping angrily out of the room with the soldiers, leaving Nathaniel and his son alone.

"Let's go," Nathaniel suggested.

Rising from the bed, Toby joined his father, heading for the outside. Jeremiah was waiting for them, following his departure from the room after returning his employer's capital to him.

Mary stood at the gate to the house, scanning the hillsides, she had been there for the best part of three hours, it had seemed like three days to her.

Cresting the vineyard slope, she spotted three riders approaching, she cried out in delight, wrenching the gate from its closed position and ran towards the party.

At the same time, Toby glimpsed the figure and knew it was his mother. He spurred the horse to gallop and rode down the intervening distance swiftly, leaping from the saddle in mid flight as he neared her.

Mother and son collapsed into each other's embrace, the horse careering on. They remained locked together until his father and Jeremiah trotted up, dismounting.

"You brought him back to us, Nathaniel," his wife wept.

"Didn't I say I would?" her husband laughed.

"And my thanks to you, Jeremiah, accept the gratitude of a mother."

"My pleasure, Mrs Davidson," replied the Manager who remounted, trotting away discreetly, leaving the family to their reunion.

"Are you alright, Toby?" his mother questioned the boy.

"Yes, Mother, it's so good to be home," he shouted.

The family walked to the house, Nathaniel stopping at the door, turning to survey the estate, realising just how fortunate his life had become. Now his son was safe the future seemed as promising as it had ever been.

CHAPTER 35

Several days had passed since Toby's recovery, periods of toil in the sun for the workers of the vineyard. Jeremiah oversaw the work to be done while Nathaniel and Toby helped with the labour under the manager's watchful eye. The owner was happy to leave the organisation and command of the work to Jeremiah, whose faultless management so far had made the company as successful as it had ever been.

The men were high on the slopes when several riders appeared on the opposite bank heading toward the house. Even at distance, they were instantly recognisable as soldiers, brasses glinting in the sunlight. Nathaniel counted seven, one officer leading and six other ranks, he surmised.

The leading man disappeared into the dwelling as Nathaniel watched. In his heart he knew why they were there. One of the house boys exited the dwelling and mounted a horse, galloping toward the slope where the father and son were employed.

"Toby," Nathaniel directed, "leave that, I think we are wanted at the house." Toby's eyes followed his father's, seeing the soldiers in the compound at the front of the dwelling.

"What is it, Father?"

"Nothing for you to worry about, my boy; I think this may be about your rescue, and I think we should return to the house and find out what these gentlemen require."

Twenty minutes later, Nathaniel and his son entered the abode, passing the lounging men at arms, who were talking amongst themselves.

In the cool of the interior a fresh faced young man sat, sipping sherry and conversing with Mary. Her eyes betrayed the fear she felt, although she entertained him without an outward sign of concern.

As the father and son entered, the officer rose from his seated position, smoothing down his dress jacket.

"Mr Davidson," his voice was clear but that of a young man on an errand he would prefer not to have undertaken. "I am Lieutenant Thompson of the general staff, the Governor would like to see you on an important matter."

There was no indication it was a request, this was an order.

"May I ask what it concerns, Lieutenant?"

The man looked bored to death. "I am led to believe that it concerns the recent abduction and rescue of your son and if this is the young man next to you," he indicated Toby with a slight inclination of the head, "then his presence is also requested."

"And may I ask where you are taking us?" asked Nathaniel.

"Initially to the Governor's residence," the man's eyes flickered away from the vineyard owner's.

"And then?" pressed Nathaniel.

"I have no information about anything, other than taking you to see the Governor," Lieutenant Thompson said, with an indication in his voice that he would not accept any further discussion on the subject.

Horses saddled, father and son joined the band of soldiers in the courtyard at the front of the house. Mary reached up, embracing her son, then turned her attention to her husband, "Look after yourselves, Nathaniel," she instructed him.

"Everything will be alright," advised Nathaniel as he sorted out the reins. "We will be back soon."

The anteroom to the Governor's office was refreshingly cool, its ornate interior exactly as Nathaniel had seen it on his last visit. He hadn't met the present Governor and regretted the fact that he would have no rapport with the man as he had with his predecessor, who had been in post when his father, Sir Toby, had been arrested and sent to Australia. He consoled himself that the man may have the good judgement of his forerunner.

From the moment Nathaniel and Toby entered the man's room, Nathaniel felt something important might happen. The man's head

250

was bowed, the close cropped hair gave a severe impression before he looked up.

"Nathaniel Davidson," the man sneered as he spoke. "And this must be your son, Toby?" he enquired.

"May I ask why we have been requested to present ourselves?" Nathaniel countered.

Sir Desmond Archer glanced at the correspondence on his desk blotter, mumbling, "You may, Mr Davidson, you may, and I will tell you all in good time, however, may I first ask you and your son to take a seat while I finish this pressing work."

Nathaniel looked impatiently, why couldn't he just get to the point, the vineyard owner thought? Presently the man rose from his sitting position, walking the room with document in hand, eyes scanning the text all the while.

"I understand your son was recently kidnapped, am I correct?" His eyes never wavered from the pages of the file.

"That is so," replied Nathaniel.

"I understand that you aided my men in the recovery of your boy," Archer continued.

"That is also true, as you well know."

"I also understand that you acquitted yourself magnificently." Archer's eyes glinted. "At one point saving the life of my Lieutenant."

Nathaniel looked modestly back at the man. "It was in my interests to do so; the men who did this assured me they would kill my son and your soldiers showed bravery; all I did was aid them in the fight."

"Nevertheless, you understand the implications of your actions, Mr Davidson, you saved an officer of the crown and that deserves recognition." Nathaniel thought the tone had changed to a deep warmness.

"Sir Desmond, put yourself in my position, I was given little time and the clearest possible indication that my son was in serious danger. Of course I would help anyone who was aiding me in getting my son back."

251

"You are to be decorated, Mr Davidson," the smile was now beaming from the Governor's face. "The group of people killed were a band of thugs, sought after for some time. Yours was the fourth case of kidnap by these people." He moved about the room again. "In the last case the young man involved lost his life; I had personally taken charge of that situation."

Nathaniel noticed a growing friendliness in the man's demeanour, the strong features seemed to have got younger as the man smiled, "I am delighted that I will be able to give you recognition for this," he said. "In normal circumstances I would do this immediately, but I am waiting for my Lieutenant's report. You have done me a great service in dealing with these men, I have given the matter great thought; you will be awarded for your actions and I will be informing the authorities back in England of your service to the Cape."

They rode back to the vineyard, Nathaniel reflecting on his good fortune. The day was warm, countryside as beautiful as ever. He could enjoy it along with the news given by Sir Desmond Archer, thanking the man profusely before setting out to give Mary the news. Jeremiah and Pierre were also to be recognised for their part in the rescue.

Reaching the house, Mary emerged, clearly relieved to see the return of her husband, embracing him warmly,

"Are things alright, Nathaniel?" she ventured.

"Yes, sweetheart, everything is fine," her husband advised before launching into a description of his meeting with the Governor. Toby joined them and Mary led Nathaniel to the kitchen of the house, preparing him a much appreciated meal after congratulating him.

With the onset of evening, Jeremiah arrived at the house after a long day supervising work on the vines. Nathaniel went through the meeting again, telling Jeremiah of his excellent news about the rescue, instructing him to tell Pierre as soon as possible about his good fortune.

"Did the Governor explain who the people were?" enquired the vineyard manager.

"It doesn't really matter who they were, we seem to have done the country a service by our actions," explained the employer.

Nathaniel busied himself with the running of the vineyard over the next few days, pleased to have an opportunity to get back into routine. He worked on the vines with Toby and Edward, recently arrived from England, on a sweltering day, Jeremiah rode up, expression betraying concern.

"Mr Davidson, we have a problem," he advised Nathaniel.

"What is it, Jeremiah?"

"Several of the workers have come down with some sort of disease, I believe it might be cholera," he cautioned.

"Are you sure, Jeremiah?" asked the owner

"I'm no doctor," continued the manager, "but it's a diarrhoeal infection and we have four victims at the moment."

"I'll call in a doctor from the city. In the meantime, isolate them, get them away from the rest of the workers," Nathaniel instructed.

"I have already done that, Mr Davidson," Jeremiah told him, "I fear it may be just a temporary stay of the problem though."

"Why?"

"The likely source of the outbreak is the well outside the accommodation. If it is infected then it is a sure bet that the others have drunk from there. We could be looking at a major outbreak," continued Jeremiah.

Nathaniel knew the implication of the man's words. They were coming to the time of the harvest. "First things first, keep everyone from the house away from the workers. Isolate them as much as possible," he instructed. "I will fetch the doctor myself." He mounted his horse and was gone, riding toward the city.

CHAPTER 36

Sitting in the lounge of the house, Nathaniel, Mary, the boys and the estate manager awaited the verdict of the doctor.

Nathaniel was usually a positive man but the events recently in his life was fermenting some doubt in his mind. If the verdict proved to be cholera and there was mass infection, there was every chance the vineyard crop would be lost by virtue of it not being picked and, although it wouldn't necessarily mean complete ruin for him, it could cause severe problems. It could also impact on future crops. Vines needed constant tending and the chance of finding replacement workers of the necessary calibre at such short notice, was remote in the extreme.

From the moment the doctor arrived, he knew the news was grave.

"Mr Davidson," the doctor began, "I'm afraid it is indeed cholera; at the moment there are six workers infected but there will undoubtedly be more; I have instructed them to drink as much clean water as possible, as dehydration is a real problem, but not from the infected well there," he looked concerned as he continued. "I would prepare yourself for at least some deaths, there is little can be done for them; I must also advise that no one from the house here visit the accommodation under any circumstances. I have told the ones who are well how to deal with their comrades, so there is no reason for anyone from here to expose themselves unnecessarily."

The subsequent days were tough on Nathaniel, Mary, Toby, Edward and Jeremiah, valiantly attempting to perform as much work as possible around the vineyards but it was clear to the owners from the start they were fighting a losing battle. Needing more manpower, Nathaniel had no time to solicit it, the vines were bursting with fruit. Great globules of filled grapes, hung pendulously from the creeping vines.

On the fourth day they woke early, hardly refreshed from their night's slumber, such was the absolute toil they had endured. Nathaniel rose first, sitting at the table in the cool kitchen, awaiting his wife and son's appearance, when he heard muffled voices outside. He rose achingly and crossed to the door, cracking it and peering outside.

The scene before him was a dream. Fifty people milled around on the parched ground, along with four of the nearby vineyard owners.

"Ah, Nathaniel," remarked Bertram Cockburn from the closest estate as he saw Davidson's ashen face peering from the doorway. "It has come to our attention that you are having some problems gathering your harvest; so we have decided to loan you some workers to tide you over."

Hardly believing his ears, he emerged into the light to shake the hands of the people prepared to help him, "How did you find out about our problems?" Nathaniel asked.

"You can thank your Estate Manager for that; Jeremiah contacted us overnight to tell us about it all," continued the cherubic Cockburn.

"I don't know what to say, gentlemen," Nathaniel stammered, "we are rivals and yet you would do this for us."

"Let's just say we've all had problems of one sort or another over the years," advised Elijah Wood of the Trenton Vineyard. "We are sure you would help us in similar circumstances."

Bounding up the stairs to the sleeping form of his wife, he gently shook her to wakefulness.

"Sweetheart, our prayers are answered," he blurted, over the next few minutes outlining what had happened.

For two weeks the temporary workforce toiled in hot conditions to gather the harvest, working every hour of daylight. Nathaniel's faith in human nature, reaffirmed as the employees of his rivals broke their backs for the cause.

It was the final day of harvesting when his two main rivals rode back to Nathaniel's vineyard. Side by side, Cockburn and Wood trotted up to the house, he watched them arrive, hot and dusty from their journey.

"My friends, come in and breakfast with us," begged the grateful owner. Mary busied herself in the kitchen of the house, the men gathering around the table in the same room, drinking coffee while waiting for the food. The man they had aided wondered how he could ever repay them, watching as his wife laid food before the businessmen.

"Gentlemen, I will never be able to thank you for your kindness; in this business we work on very tight margins, if you had not come to my rescue, there is no doubt I would have lost my concern."

Wood smiled broadly, "Forget it, Nathaniel, we may be in need of your services in times to come and we know you won't let us down."

"How are your workers doing, Nathaniel?" inquired Cockburn, forking food into his mouth, his reputation for being a glutton preceded him, his thick girth betraying the fact that nourishment was his main interest.

"The doctor says we will lose seventy per cent of them before the sickness ends," advised Nathaniel, "but I have taken steps to recruit others to replace them."

"A wise decision," continued Cockburn. "It will take time to teach them how to manage a vineyard, the longer you can train them, the better."

Following breakfast, the men rode out into the vines, surveying the work done, Cockburn and Wood taking an inordinate pleasure in the fact that they had saved their rival's business. Stripped bare, the vines looked almost forlorn. They hung in sad looking strands awaiting the next growing period. Aglow in the shimmering sunlight, the workers' accommodation's white walls shone with an intensity painful to the eye.

"I wish there was more I could do for those poor people," exclaimed Nathaniel, pointing at the block with his riding crop.

"No more could be done than you already have; you have provided the best medical provision you could and there is nothing to reproach yourself for," mumbled Wood.

"At least the damned well has been filled in and I will sink a safe new water source for my future employees," insisted Nathaniel.

Wood and Cockburn exchanged glances, knowing their new made friend was suffering pangs of guilt for the situation which were misplaced. Nothing could have prevented the occurrence, but Nathaniel's inner humanity made him blame himself for what happened.

They headed back to the house, where the interim workforce had gathered on Nathaniel's instruction, given the day previously.

Jeremiah stood at the forefront of the coloured faces, face spread in an expansive grin, his representation had solved Nathaniel's problem and it provided him with a great deal of pleasure.

Nathaniel stood before the gathered throng.

"I wanted to say a few words to you all," he began. "You have laboured for days, gathering the harvest of this vineyard and for that I thank you all and also your employers for aiding me so ably at a trying time," he paused. "I would like you to join me in some food and wine to celebrate the successful gathering of the fruit," he looked at Jeremiah. "Bring them round to the paddock."

Tables were set out groaning with fare. Chickens, geese, slabs of steaming beef, all vied for culinary prominence, along with a variety of vegetables glazed in melted butter.

The workers attacked it all ravenously, laughing and dancing around the tables as they accepted the hospitality gratefully, tiredness temporarily forgotten.

Wood, Cockburn, Nathaniel and Jeremiah sat at a small table away from the main throng, eating, watching the scene before them with a sense of pleasure.

"Quite magnificent food," muttered Cockburn, his mouth coated in shining butter. "Glad we could be of help to you, Nathaniel."

Next to the scene, Nathaniel's second son, Edward, stood quietly, the boy watching quietly, oblivious to the noise and laughter. He looked at the young lad with pride, his birth had been a difficult one for Mary, so many years before, but despite that, he had grown to a fine young man. Nathaniel's first son doted on his younger brother. For a moment his thoughts went out to Ebenezer. They had received word that he and Sally had been blessed with a daughter soon after Edward's birth, calling her Margaret.

Wood watched him looking at his son. "Fine young man," he ventured, "a credit to you and your good lady."

They watched the workers enjoying themselves, tearing into the food on offer, the songs they sang held the mystery of Africa in their words, native tribal anthems which were a mystery to Nathaniel. The afternoon progressed, heat diminishing as evening marched inexorably toward the scene.

Carts were brought up to the house as the celebration ended. The workers replete and dozing from the wine, finding it difficult to climb aboard the transport.

Mary joined Nathaniel, waving off his fellow vineyard owners and their labourers, songs still ringing out as the vehicles trundled away over the countryside.

CHAPTER 37

Sunsets were spectacular in the continent, but the one which descended as Nathaniel and his wife sat on their porch was stirring in its grandeur, the small amount of cloud, streaked over the sky was flushed orange as the orb of the sun seemed sliced in two by the shadowed mountainside.

Edward had long since taken to his bed, tactfully leaving, giving Nathaniel and Mary some time to themselves, time which had become more and more precious as the illness of his own workers had developed.

"A lady to see you, sir," the house girl had returned.

"Who is it?" asked Nathaniel.

"Mrs Smith," stated the girl. "She waits in the house, sir."

Mary rose quickly.

"Sally, here, is her husband with her?"

"No gentleman, ma'am," replied the maid.

They rushed into the house, delighted to be seeing Ebenezer's wife once more but the expression on her face provided a presentiment of bad news. As Sally saw them, she broke down, wailing uncontrollably, Mary moving to her side, slipping a solicitous arm around the woman's shoulders.

"For God's sake Sally, what is it?" she implored her. The woman was finding it hard to get her words out, familiar friendly faces finally causing an outpouring of emotion she had not permitted herself before.

"Ebenezer is dead."

The news pole axed Nathaniel, feeling nauseous as the realisation of what Sally had said invaded his consciousness. He couldn't take in the enormity of it. After Christian Davenport, Ebenezer had filled the void of his best friend, although they saw each other spasmodically. He had felt enormous regard for the man who married his first love and taken on the child denied to him from his encounter with Sally all those years ago.

Mary enfolded the shrunken form of Sally in her arms, emitting solicitous endearments into her ear. It had precious little effect on the woman who held tightly to her friend, not wanting to let go.

His wife turned to him, "Get the maid, Nathaniel, see that the visitor room's bed is aired, she's exhausted."

Twenty minutes later, Sally was settled in the chamber, having fallen into a tormented sleep, mouthing incoherent words as the dreams overtook her troubled mind.

"We had better sit and watch her, Nathaniel," Mary voiced maternally.

"I'll take the first period," confirmed Nathaniel looking at the sleeping form. He sat at the side of the bed reading, concentration wavering. He fondly remembered his encounter with Sally so many years before. It played an important part of his life. He had enormous respect for the woman lying so distressed before him. She looked aged before her time like a wizened old woman about to die. Even in sleep, grief etched her face, as if an artists finger was painting on lines of misery by the minute.

Like hundreds of people observing a vigil over the years, Nathaniel had fallen into the arms of Morpheus himself, shaken to wakefulness gently by Mary. Night had invaded the room but lit candles gave it a cheery, if dim glow.

Sally continued to sleep, caught in a web of dreams and nightmares, although now quiet, Mary moving to tuck in the bedclothes which her earlier thrashings had worked free.

"Sweetheart, go down and eat," instructed Mary. "There is hot food ready for you."

"No, I'm not hungry; I'll stay a while, I want to find out exactly what happened to Ebenezer."

Shrugging her shoulders, she headed for the door, pausing to look at the back of her husband who was bending attentively towards their friend.

As the door closed, Nathaniel picked up the book he had placed on the bedside table and began to read once more, paying little attention to the words or their meaning.

The clock counted off the minutes with resounding ticks in the room, the sounds of night filtering into the chamber. Daylight heat gave way to the plummeting temperature of evening, Nathaniel trimming the candles, enshrouding the bedroom with an eerie yellow brightness. Dancing shadows flickered on the walls at the bidding of the guttering flames.

"Nathaniel," the voice was feeble at best, "thank you for being here." Looking up from the pages of the book at the sound of her voice, he rose, standing over her shrunken form. She seemed even more lost than his first sight of her earlier in the evening.

"How are you feeling, Sally?" he asked.

"May I have some water, my mouth is so dry?"

He picked up the jug from the bedside table, thoughtfully provided by Mary, pouring the Adams Ale into a glass, passing it to the woman in the bed.

Sally gulped down the liquid as though she had never tasted it before, holding her glass out for more. When she had finished, Nathaniel felt confident enough to question her about the death of her husband. The face before him darkened at his enquiry, he wondered whether he had chosen the right moment to broach the subject.

"Ebenezer commanded a ship to Jamaica to collect a cargo of rum," she began. "While there he contracted Typhoid fever; the doctor on the ship tended him, treating him to the best of his limited ability, but it was to no avail and my poor Ebenezer died soon after contracting the fever." Her face seemed to crumple with emotion as she continued. "We had argued just prior to his leaving, Nathaniel, and the last words we spoke to each other were bitter and acrimonious; I can't live with the fact that he may have thought I didn't love him, that is so far from the truth."

"I knew Ebenezer as well as anyone might," he advised Sally, "and I know that he was deeply in love with you too. I assure you he knew you loved him. There is no question that wherever his soul resides now, he knows your feelings full well."

Her face brightened considerably, the ease in the features obvious.

"Thank you my friend," she spoke softly.

"Your loss hurts me just as much as you, Sally, I assure you, Ebenezer was one of only two true friends I have ever known, now both he and Christian Davenport are dead." His face darkened.

"God seems to have it in for me, but He can't take away the memory of two individuals who showed nothing but loyalty and enduring friendship." His voice cracked with sentiment.

"They were the best of men and the world is a much darker place with their demise." His thoughts had been occupied with the news of his friend's death, now he realised that Sally's daughter, Margaret was not with her.

"Where is Margaret?" he asked. "Is she well?"

For the first time since she entered the house, a smile played on the lips of the woman before him at the mention of her daughter.

"My thanks to you for asking, Nathaniel, she remains in England; yes she is well physically but her father's death has devastated her."

The concern in Sally's face amply demonstrated he had said the wrong thing, he quickly changed tack.

"If you feel up to it, Sally, maybe you would like to eat now?"

"I think I could manage something," she advised him. Descending the stairs, he questioned her about her son.

"How is Jonathan?"

Her face softened further. "He is well too, although Ebenezer's death has affected him greatly also," she paused. "Since the loss of my husband, I have told him who his real father is, I thought it only fair."

She observed the panic in Nathaniel's eyes and continued quickly.

"There is no need to worry. He realises Mary is unaware of the situation and will keep his own counsel. Jonathan will never say or

do anything to disturb you and your wife, of that you can be sure."
As he considered the news, Nathaniel was relieved to know that the
boy finally knew the truth about his natural father.

"How did he take it?" he asked.

"Surprisingly well, considering that he had always thought
Ebenezer to be his real parent," she replied.

They entered the living room. Mary sat hunched over her
embroidery, her eyes aching from the candlelight. At the sound of
their arrival, she laid down the frame and smiled in their direction.

"How are you feeling, Sally?" she asked, rising from the chair
and crossing to hug the woman.

"Much better," she replied, "I really needed to come and break
the news to you both personally, I hope you don't resent my
unannounced visit."

A broad smile encompassed Mary's features, "How could you
ever think you were anything but welcome in our house, Sally, we
are just sorry it has to be in such sad circumstances, aren't we my
dear?"

"Sally, you will always be welcome here," he told her.

They ate and saw out the evening in conversation, talking
mostly about Ebenezer, and eventually, at one in the morning, they
retired, exhausted to bed.

CHAPTER 38

Weeks passed, Sally staying and helping in the vineyard. As time progressed she became much like her old self. Perhaps it was the tranquillity of the setting or the exposure to loving friends that repaired her fragile mental state, whatever the panacea, the effect was remarkable on the woman.

Nathaniel and Mary came to accept Sally as one of the family, so it was with some disappointment that one day she returned from the slopes to announce that she was returning to England.

"I cannot thank you enough for your hospitality and goodwill, my friends," she said through tears. "I have so enjoyed my time with you, but I have a home to return to and I need to see my children."

"When will you leave?" enquired Nathaniel.

"Within the week," she advised him.

Sally and Mary fell into conversation, Nathaniel leaving them to their discourse, preferring to walk in the twilight of the nearest lines of vines. Sally, no longer someone he loved in the physical sense, was someone he cherished desperately as a friend, he knew he would miss her presence in Africa greatly.

Lying in bed that night, watching Mary, sleep, he thought of ways to keep his old friend in the African continent.

Quite why Sally had picked this moment to leave puzzled him, he could see how she would miss her children, but with Ebenezer gone there were no other ties to England.

Nathaniel had hoped to persuade her to stay and make her home in Africa, but she seemed adamant to go.

There was a loud banging on the door, the sound echoing eerily through the silent house. The raps were urgent and rapid. Nathaniel climbed out of bed, draping himself in his dressing gown, heading for the front door.

Jeremiah stood swaying in the cold night air, pupils dilated from alcohol.

"How can I help you, Jeremiah?" questioned his employer.

"You have to stop this, Mr Davidson," the man slurred.

"I'd be delighted to, if I knew what it is I am supposed to prevent," Nathaniel advised him.

Taking the vineyard Manager into the house, he guided him to a chair seeing him safely ensconced, before slumping wearily into another opposite the man.

"Now, how can I help you, Jeremiah?" he began.

"You must stop Sally from leaving, Nathaniel."

Realisation dawned on the employer. When he thought about it, he recalled his Manager and Sally had spent every moment in the vineyard together. Clearly for Jeremiah the relationship had blossomed into one of real affection.

"I'm sorry, my friend, but I have no control over Sally, she is free to go wherever she wishes."

Jeremiah looked crestfallen, head slumping forward onto his chest, a sigh escaping his lips.

"Does Sally know of your feelings?" inquired Nathaniel.

"That's the trouble, Mr Davidson, I told her how I felt two days ago and now she is leaving. I am the cause. I had hoped she may harbour some feelings for me also, clearly she does not."

Nathaniel sympathised with the man's pain, realising how much Ebenezer had meant to his wife. "Sally is going through a difficult period and I don't think she would welcome advances from any man at the moment," Nathaniel said. "Perhaps you should give her some time before you declare yourself as you have."

Looking at the man's expression, Davidson could see that he was devastated. It was a very unusual thing to see his reliable manager in such a state.

"Why not go home now; I'll talk to Sally in the morning and see how she feels about all this." Dragging his bulky frame from the seat, Jeremiah headed for the door, Nathaniel following, close on his heels. Opening the portal, Nathaniel addressed Jeremiah, "Goodnight, my friend, try to get a good night's sleep."

He climbed gratefully back into bed, Mary sitting up fully awake, having been roused by the banging on the door and the voices. Nathaniel briefly outlined the conversation with the manager. His wife agreed with the advice he had given to the manager, telling him to sleep on it himself before talking to Sally.

Flecks of red punctuated the swathes of morning cloud as the next day's sun rose. The air was crisp with a biting early morning coolness as he left the house.

Sally was not in the residence when he got up and he went in search of her, hoping to persuade her to stay.

Just beyond the limits of the house's grounds, he saw her milling around in the first line of vine, calling her name, she turned to face him, waiting for him to catch her up.

An intermittent mist swirled around the foot of the creepers as the ground heated up from the first rays of the sun.

"I'm pleased I've found you, Sally," he opened. "I wanted to talk to you alone."

"If it's about Jeremiah, there is nothing to talk about, Nathaniel," she said adamantly.

"How do you know that's what I'm here about, Sally?" remarked her friend.

She gave out a resigned sigh, "You are his friend, Nathaniel, as well as his employer, who would he come to when the object of his affection has decided to leave?" She turned, walking on and he trailed her through the vines.

"I know that Ebenezer is not long dead, Sally, but the man really does have deep feelings for you, that is obvious," advised Davidson.

"Another time, in another place things might be different, Nathaniel," she inferred, "but at this moment I cannot think about anyone else sharing my life."

Nathaniel grasped her arm, turning her to face him. "What do you feel about this man, Sally, do you have any emotion for him at all?"

She looked uncomfortable at the question, hesitating before speaking, "I can't deny he is a very engaging man and in other circumstances there could have been an empathy between us, but at this moment in time, I cannot think about love for anyone."

"Sally, I have a proposal to put to you. I have thought about it since you came here," advised her friend. "There is nothing to bind you to England now with your husband gone, so my idea was for you to come and live here with Margaret since Jonathan is already married and settled." Her eyes glazed over at his invitation, she could hardly believe the depth of generosity he was showing to her children and herself.

"Oh, Nathaniel," she murmured, "that is the most charitable of offers, you have overwhelmed me."

"Then say you will take up the proposal, come and live here with us; over time you might learn to love Jeremiah. I know Ebenezer would want you to find happiness once more."

It took her no time at all to decide. "How can I say no?" she laughed.

With everything agreed they walked back to the house in the increasingly pleasant morning air. Sunlight bathed the vines with a hazy glow, promoting health in the creepers. They could see the first workers heading into the lines of fruit to begin their daily work. Nathaniel felt life could not get any better.

CHAPTER 39

It took several months for Sally to settle her affairs and bring Margaret to the vineyard. Jonathan had expressed a particular doubt about the arrangement and it took his mother some persuading to finally change his mind.

Margaret had become a beautiful young woman, with silky brown hair and piercing blue eyes of the most disconcerting nature. As he looked on her, Nathaniel realised that young men throughout the continent would fall helplessly in love with such a stunning woman.

The family climbed from the carriage to be greeted by the vineyard owner and his wife, who hugged them both in turn. From a vantage point in the lines of vine, Jeremiah gazed down on the unfolding scene. Following Nathaniel's representation, Sally had spoken to the manager, telling him if he was prepared to wait, he may have possible cause to hope for a softening of her emotions towards him. From that moment he had resolved to work toward marriage. She had warned him that her children would be paramount in any decision she would make about her future, and that was the only thing which gave Jeremiah cause for concern, although Nathaniel had allayed his fears as best he could.

"How was your journey, Sally?" inquired Nathaniel as they entered the house.

"The sea was rough in parts, but it was not too bad," stated his friend. Mary maternally herded Sally and Margaret like straggling sheep into the house, apportioning bedrooms and settling them down in their new home. She acted like a mother hen, personally taking charge of the situation. Looking on the scene before him, Nathaniel realised his home life would never be the same again.

An hour later when Margaret had familiarised herself with their surroundings, the house girl called everyone to dinner. The conversation was stilted at the outset and scarce, but as the wine flowed with each course, the mood lightened, it was Margaret who brought the discourse to life.

"Nathaniel, may I ask an enormous favour?" the voice was rich and confident.

"If it is in my power to grant it," he returned

She continued on. He noticed great passion flashing in her azure blue eyes. "It has long been my ambition to embark on an African safari; now that I reside in the continent, I wondered if you might arrange it for me?"

"Margaret, we discussed this on the voyage here," chided Sally. "Safari is a very dangerous activity, I would prefer you did not involve yourself with it."

"Your mother is right, my dear, safari is not for the faint hearted," Nathaniel stated. "It's a most unladylike activity. It involves a great deal of hardship and roughing it, in the most inhospitable of conditions."

"Nevertheless, I would like to try it for myself; I hoped that you and Jeremiah might introduce me to its delights."

There was a stubbornness in her manner which rivalled her determination in intensity, Nathaniel realising she would go on safari with or without their help.

"If your mother agrees, I will take you as you wish, but I reiterate to you, Margaret, this is not an activity appropriate to a woman."

Even as he said it, he knew that Margaret represented a change in womanhood which was irreversible. His eyes, as he looked at Sally, showed her that he thought she should acquiesce.

"Very well," Sally relented. "So long as Nathaniel is prepared to take you and look after you, I won't stand in your way but I register my protest."

The meal continued in a more sombre mood following the exchanges and Nathaniel watched Margaret closely, noticing a self-satisfied look on her face.

At breakfast the following day, he noticed there was still an atmosphere between Sally and her daughter. Immediately following the meal, he invited the mother to walk with him so that he could explain his thinking in more detail. They stood and looked out over the vineyard, Nathaniel searching for a way to begin.

"Margaret is her own person, Sally, she will have her way whatever you say; I think you know that. Young people today are changing and we have to come to terms with that."

She gave out a huge sigh, "I know, Nathaniel, she is her father's daughter without doubt, she has picked up his spirit of adventure, but she is my daughter too and I am a mother first and foremost. I don't want anything to happen to her."

"I cannot promise that her safety will not be threatened if she does this," he advised. "All I can say is that I will do everything in my power to minimise the risk and treat her as if she were my own daughter."

"I can't ask any more than that of you." A hot wind sprang up as they returned to the house.

"If I could make a suggestion," Nathaniel stated. "Say nothing more about it; allow her to know that you see her as a responsible person with confidence in her own ability to achieve her own destiny; she will certainly need that if she is to survive in this continent."

"I'm sure you're right my, friend just get this safari over as soon as possible so that I can sleep safer in my bed knowing she has returned safely."

CHAPTER 40

The preparations for the expedition were completed seven days later. Arrangements were made for the smooth running of the vineyard in the absence of the owner and manager, over the period they would be in the bush.

The horses stood in the early morning air, breath clouding as it left their bodies. Nathaniel and Jeremiah supervised the packing of the animals and the cart they would be using, while Margaret took leave of her mother in the house.

Nathaniel's son Edward insisted on joining the party, his father allowing it, judging Margaret would feel more comfortable with someone close to her own age accompanying her.

He was tightening the straps to his horse as the door opened, the youngsters exiting, Mary and Sally following, their eyes glistening at the prospect of losing their offspring for six weeks.

Jeremiah could see the awkwardness of the situation, moving toward the party.

"Come on, you two," he instructed. "A safari is what you wanted and the quicker we get there, the quicker you will see some animals."

Mary turned back to the house and Sally moved toward Jeremiah, the youngsters heading for their mounts.

"Look after Margaret," she pleaded. "And when you get back perhaps we could talk about us." The Manager's face cracked into a grin. "You mean it?" he asked.

"Yes, I mean it," she returned, her face showing the hint of a smile.

"Nothing will happen to her, I swear," advised Jeremiah. "If my future with you is dependant on her safety, you can plan our wedding now."

"Go on, get off with you," she said, pushing him towards his steed.

Trotting away from the vineyard, Nathaniel turned to the Manager, "It seemed to me Sally was sorry to see you go," he smiled.

"You could say that," replied Jeremiah, looking smug in his saddle. Edward steered the cart with the supplies behind his father and the vineyard manager, Margaret riding alongside him. Nathaniel could hear their excited chatter about the expedition, realising both would grow up considerably over the next six weeks. Neither had lived rough or had to work hard, he knew the expedition would be the making or otherwise of them.

It would take five days of gruelling travel to get to the site of the safari, followed by over two weeks of intense work and then another five days to return. Pitching tents on the first night gave the guardians an inkling of the time ahead. Neither Margaret nor Edward had any idea how to put the shelters up. It took two hours to teach them the rudiments in the gathering gloom.

Licks of orange flame lit up the area of the campsite, the fire crackling and spluttering the occasional shower of sparks. Margaret, keen to do her share of the work, prepared the evening meal. Despite it being fairly unappetising, the men ate the fare without complaint, such was their hunger.

Settling by the fire after the meal, Nathaniel and the manager sipped at some whisky, Jeremiah had thoughtfully packed,

"So how was your first day, you two?" questioned Nathaniel.

Margaret was consumed with enthusiasm as she replied, "Absolutely wonderful, Nathaniel, I can't wait to get to our destination."

He wondered how wonderful she would think it was in another three or four days.

"And you, Edward?" Jeremiah kept up the assault.

"I miss my bed," said the boy grumpily. In that instant, Nathaniel knew his son would survive the trip better. The boy had known there would be hardship, yet had still made the effort to come.

Edward and his father had never been that close, Nathaniel hoped this experience might engender a deeper bond between them. They talked into the night before retiring, exhausted but content, with the night sounds of the bush echoing around the area.

The next four days proceeded as the first, except by the third morning, the travelling had become tedious and the conversation had dried up.

CHAPTER 41

Mid morning on the fifth day saw them crest a hill, looking down on a plain stretching away into the distance. Animals represented by varying size dots, grazed the vegetation in searing heat and a river glinted in the intense sunlight, being lapped at its banks by yet more species.

"There we are," Nathaniel pointed out, "that's the area of our safari." Margaret and Edward stared at the scene below, caught up in the majesty of it.

"It's beautiful," breathed the girl.

"Indeed it is," agreed Nathaniel, "but we have more ground to cover until we reach it; we need to find a way down."

Sloping away from the drop, the hill descended at a steep angle, which made it difficult for the cart to negotiate. Edward was thankful when the tilt became less pronounced and all he had to negotiate was the occasional acacia tree and low bushes. As the hill fell away to the flatness of the plain, Nathaniel rode away from the party, searching for a suitable campsite. One which would afford protection, and would also give them the earliest warning of animal attack.

Eventually he found what he was looking for, a piece of ground enclosed on three sides by bushes, fairly impenetrable but far enough from the centre of the site to give ample time to react in case of incursion.

Returning, he found the party drinking wine and chatting idly.

"Nice to see you are working as hard as me," he grinned.

"You're welcome," returned Jeremiah, handing Davidson a cup of the red liquid.

Pitching of tents was now smooth as silk, the site erected in half an hour. The youngsters had learned well.

"I think it would be wise if we scout around for the rest of the day and reconnoitre the area," suggested Nathaniel.

"Yes, please," pleaded the girl, desperate to start the adventure as quickly as possible.

Giraffe and elephant mingled near the sparse acacias, stretching up to glean as much nutrient from the trees as they could. In the distance they could see a pride of lions, lazing in the shadows of yet more trees, hiding from the fierce heat of the early afternoon.

The baking heat was too much even for Nathaniel who had hunted elephant years before.

"Let's take shelter from the sun for a while," he suggested to the others, who accepted the idea gratefully.

They lay in the cool of the shadows, horses grazing quietly, Nathaniel outlining the work over the next two weeks.

"I should tell you, the toil we are facing is difficult and dangerous and I insist that you follow my instructions to the letter; you will see many animals, some of which you know to be dangerous and some you may deem less so, but you must treat every species with equal caution or you may find you will regret it."

The youngsters looked on with rapt attention, but he felt uneasy about how much they were taking in and whether they would follow his advice, so he attempted to hammer home the message.

"I have seen the torn bodies of men who judged themselves arrogant enough to ignore the dangers, whose gored cadavers were testament to their stupidity and I want you to consider that carefully; you are not invincible."

He looked at them, seeing them smile at the intensity of his remarks. It was clear the only way they would learn was by experience. He hoped they would not have to learn a salutary lesson.

Jeremiah sat on the ground watching the scene, understanding Nathaniel's objective, realising at the same time the futility of his pontificating.

Nathaniel continued on, "We need to establish a pattern of work each day, who makes meals and such like. If we get into a routine like that, it will make our stay here much easier. We will rise at dawn each day and leave as soon as we have eaten to maximise the daylight hours."

Edward looked up from his recumbent position, "How do we eat through the day, Father?" he inquired.

"We kill and cook something in the bush; that way we have less to carry with us," Nathaniel replied.

Outlining what was expected of them in detail, he left no room for doubt in their minds he would countenance no shirking. When he concluded, he looked out over the plain, seeing the sun had well passed its zenith, reducing its heat to a comfortable level. He rose from his seated position.

"Let's mount up and see some animals," he suggested.

They hadn't gone far before they came across a herd of elephant with an imposing bull leading several cows and a number of teetering youngsters, looking as though they were taking their first faltering steps.

The leviathan's grey hide was punctuated by dry brown patches of mud, showing it had recently wallowed, the earth adhering the skin, cracked and peeling off as the great bull moved tortoise slowly around his companions. One tusk was cracked off about a third of the way from the point from some old confrontation with another male.

"They are magnificent," commented Margaret. "Can we get closer, please?" Nathaniel leant and grasped her horses rein, holding it so the animal could not move off,.

"No" he said. "With cows and infants about, one of the mothers may challenge us; believe me, Margaret, you don't want to see a rampaging elephant."

"Perhaps we should be on our way?" mumbled Jeremiah. "The male has seen us and he looks agitated."

The bull's feet were sweeping the floor, knocking up clouds of powdered dirt as Jeremiah spoke, the animal turned head on, looking directly at the party of humans through piggy eyes.

"Turn your animals and ride slowly away, don't rush," instructed Nathaniel.

Edward and Margaret followed his advice, seeing the animal's ears twitching back and forth in challenge. Nathaniel and the manager brought up the rear as they retreated from the scene, glancing back periodically to ensure the animal wasn't following. The vineyard owner's hand rested on the butt of the rifle, sticking out from its cover attached to the saddle. It wasn't an elephant gun and a single shot probably wouldn't bring the elephant down, but it was the only protection they had.

He needn't have worried, the moment they backed from the scene the herd quietened, the male turning his attention to the acacia pods, which had been the focus of his attention before the party had appeared in the area.

Margaret was ecstatic about the experience. "Did you see him, Edward?" she cried. "What a size and how proud he was."

"Frankly, he scared me to death," replied the young man.

"But how he protected the others," she continued to babble, "I hope we see a lot more elephants."

Nathaniel and Jeremiah exchanged disinterested glances, hoping the woman would become less demonstrative as time went on. Margaret was too flighty in Nathaniel's eyes, that kind of attitude could see her make mistakes which might be costly to herself and to the others.

Although the heat was less ferocious, the baked earth was testament to thousands of years of harsh exposure to the sun. Cloying dust kicked up by the horses assaulted their throats, the water supply diminishing rapidly as the party fought to combat the dryness.

Nathaniel looked into the distance, shimmering heat haze rising from the ground, distorting distant objects into grotesque shapes. Trees appeared to possess disjointed limbs, the extremities seemed to dance in a macabre fashion as the heat haze worked its eerie magic on them. In the immediate foreground everything was normal, making the far off scene even more weird.

Many animals were observed by the party, but they did not come as close to any as they had the elephant. The river bank was congregated by many species; Thompson's gazelle, wildebeest and zebra jostled for position at the water's edge, lapping at the liquid. Well before the party arrived, the animals sensed their impending appearance, scattering nervously.

It was late in the day, the angle of the sun dipping towards the horizon. Nathaniel raised his hand to stop his companions.

"It's time we headed back now," he instructed. "For a first foray into the bush, it's been reasonably successful."

"Father, my horse seems to be struggling," informed Edward, dismounting the steed and lifting a hind leg. "I think it's lame," he announced. His father dropped to the floor, joining him at the animal's rear quarters.

The young man was right, his mount would not be able to carry him further. All that could be done was to lead the animal slowly back to the campsite. Nathaniel took his son with him on his own horse. It would make the journey slower he thought, relieved to have brought a spare animal, tied to the back of the cart at the camp.

Arriving back in gathering twilight, they tethered the hobbling animal, while Jeremiah administered a bandage to the leg, bound tightly for support.

Margaret and Edward were exhausted, retiring to their shelters to nap. The two men busied themselves, tending to the horses and preparing a meal.

"I'm concerned about Margaret," began Jeremiah, squatting over the pan perched precariously over the fire. "She's very immature for this kind of adventure," he whispered.

"I agree," returned the man's employer. "We just have to hope she will learn to adapt rapidly."

They talked of the day's progress for the next half hour, tending to the stew and planning the next day's foray.

Margaret appeared from her tent, clearly rested, looking as alert as she had in the morning.

"The food smells wonderful," she remarked, bending her head over the saucepan, inhaling the aroma of meat and vegetables.

Edward joined them soon afterwards, the four eating their food gratefully.

"Edward and I were talking today and we wondered if we could go as far as the river tomorrow?" the girl ventured.

"Had you a reason in mind?" asked Nathaniel.

Edward joined the conversation, "We thought it might be fun to build a raft and sail on the water," he explained.

Nathaniel looked toward his manager. "What do you think, Jeremiah?" Pausing with a forkful of stew halfway to his mouth, the man considered the question.

"It could be dangerous but I suppose if we sail with them they should come to no harm."

"Very well, Nathaniel acquiesced. "That's what we will do in the morning."

For the rest of the evening, they sat close to the dancing flames of the fire, as the temperature tumbled, talking idle banter about the day's events, before heading to their beds late in the night.

Nathaniel held back as his companions retired, tending to the conflagration by replenishing the wood. Fire, their main protector needed to stay alight at all costs. It reminded him of the times when he and Christian Davenport searched for elephant years before and he became maudlin as he thought of his long dead friend. Not knowing why, he retrieved the bottle of whisky from the saddle bag and toasted the man's memory with an enormous swig.

After all this time, he still missed the man badly. Ebenezer Smith had been a good friend but Christian would always hold the greatest affection in Nathaniel's soul. His mood deepening he found himself drinking more and more of the biting alcohol, putting himself into an inebriated state. Fortunately before unconsciousness overtook him, he made unsteadily for his shelter, asleep the instant his head touched the bedding.

Singing coming from outside his tent awoke him. With a pounding head he reached for his water bottle and drained it of the cool water.

Margaret was busying herself in the campsite, preparing the early morning meal, her joyous tunes lilting in the early morning air. First light was barely up but she was astonishingly awake and disgustingly chirpy, seeing him emerge delicately from his tent, holding his head to try and stop the incessant hammering.

"Good morning, Nathaniel," the woman called in her high pitched tone, grating through him in his unhealthy state.

Bending and stretching in the morning light, he managed a gruff greeting and headed for more water, drinking copiously to assuage his raging thirst.

The next five minutes saw Jeremiah and Edward emerge and begin moving about the camp. Jeremiah approached his employer.

"My God, you look awful," he laughed. "Alcohol I presume?"

"Indeed," was all Nathaniel could manage, stomach heaving as the effect of his indulgence gripped his body even more ferociously.

Suddenly he lurched toward one line of bushes, crashing through and falling to his knees to vomit on the ground, out of sight of the others. Returning, his ashen features were plain to all, Margaret thrusting a cup of steaming tea into his grateful hands.

Nothing more was said about his physical state and he declined breakfast, even though he felt hungry. The queasiness in his stomach was warning enough as to what would happen again if he ate at this moment.

Nathaniel's head continued to pound as they prepared the horses for the day's exploits, his companions allowing him to go about his business without talking to him, he was grateful for the thought. His indisposition was getting progressively worse as the party rode out for the day.

It took an hour to reach the river, the banks deserted. The animals had drunk their early morning fill and were out foraging for food. An occasional bird dotted the waters edge, picking at possible sources of nourishment, preening their feathers in the sunshine. Several crocodiles were basking some way down the bank, opening their jaws intermittently in the semblance of a yawn. In the distance a gathering of hippo moved slowly around the bush.

"Let's start building the raft," commanded Margaret, full of enthusiasm for the day's events.

"Jeremiah and I will take a look around the area and check that it's safe first," suggested Nathaniel.

Twenty minutes later, Edward and Margaret were gathering suitable material for the building of the craft. By the time they had sourced the wood, the pair were soaked to the skin with sweat, needing to rest before they began construction. Edward's father and Jeremiah allowed them full control of the project, preferring to lay in the sunshine. The vineyard owner hoped that his under the weather state, would have diminished by this moment but it was as unpleasant as ever. Once they had rested and eaten, the younger pair set about the building of the raft, the older men looking on.

Edward's father had dropped off to sleep in the warm sunshine when the boy came to him.

"Father," he said, prodding the man awake. "The raft is ready, I know you wanted to inspect it before we took to the water."

The man clambered to his feet. "Yes, I do want to look at it," he countered.

If he had hoped that it would be a failure, Nathaniel was disappointed. It was well put together, the rope bindings tight and securely lashed. The knots, competently tied, he had no criticism to make. It irked him, he was hoping he wouldn't have to test it but knew he had to.

"You've done a fine job," he announced. "You should be proud of yourself, but we still need to test it. It must be you and I who does that, Edward."

The four carried the vessel to the river bank, lowering it into the current, holding it to allow first the son and then the father to board with long poles to propel and steer it.

Jeremiah and Margaret stepped back up the gentle bank, watching as Edward pushed the wooden structure away into the flowing water. Surprisingly watertight and manoeuvrable, the two men took turns in steering the raft down stream. Nathaniel wanted to ensure it was going to stand up to any rigours it might come across. He decided on as thorough testing as he could give it, rocking it for all he was worth to judge how stable she was. It seemed perfectly acceptable in that state so he decided to try her out for speed. He and his son moved to the rear of the structure, plunging the long poles into the river bed in unison. The raft picked up speed and remained secure in balance.

They proceeded down the watercourse, leaving Jeremiah and Margaret as ever diminishing specks, Nathaniel's confidence in the vessel ensured, he began to enjoy the journey. They were involved with the propelling and steering of the raft when Nathaniel suddenly observed bubbles rising from the surface immediately before the front of it.

"Do you see that?" he commented to his son.

By the time the father had drawn Edward's attention to the surface disturbance, the raft had moved over it. Boiling water surrounded the wooden vessel which slowed slightly as the men stopped punting for a few seconds, murky water churning into a seething mass of mud and vegetation. A form began to rise up from below, massive in size and awesome in strength.

The hippo broke the surface, forcing the raft upward, pitching the occupants high into the air, depositing them into the maelstrom of the water. The great mouth opened, showing discoloured tusks draped in weed from the base of the river. As Nathaniel watched, the animal's head turned in the direction of Edward, thrashing about.

With a terrible realisation, Nathaniel knew the hippo's intention. All he could think of was saving his son, he grabbed the pole floating next to him.

The giant creature was moving toward Edward. With little time to react, Nathaniel forced the pole forward with a huge effort. By the luckiest of chances he caught the beast in its most vulnerable place, the wood catching the hippo in the glutinous membrane of the eye blinding it permanently as the timber displaced it from its socket.

A roar of unimaginable intensity escaped the animal as it thrashed about, infuriated. It turned in the direction of the attack and with its functioning orb detected its assailant. The focus of its attention turned to Nathaniel and the beast moved in his direction.

From the corner of his eye, Nathaniel could see his son swimming panic stricken toward the bank, feeling relief as he saw him straggling up the incline.

The animal was on him now, about to tear him with its open jaws. Still holding the pole, Nathaniel judged the time well. As the mouth gaped, he forced the wood into the aperture, thrusting with manic strength. It collided with the soft fleshy skin of the throat, infuriating the animal once more. With an involuntary reflex the jaws closed, splintering the pole apart, expelling the residue.

Hitting him in the midriff, the massive head knocked the breath from his body, leaving him gasping to stay afloat on the surface. Nathaniel watched as the great jaws opened afresh, waiting for the tusks to wreak their havoc on his body.

A shot rang out, followed quickly by another. With a heave the Hippo rose, belying its size and weight, blood spewing from holes in its head. It fell back, head catching Nathaniel once again, compounding the first injury. This time he could not cling on to the surface, dropping into the mixture of silt and slimy weed.

Nathaniel was losing consciousness, when a hand grasped him from above and heaved him into the air. He had time to see the face of Jeremiah seconds before blacking out.

The next thing he knew, was coming to on the bank, his three companions bending solicitously over him.

"Are you alright?" demanded Margaret as she wiped away the residue of weed and mud from his face.

"In better condition than the hippo, I suspect," Nathaniel smiled back at her, before retching dirty liquid on the floor.

"Thank God you were all there when I needed you," he declared as the vomiting finished.

They helped him to his feet and he looked into the river to see the lifeless body of the animal stuck on mud near the edge. Jeremiah suggested a swig of whisky, his employer declining. Although his delicate condition was now firmly at the back of his mind, he felt less than healthy.

"You have Margaret to thank for your life, Nathaniel," announced Jeremiah. "She reacted first."

"Thank you, my dear," he aimed at the young woman, before looking back to his manager because the girl had moved off to wet her cleaning cloth once more.

"How did she do it, Jeremiah?"

"I was lying in the sun," he advised. "She was watching your progress and saw the raft upturn, she jumped for the horse immediately, tearing down the bank, shooting the animal on the ride. Believe me it was very, very impressive."

"Good God," replied Nathaniel.

"I followed up and fired the second shot as a precaution but it was Margaret who undoubtedly saved you," confirmed Jeremiah.

She returned from the river bank, continuing to mop at his face, clearing the last remnants from his features. He took her by the wrist and looked up into her eyes.

"You are a truly remarkable young woman, Margaret," he exclaimed.

Her job finished, she walked away to retrieve the horse which had bolted a little way, when she had slipped from the saddle. Jeremiah and Edward eased Nathaniel to his feet where he stood uneasily, a sharp pain began to course down his side. It was clear he would not be able to walk, the men brought up a second horse, lifting him onto its back with some discomfort to the man.

Presently, Margaret returned and the party headed back where the other two animals were tethered. The journey was a real distress to the injured man. His chest screamed in agony each time the horse placed its hooves on the floor, Nathaniel knowing he had broken at least one rib in his encounter with the hippopotamus.

What had been an hour journey on the way out to the river, became more than a three hour one going back. Despite the pain,

Nathaniel had not cried out once, despite an overwhelming wish to do so.

It was a godsend when they arrived back at the campsite, the party gently extricating him from the horse, placing him on his back in the tent. Even the act of eating was torture when they brought him food, each swallow acting like a hammer in his chest but he managed to get some of the meat down.

For the second time in as many days, Jeremiah's bandaging skills were called on as he bound Nathaniel's chest tightly for support. Dinner was a sombre affair for the others, sitting in the light of the fire, eating silently. Margaret was first to break the hush once again.

"I daresay that is the end of the safari," she ventured. Jeremiah looked at her with sympathy in his eyes, knowing how much she had wanted this experience.

"Yes, I'm afraid it is," he said.

"No matter," she replied, "we must get Nathaniel back home, I know that."

Jeremiah looked at her with new found respect. He wouldn't have believed how much change there could be in a person over a twenty-four hour period. From a scatterbrained girl she had become a mature woman, saving his friend from certain death with a breathtaking logical manner a man twice her age would have struggled to achieve.

The danger for Nathaniel wasn't over. A journey much longer faced the man, who would have to be treated with kid gloves.

Edward finished his meal quickly, leaving the area of the fire, seeking out his father's shelter. Nathaniel was napping when he entered, the young man shaking him gently until he woke with a start.

"Edward, my boy, what can I do for you?" Never having been a demonstrative person, Edward found it difficult to open up to his father, but his conscience dictated he must in this case.

"Father," he faltered, "I wanted to thank you for what you did today, if you hadn't taken on that animal, then I probably would have been killed."

Nathaniel's face showed pride for the boy, watching his son wrestle with his personality and voice his gratitude.

"Edward, I may not have devoted as much time as I should have to your childhood, what with the development of my business and other things; I want you to know that I am proud of you and that you mean the world to me. I am as proud as any father could be of his child."

Despite the pain, Nathaniel leaned over, placing his arm around his son's shoulder, pulling him towards him, where they hugged each other fondly. The boy pulled himself away from the embrace, the moment overwhelming him, exiting the tent rapidly, heading back to Jeremiah and Margaret.

Nathaniel lay thinking about the encounter, realising that the relationship with his son would change inevitably. He dropped off to sleep again, contented but in much pain.

CHAPTER 42

He awoke to voices in the campsite, where his companions had been up for more than an hour. Margaret thrust her head through the flap of the tent.

"Good morning, Nathaniel, how are you today?" she inquired. Since waking, each breath he had taken was hell, pain shooting through his upper body on each inhalation and he told her of the fact.

"We're leaving for home today," she told him.

Minutes after she left, Jeremiah and Edward entered. "Nathaniel, we need to get you outside, do you feel up to it?" asked Jeremiah.

"I suppose so," he replied, "but you will have to be gentle."

It was an effort getting him to his feet, each movement promoted a sharp intake of breath from the man, the colour draining from his face with each step.

Heavy clouds littered the sky, a drizzling rain invading everyone's clothes. Outside the tent, a stretcher like structure lay on the damp floor, awaiting Nathaniel's form. With care they gently deposited him on it, pain excruciatingly severe as they laid him down. Two of the horses stood close by with strange additions to their harnesses, being held steady by the young woman.

Jeremiah and Nathaniel's son took the front and rear poles of the improvised structure, lifting it from the ground, manoeuvring themselves to a position between the animals.

Margaret left her position at the head of the horses and joined them, firstly at the head of the structure where she guided the poles into the specially rigged straps at the front of the harness, repeating the feat at the rear. The stretcher hung sturdy between the beasts, just as Jeremiah had predicted it would.

It was a surprisingly comfortable improvisation as the creatures slowly moved off with the men riding them. After a while, deep sleep which had evaded him overnight because of the pain overtook Nathaniel, prompted by the gentle rocking of the makeshift stretcher. Presently he began to snore loudly.

It was mid morning by the time his eyes flickered open. The clouded over sky had disappeared, leaving him staring up at an azure blue heaven.

"Back to the land of the living?" Jeremiah said, looking down on his employer.

"Yes, unfortunately, if I was still in the land of nod, I wouldn't have to look at your ugly face," he smiled playfully.

The day wore on as they moved gradually across the terrain, early conversation dissipated into total silence as they negotiated the bush. As the journey was taking so long, they decided to dispense with lunch, preferring to see as many miles behind them as they could in the daylight hours.

Each day took on a similar pattern, tediousness growing along with frustration at the slowness of progress. The outward journey had taken five days and it was mid morning of the eighth on the return when the vineyard finally appeared hazily before them. Their spirits soared, realising there was only one or two miles more to negotiate.

"Thank God for that," sighed Margaret, riding at the rear of the two horses carrying the invalid between them.

"Ride forward, Margaret; tell them we're coming," instructed Nathaniel from his prone position on the stretcher between the creatures.

She spurred her mount, kicking up powdered dust in her wake, galloping off into the distance, expertly negotiating low slung bushes as she went.

Even though they had abandoned the cart before the journey began with a cracked wheel and in danger of collapse, the trek had taken much longer because of Nathaniel's injuries. It was with relief they entered the area of the house and stopped right in front of the door.

Mary tore from the interior heading for her husband.

"As soon as I let you out of my sight, you get into trouble," she chided him. "What am I going to do with you?"

She leant over to kiss him, concern etched in her features.

"Let's get you inside," she ordered, two of the vineyard workers moving in to remove the structure from between the beasts. They carried the vineyard owner gently into the house and up to his bedroom.

Sally had followed her friend out of the house, approaching Jeremiah with a look of pleasure and welcome in her eyes. "I asked you to look after Margaret, and you were as good as your word, welcome back, Jeremiah," she said, placing her hand over his on the rein.

The tall manager slid from his saddle, standing next to the diminutive woman. He wanted desperately to hold her, suspecting the same thought had crossed her mind, but he satisfied himself by observing.

"I missed you, Sally, you don't know how much I missed you."

"You were in my thoughts too," she advised him, smiling lovingly up at him.

As Nathaniel, Mary and Edward disappeared out of sight into the house, Jeremiah's resolve cracked, dragging Sally round to face him, bending down to lock his lips on the woman's. There was no restraint in her welcoming reaction as their mouths crushed together for what seemed like an age.

"You must marry me," he almost ordered her. "If I don't have you, then I don't want to live," he stated dramatically.

"Of course I'll marry you," she replied. "I know I expressed concern before but I had to be true to Ebenezer, but while you were gone it gave me time to think and I know he would want me to be happy." Jeremiah was overwhelmed as the two of them walked off to discuss their future together.

Mary sent one of the workers to fetch the doctor for Nathaniel but the man returned to say the medical practitioner would not be able to attend until the following morning. A particularly difficult labour required his full attention and he promised he would attend the patient next day.

They lay next to each other in bed, Mary sleeping soundly, Nathaniel looking at his wife in the moonlight, realising just how much she meant to him. He could search a million years and never find anyone half as important as she was.

An excruciating pain engulfed his chest as he attempted to move position, he gasped with pain. He would be delighted when the doctor finally put in an appearance. Finally, after moving himself gingerly to an acceptable place, he dropped off to a fitful slumber, punctuated with dreams of his encounter with the hippo.

It was disgustingly early when the physician finally arrived at the house directly from his problem birth, which had finally concluded at six in the morning.

"Morning, Mr Davidson," uttered the doctor, looking down upon Nathaniel in his supine state.

The only way he could get any degree of relief was to lie flat on his back. It diminished the pain but affected his breathing.

"I am so pleased to see you, Doctor," Nathaniel replied.

"Well I would save your pleasure for a little while, as it's probably going to hurt a bit when I examine you," advised the medical man.

He was right. Firstly the doctor sat him up and it seemed like all the relief of lying on his back evaporated. The pain concentrated into one huge bout when the doctor helped him up, Nathaniel screaming in agony.

It took twenty minutes for the examination, the pain, seemed to be weakening massively the moment the chest binding was removed.

"It would appear the person who bandaged you had little medical skill," the man stated. "The binding has caused you more pain by its amateurish application than you needed to experience."

At the end of his investigation, the doctor confirmed a broken rib and rebound the invalid less tightly than before.

"It will take some time for the healing process to take over and knit the bone, but you should feel less pain and your breathing should be much less laboured now," he advised. He closed his bag, heading out, pausing at the door. "Rest as much as you can but don't restrict yourself to bed, I don't feel that is beneficial when it's avoidable and in your case it is, good morning."

Shutting the door behind him, the doctor left, taking his brusque bedside manner with him, leaving Nathaniel to struggle out of bed and begin dressing. He was midway through the task when Mary entered.

"Why didn't you wait for me to help you?" she asked her husband.

"Our good friend the physician seems to think I should help myself as much as possible," he informed her, wincing slightly at a twinge but nothing anywhere near as painful as he had recently experienced.

"I have some news, Jeremiah and Sally are to get married," she grinned.

"Not before time, everyone knew it was inevitable," replied her husband.

"Try to be a little more enthusiastic about it my dear," Mary admonished him. "It's a big thing for them and it will be nice to hold a wedding here."

Nathaniel suspected his wife would have little time for him up to the wedding day. She and Sally would be totally engrossed in making the arrangements and ensuring the day went off without a hitch. He would be a bit part player in the drama of it all. That was women though, emotional times like this, meat and drink to their feminine souls.

He followed Mary downstairs, Jeremiah lying in wait for him at the bottom, like a wild animal ready to pounce on its prey.

"Hello, Jeremiah, I understand that congratulations are in order," observed Nathaniel.

For a man about to marry the object of his desire, the manager looked nervous and ill at ease, "May I speak with you?" he asked nervously.

Mary took leave of them, searching out the bride to be to discuss the arrangements from the woman's perspective, while Nathaniel and his manager exited the house for the warm sunshine of the morning.

"How can I help you?" Jeremiah's employer asked when they had moved away from the house.

"How are you feeling?" enquired the man, giving Nathaniel the impression he didn't want to come to the point or was putting it off as long as he could.

"I'm fine," he replied, remaining silent afterward in the hope that the quietness would bring Jeremiah to his question. With an effort, Jeremiah's resolve hardened.

"I wondered if you would consent to be my best man?" he spluttered.

It was so unlike the man to be reticent and Nathaniel laughed out loud at his discomfort.

"Of course I will," he confirmed, slapping his friend on the back and then pumping the man's hand vigorously. "I'd be absolutely delighted to do it."

Jeremiah's face lost all appearance of the worried frown, was now wreathed in smiles at the news. The concern had grown since he first mooted the idea to his future wife. She had assured him that Nathaniel would do it, but nevertheless it worried him more than anything had in his life.

"The women think they have the lion's share of the arrangements, but you and I may just introduce some surprises they aren't expecting," Nathaniel suggested.

Why his manager had been so reticent about asking him to be best man was beyond him. He thought back to his own nervousness at the time of his own marriage, realising the illogic vein of thought which could come over you at such a joyous time. It was almost as if you expected something to go wrong. As a consequence, tiny things blew out of all proportion.

That night, as they sat in the warm glow of the fire, Nathaniel turned to Mary. "I've never seen Jeremiah so off balance as he was this morning," he stated.

"Sally was the same," confessed his wife. "The way they are going they'll both have heart failure and never see their big day." She snuggled up to him. "Do you remember our day?" she asked.

"Of course I do, I remember wondering how I could get out of it and thinking how all the other women in my life would cope now that they had no chance of capturing the best man available," he teased.

She hit him with the pillow playfully and they collapsed into each other's arms, their lips joining in passionate embrace. It was amazing how it still made him tingle when they kissed, even after all these years. Making love was inevitable. They enjoyed each other for the next hour before falling exhausted into a deep sleep.

The wedding was arranged for the following week, the women working hard on making the house and surrounds presentable. Jeremiah and Nathaniel were surplus to requirements, so the vineyard owner took the groom into the city two days prior to the nuptials. He had booked a room for them to stay until the morning of the wedding, the men seeking out a watering hole to celebrate Jeremiah's imminent marriage.

Nearly two bottles of whisky later, it was clear to the other amused clientele the pair would not be able to walk if they stood up. Neither male was used to the level of alcohol they had imbibed.

Jeremiah threw his head back and drained yet another glass of the golden malt liquid.

"Nathaniel, I want you to know that I think the world of you and Mary, you have made me so welcome at the vineyard," he was slurring and dribbling at the same time.

The landlord crossed to the table when Nathaniel called for yet another bottle of whisky. "I think you have had sufficient," the man advised, "perhaps you should go and sleep it off."

"Let's go my friend," exclaimed Nathaniel, "it appears our presence in this establishment is no longer acceptable."

To the ringing laughter of other customers, Nathaniel and Jeremiah rose with much difficulty and, holding firmly to one another, extricated themselves from the building but not before crashing into two tables as they stumbled about.

Outside, the air hit them with the force of a sledgehammer cracking a walnut. Jeremiah collapsed, giggling to the floor while his colleague tried desperately to help him to his feet, dragging himself to the ground in the process, floundering there for a few minutes until Nathaniel regained some composure and rose unsteadily to a standing position. He tried again to hoist his friend to his feet and this time managed it with a great effort.

In a drunken stupor the men lurched down the road, searching out their hotel. Neither could remember the name and that became a source of even more merriment.

"Now look," said Nathaniel, almost incoherently. "On which street was the hotel situated?" Jeremiah sniggered, pointing across the street. There it was, right in front of them, the most imposing building in the area and looking welcoming. Struggling to its front door, they crashed through into the lobby and up to the desk.

"The keys to 27 and 28 if you please?" Nathaniel requested.

Fortunately, the rooms were situated on the ground floor, so they had no stairs to negotiate. It took twice as long as it normally would have to reach Jeremiah's chamber. Inside his friend threw the manager onto the bed, just in time before he passed out. Nathaniel arranged his body so that it would be comfortable when he awoke and then headed for his own room.

The room was spinning as he lay down. Before he dropped off to sleep he had a premonition of how he was going to feel the next day and he dreaded it.

CHAPTER 43

Nathaniel and Jeremiah rode out early to reach the vineyard on the morning of the wedding. The previous day had been a write off following their excessive drinking session, today, however, both were feeling on top of the world.

They neared the estate, overwhelmed by the display at the house. Garlands of flowers twined around the fences and adorned the porch around the door. A wonderful pungent aroma of Cape cowslips, Lachenalias and roses swept over the men as they crossed into the garden before the house.

Long tables were placed strategically around the area, waiting to be adorned with tablecloth and food, the smell of which wafted from the interior of the house. On entering, Mary hurried towards Nathaniel, kissing him perfunctorily before sweeping majestically off to carry on with the arrangements for the day.

The wedding was due for 1.00pm, a good four hours away, so the vineyard owner suggested Jeremiah partake of a long soak before dressing.

"Nathaniel, please do something and get from under my feet," scolded his wife as she dashed by with some sort of foodstuff in her hands.

"Just a minute," he shouted, grabbing her arm. "I'd like to kiss my wife if that's alright, I have just been away for two nights."

The peck that she allowed him was hardly passionate, she was gone before he could protest. Suddenly the room was empty and relatively quiet. Jeremiah had taken his advice. Sally he presumed, was in her room and his wife was taking on the entire organisation of the day. With nothing to occupy himself, he flopped into his favourite chair, slipping into sleep, catching up on some of the slumber he needed after the drinking bout.

He woke with a start, Mary prodding him to raise him from his unconscious state.

"Come on, Nathaniel, it's time to get ready," she instructed.

Reluctantly dragging himself from the comfort of the chair, he went to bathe. The house boy had already filled his bath with steaming water, almost too scalding to bear, as he gingerly lowered himself into the relaxing water.

An hour and a half later, he was dressed in his finery, talking to the groom in the lounge. If anything, Jeremiah was more nervous now than he had been over the last few days. Nathaniel found it difficult to believe that was possible but here it was.

They walked into the garden just in time to greet the minister, descending from his carriage, already liveried up for the ceremony.

"A lovely day for it," the religious representative observed. Jeremiah was looking ashen. The whiteness of his face concerned Nathaniel.

"Are you alright?" he inquired.

"Not really," replied the man, "I think I'm going to be sick."

They walked away from the house, just as the guests were arriving. Not many as neither Jeremiah or Sally had a lot of friends but the vineyard owners were in attendance, who had helped Nathaniel out of his spot when his own workers were indisposed with sickness. Their wives joined them, each seeming to vie with the rest to outdo the other's dresses.

Ten minutes later, Nathaniel suggested to the groom that it might be a good time to return for the ceremony. He hadn't been sick and his colour looked much better, the best man hoping for a smooth ceremony.

They rounded the corner of the house, the scene before them magnificent. Chairs had been arranged on the lawn in rows, the minister standing in his painfully white surplus at the head of the makeshift aisle.

"Here we go," smiled Nathaniel, "time to marry your beautiful fiancée."

With a beatific smile the minister arranged them correctly in their places; they waited patiently for Sally.

When she came around the same corner of the house, everyone craned to see her. As he watched her stately movement between the chairs, Nathaniel remembered the fresh faced young servant who had afforded him the first pleasure of a woman all those many years ago. A lot older now, but the years had been kind to her. She still had that mischievous demeanour that she'd shown in the stable stall, when she had giggled at his examination of his torso. Perhaps if things had worked out differently he would have married Sally himself, but he knew that Mary was his soul mate. No one could replace her and he looked proudly on his spouse, acting out the role of Matron of Honour. She was quite simply the only woman he had ever truly been in love with. A love that was still a furnace in his soul. It couldn't be extinguished even if he had wanted that, which he never would.

Twenty minutes later the ceremony was concluded, he had even remembered the ring. Jeremiah was hugging everyone in sight, keeping the most important one till last, approaching Nathaniel and engulfing him in a bear hug, which crushed the breath from his frame.

"You are the best of men, Jeremiah spouted fondly, "and the finest friend anyone can wish for, thank you so much for today."

"You haven't heard the speech yet," warned the man's employer.

"Whatever you say couldn't ruin today, Nathaniel, I have married the best woman in the world; nothing could destroy my happiness."

"You really look like the cat who's got the cream don't you, you are disgustingly happy, Jeremiah," said Nathaniel as he looked at the crescent moon grin on the man's features.

The sumptuous wedding breakfast was called and for the first time in the day, Nathaniel finally got to be and talk with his wife as they sat down to eat. She straightened his hair as he sat down beside her, giving him a look of unadulterated pleasure, squeezing his hand under the table. It was like coming home to a familiar house, warming and safe. They ate and talked intimately between themselves.

Nathaniel's best man speech, funny and informative, entertained the guests royally. They laughed at the relevant moments and rose as one as he lifted his glass.

"To the happy couple, may they be as happy as I have been with my magnificent wife, Jeremiah and Sally."

Presents were presented to them by the guests as they left, extraordinary in their generosity and welcomed with genuine affection by the couple.

When everyone had departed, Mary told the men that she was taking Sally upstairs to help her disrobe from the wedding dress. In the late afternoon, Nathaniel and Jeremiah took one last drink, watching the sun arcing to its setting, encompassing the sky in an orange glow.

"Here's to your night ahead and a wonderful life," said Nathaniel.

Presently Mary arrived. "Your wife is waiting for you, Jeremiah," she declared, kissing him fondly on the cheek. He looked even more terrified at the news, making Nathaniel smirk as he watched the man head toward the house.

"Jeremiah," he called after the man who turned. "Don't worry, it's hardly manual labour."

Mary dug him in the ribs at the coarseness of his comment. "That's quite enough of that," chided the woman.

"Let's walk," her husband suggested, grasping his wife around the waist and leading her toward the nearest line of vines.

In the confines of the creepers with her head on his shoulder, he asked her a question which had bothered him for a long time. "Have I made you happy, Mary?"

"Truthfully, no," she said. It made him pause and turn her towards him. She was laughing. "Of course you have, Nathaniel, I couldn't be anymore content than I am."

"Then why did you say I hadn't?" he pursued.

"It never does any harm to keep your husband on his toes." She ran off as she saw the look in his face and he chased her deep into the plant lines where he caught her and kissed her.

In the twilight of the warm evening, they enjoyed each other as they hadn't for some time, spontaneity stretching them to heights unparalleled,

"I love you so much, Nathaniel," she breathed as they collapsed exhausted on the ground.

Mary fell asleep on the warm earth, her husband looking up into the gathering twilight, thinking back over his life. He had cause to be grateful with astonishing friends like Christian, Ebenezer and Jeremiah, but their influence as friends paled against what the beautiful woman who lay next to him now, had given him. She was his friend, his wife, his lover, his business partner. All he had achieved was down to her. It terrified him to think he might have missed out on her but for a chance meeting.

Thistlebrough and his father seemed so long ago, he was finding it difficult to remember either of them with any degree of accuracy, his life had changed so much.

He pulled his wife close, and, lying beside her, he wondered what the rest of his life would bring.